CONTRACT OF WAR

SPECTRAS ARISE
BOOK 3

TAMMY SALYER

CONTRACT OF WAR

INTRODUCTION

Hello and thank you for being here! Should you enjoy the words on these pages (and I hope you do!), I encourage you to join my Book Club and visit me at:

www.tammysalyer.com

I occasionally send newsletters to my Book Club with new releases, special offers, and other bits of news. As a special thanks to new members, please enjoy a handful of novellas and short stories from my many and sundry universes FOR FREE.

PROLOGUE

From the Journal of Doctor Eleanor Vitruzzi, year 2727

Yesterday marked 460 days since the system's civil war began, but sometimes I feel like I've been at war my whole life. Only eight years have passed since the Soldier's Rebellion, and in that time, I now realize, *peace* was the illusion. When I look up at a rust-red sky filled with grit and chaff from the latest strafing, the smell of burning things, burning bodies . . . on days like those I can't remember what life was like before the suffering and fighting. There's been more death since this all began than anyone will ever be able to tally. Still, how could it have been any different?

When Rajcik dropped the Richter Mini-Nova on Tunis City, the war was inevitable. Cits and non-cits predictably divided straight down the middle, but that first year was devastating for those who still called themselves citizens. They were people who'd never known the harsh realities of noncivilized worlds, never had to adapt to bad air and a shortage of food. Except for the ones who'd been soldiers or engineers, they didn't even know how to get around the DNA signatures that would enable Admin-manufactured weapons to be fired. They dropped like headstones in an earthquake, and for a while it looked like the non-cits, with the help of the former-Corps-now-anti-Admin forces, were going to overrun all the Obal planets with ease.

The soldiers fighting from inside the fleet were another story, however. With Tunis City obliterated and the acceleration of Obal 10's magnetic reversal causing mass extinction and climate disruption, most of the Admin's political and military leaders died or disappeared. Like a chicken without a head, order and discipline disintegrated, and the rest of the Corps advanced rapidly into complete self-destruction. Soldiers who had been loyal to the Admin their whole lives suddenly switched sides and started mutinies within their divisions. Others who'd always been fast and loose with their beliefs locked onto the Admin rhetoric and dug in against the mutineers with a vengeance. Battles were waged within ships and between squadrons that most often ended with the deaths of everyone involved. For the first year, the chaos unfolding within the ranks kept the Corps and their weapons and ships too busy with each other to do much about what was happening on the ground. And we stayed busy.

And what's it all been for? For years non-cits have been thrown to the wolves on the edges of the system, left defenseless and completely at the Admin's mercy—expendable. There was more than enough festering hatred built up in the hearts of the people living on the system's eight Spectra planets; when the transmission was broadcast detailing the Admin's human experimentation, their diseases and plagues, and their utter contempt for human life, it was all the spark that was needed. Non-cits and criminals teamed up on every planet, galvanized by a shared motivation for revenge, and the citizens on the Obals, who never even knew of their own complicity, were systematically, ruthlessly slaughtered.

A few levelheaded leaders have risen, people who still have the capacity for reason and compassion. But they're becoming fewer and fewer. Even Command General Medina, leader of this fleet cruiser, the *Celestial*, seems to be losing sight of the goals. We need to bring order and meaning to the lives that are left. Halt the slaughter and begin bringing others onto our side, the side that fights for freedom before all. The people who were once citizens, as I once was, who had it easy before the war and thought they were being looked after by the Admin—like children—they have to know deep inside that their lives were so simple and sedate only because they consented to well-masked tyranny. And some already have. Whether it was their wounded dignity that forced them to step over, or something deeper and more noble, something like an innate understanding that there is nothing more important than freedom and self-governance, a great number of these people have quit cowering and picked up the banner of anti-Admin sentiment.

Yet the fighting continues.

ONE

For the love of all that is holy. If they'd shut up, I could sleep.

This grating thought finally brings me fully back from the nearly comatose sleep of complete exhaustion. Two and a half days rendering round-the-clock maintenance on the *Nebula* and *Orika*, our two largest scouts, prepping them for the next retrieval and salvage run has completely done me in. Once I found time to take a break, I would have jumped to my death off Keum Libre's oceanic landing platform just to get some much-needed shut-eye if I hadn't known I'd be able to bunk up in Venus's maintenance shed before heading back to the colony. Awake once more, groggy, cranky, and covered in oil and carbon dust, I don't think I've been asleep for more than a couple of hours. But now I have to listen to whoever's outside bitching at each other?

I'll give them something to yell about. Sitting up, I have to jam my hands into the small of my back, trying to rub away the stiffness nesting there. Cramp inducing or not, the purgatory of sleeping on Venus's tucked-away cot still beats the crowded, open-bay barracks of Keum Libre's old penal colony. Until *now*. And I don't like staying alone in the one-room outbuilding Karl and I share when he's not there.

The argument that awakened me continues.

"Doctor, the only thing you are in charge of on this rock is your pointless convalescent house for the broken and dying people you treat. You don't decide for me or anyone else what goes." Quantum's voice, his usual lack of tact making it unmistakable.

"You're wrong," Vitruzzi answers. "This colony has chosen a system of leadership. And that means Brady and me."

"*Chosen*. Don't make me laugh. You mean your demagoguery and threats have made everyone your puppets."

These two again. Quantum and Vitruzzi have been going rounds lately, but I haven't been able to find out what exactly their disagreement is about. I don't care really; I just want to stay focused on making our regular salvage runs around the system and lying low. Anything to keep from being sucked back into playing medic to the injured people inhabiting the colony's makeshift field hospital—the broken and dying people Quantum's talking about—even if it means thirty-six hours as slave labor, forced to beat the dents out of our busted-up scout ships.

"Quantum, I've already told you, and I'm getting tired of doing it, that you're more than welcome to leave. I can have Erikson or Strahan drop you at any point you'd like on their next run."

"And I will. When you give me access to the soil compound."

Soil compound? What the hell?

A long pause, then Vitruzzi: "You can't just let that stuff loose anywhere you want. There are still people living on most of the planets. The compound isn't an asset; it's a poison."

Quantum responds, "A few people maybe dying is a price I'm willing to pay for the chance—"

Voice pitched low, she cuts him off. "There's been enough death; we don't need to add to it. It's time to rebuild, not continue the destruction. If you're seriously thinking about using that compound . . . you're talking about genocide."

Quantum's voice, however, hasn't lost any of its volume. "You would know," he responds.

Footsteps, only one set, recede, and then the maintenance bay's door slams shut.

The fact is that a number of quarrels and scuffles have broken out between settlers over the last few months—even among people you'd never expect to be short-tempered or malcontent. My brother David and I have talked about it a couple of times, and it seems to boil down to two things. First, simply put, people are going stir-crazy. Nothing about trying to make this tiny settlement with less than two hundred inhabitants livable and viable has been easy, and those of us who don't get off planet much are stuck with a radically reduced—everything. Space, resources, new faces, they are all in short supply on Keum Libre. Second, people are having a hard time trying to adjust to the way things are now that there's no longer anything remotely close to a central government to govern the worlds out of chaos, along with the fact that half the Obals are wastelands. It *used* to be a big system. Now we're all just the last threads of a tattered spider web still clinging to the gutter after a cataclysmic storm. Personally, though, there's not a damn thing I miss about the Admin.

It's still quiet on the other side of the maintenance shed's door. Remaining seated, I listen awhile longer, more rattled by V and Quantum's conversation than I want to admit. Venus is out on the platform, working on the damaged scout Karl, David, and I had been hopping around the quadrant in before three of its four stabilizers had gone tits up. No one else is in the shed now besides me and whoever stayed behind after their argument.

Concluding they may both be gone, I lie back down, already feeling the heaviness of craved-for sleep pressing against my eyelids. My thoughts return to the overheard discussion and the soil compound. We'd found thousands of kilograms of it stored on the bottom level of the landing platform. The Admin had engineered the stuff to chemically alter a planet's soil and make it more fertile in a matter of only a couple decades, thus giving them the power to terraform more planets and make them not only more productive, but more livable. Keum Libre had been the experiment that proved its efficacy.

And, we've learned from the survivors, its deadliness.

After synthesizing and analyzing the data stored out here on the platform, as well as what we could retrieve of the data Bodie, my old friend who'd been killed by the Admin, had taken from the Fortress over two years ago, we know phase one of the compound's cycle is to wipe out everything living. By introducing a poisonous catalyst, which is beyond my rudimentary chemistry knowledge to understand, it clears an area completely of organic life, and essentially lets newly introduced flora and fauna regrow new ecological foundations from scratch. Perfect if you move into a place ten years after the compound's deployment. Not so great if you happen to be an organic life-form that's there from inception.

It sounds like Quantum wants access to it, but what for? Keum Libre has room enough to sustain our current population, as well as plenty more for expansion. The compound is dangerous, and no one here is an expert on chemical or planetary engineering, so we don't even have a full understanding of how it works. The data on the KL data-storage blocks has shown us all we really need to know: keep it locked up and don't let anyone near it.

Despite my tiredness, the questions evoked by their argument don't let me sleep. I'm trying to shut my mind off by reciting nav-chart coordinates (a technique I'd practiced to perfection when I was still enlisted—anything to push out the constant replay of past firefights) when something starts to feel off. A slight vibration works its way up the cot's legs, then through its thin fabric and into my back. A low droning noise leaks through the walls, like a million hummingbirds' wings flapping, deepening slowly until it becomes a buzzing roar outside. They must be testing something on our broken scout, the *Nebula*, and have the engines cycling. Fantastic. Naptime is officially over.

Standing up with a groan and a rapidly devolving unzenlike attitude, I walk to the wall and pull my jacket and arms-belt from their hooks. My boots hadn't made it off my feet before I'd passed out.

I step out of the cot room and see Vitruzzi seated on a stool inside the maintenance bay, which is really nothing but the psychotically disordered interior of Venus's old dwelling at Agate Beach, increased by a factor of ten. As Queen of All Things That Fly, Venus is the unquestioned ruler out here, and when I say *disordered* I'm not being entirely honest. The bay looks like Satan's funhouse to me and every other "normal" person who dares to enter, but Venus can tell you the location of every part, piece, wire, and nut and bolt it contains, down to the centimeter. And she gets *hostile* if you move something without telling her. To her radically enhanced brain cycles, this is just an excellent storehouse for the tools of her trade. My nearly three months of living with her at the Beach have inured me somewhat to the chaos, which is my ace in the hole when I need to borrow her quiet little corner of serenity. No one else comes in here without a very specific, and very brief, need.

I nod at the doc but have to shout to make myself heard. "Everything okay, V?"

The level of weariness in her eyes is almost shocking. And—there's something deeper there. Something that reminds me, in the quieter corners of my mind, of the look I'd catch in Rajcik's eyes, my former black-market arms-smuggling boss, when he was about to do something totally insane.

She jumps a fraction—so unlike her usual unflappability—then returns my nod. "Didn't know you were in there, Aly."

She says more, but I can't hear a thing over the *Nebula*'s engines. Hand-signing that I'm heading back to the colony, I leave her behind. As mentioned, whatever the disagreement is between her and Quantum, it's none of my business. And I'm happy to keep it that way.

I run into Venus at the skiff that will take us the six kilometers from the platform to the colony. Looking like a windblown cheetah, she's shifting her weight from side to side like a little girl who has to pee as she stands at the boat's release console.

"You heading back to the mainland?" I ask, walking up beside her.

"Yep! Jer is making cake for me! My birthday dinner!"

With the addition of flecks of engine oil, dust, and salty ocean spray covering her, the violence of curls haloing her head, their shade somewhere between the inside of a cantaloupe and the red skin of an apple, only looks more ferocious and indomitable. When I'd met Venus, her hair had been clipped short almost to her scalp, but now, two years later, it's grown out to her shoulders. Or it *would* reach her shoulders, except for the nearly afro-tight curls that explode from her head as if filled with electricity. Like everything else about her, from her phosphorescent green eyes to her overcharged brain to her savant flying skills, even her hair is almost impossible to believe. Venus is basically an exclamation point on legs.

"But I thought your birthday was last month."

"It was, but now we're going to celebrate it every month. Did you try that cake he made me last time?"

"I didn't get—"

"Well, if you had, you'd understand. It tastes just like an orgasm in your mouth, Aly. Really."

"Okay, fantastic, that's all I need to know."

Jeremy La Mer, much like Venus, is full of surprises. At first, we'd all assumed he was just a highly talented wire-rat. But he's proved in these past few months that he can make just about anything sing and dance for him, including cooking and gardening. I guess when civilization takes the kind of nosedive we've just experienced, all kinds of hidden talents people didn't know they had or had never cultivated before suddenly become not just talents, but essential skills.

Venus finishes the unmooring sequence, and the bay door at the end of the docking hangar begins grinding open. We jump inside the skiff together and she takes the pilot's seat.

"It sounded like the *Nebula* was back in action," I comment.

As she double-checks the boat's systems, she nods. "She's in good shape. Goodish. We need to replace a bunch of stuff inside the controls and reactors, but she'll fly fine for now."

I don't like any sentence that ends with the words *for now*, but I have nothing to respond with. On a planet without a manufacturing plant of any sort, or even people with the skills to construct whatever components we may need, you learn to live with *for now* until . . . you can't.

"Can you get David or me a list so we can look for derelicts to take parts from on our next run?"

"Consider it done. And don't forget. You're on med-bay duty tonight after the town hall."

Town hall? Med-bay duty? "Jesus, Venus, what am I, a robot? When am I supposed to sleep?"

"Hey, Aly-oop. You volunteered, remember?"

Even the war was less exhausting.

TWO

Q uantum and several others have requested they be given one of our three scout ships to join the colony called Bogotan on Obal 6."

Rumbles and the occasional epithet follow Brady's first order of town hall business. He stands in the center of the desalination plant's largest filtering room, which may be the only functioning industrial facility remaining in this quadrant, and grits his teeth. He enjoys this about as much as I do. Another town hall and more arguments, or, as I like to call it, another night of slinging bullshit.

"We only have three! Why give one up?"

"How does it help our own colony to give away our few resources?"

"We need all our ships!"

Brady lets the hollering die down before relaxing his scowl. Deep lines spread out from the edges of his mouth and eyes, making him look twenty years older than he did the short two years ago that I'd met him. He must be somewhere in his midforties, maybe late forties, and still strong. But those lines show many more years of pain and hardship than that. Too many.

"This is a town hall. I'm only going to remind everyone one time that you wait to be called on. I'm chairing tonight, which makes me in charge."

Quantum, who stands near the right front flank of the semicircle of colonists, fronts his own hard scowl on his squished, round face. I can almost read his mind. The only reason we're here right now is because of him. When the *Boelke*'s—a light bomber and transport craft we'd commandeered when we left Medina and the PCA *Celestial* —navigation sequences performed the equivalent of a programming seppuku and left us flying blind just before reaching the moon, he had fixed our radar and visuals with his almost freakish wire-rat skill set as we broke through the atmosphere, giving the engineering team the information they needed to land the cruiser without killing anyone. The *Boelke* won't ever fly again, at least not with our current limitations on engineering and mechanical materials, but the sixty passengers and crew aboard it had all survived. Why shouldn't he get his own long-range ship? The colony has three.

Narumi, a hardworking aide to Vitruzzi, raises her one hand. The other was blown off at the wrist during the war. A replacement could easily have been created for her under normal circumstances, and no one could have done a better job of it than Vitruzzi herself. But circumstances aren't normal, and Narumi gets around with only a primitive, nonrobotic prosthetic. Despite this, she gets as much done as anyone else in the colony, and maybe because of it, she's particularly empathetic with some of the other victims of disfigurement and amputations who've found their home on KL. Brady nods in her direction.

"As everyone knows, Jillian, Tomaz, and I all came from the Obal 6 colony four months ago. Why did we leave? Because they wouldn't let me stay—they said resources were in too short supply to help a cripple. Why would we give them a ship when they won't even help a woman who's missing a hand?"

Grumbles of agreement, then Dan Hoogs, another ex-Corpsmember (but aren't most of us now?), steps forward with a hand in the air. Brady nods a go-ahead and Hoogs says, "The more of our own resources we give up, and the more they get, the less secure we are. If Quantum wants to live with them, we can drop him off nearby and he can wait to be found. Our assets are limited, and we're not doing ourselves any favors if we start letting others know what we do—and don't—have."

Almost every face in the room shares expressions of agreement. I glance back toward Quantum. Someone has draped and fastened an old canvas across the wall behind where he stands with the words ADAPT OR DIE carefully stenciled across it in letters a meter high. It's become the motto of our settlement, replacing "Fight or Die" now that the war is essentially over. Yet some of us have had more trouble than others embracing the newer philosophy. Looking at some of the hardened and angry faces in the room, I wonder if we ever will.

It's Quantum's turn to step forward, but he doesn't wait for Brady to approve before he speaks. "We're not suggesting we just hand over one of KL's ships. Brady"—he flicks a sneer at Brady that's pretty ballsy, given the crowd—"hasn't been clear. We would like to borrow a ship to visit Obal 6's leading city and begin negotiations for joining our two colonies in trade."

"What makes you any kind of spokes—?" someone blurts, but Brady's on it.

"No talking out of turn, dammit. Or I'll adjourn the meeting right now."

The voices of the crowd hush, but the restless and agitated fidgeting going on around me doesn't let up. These people feel more and more like they're being pushed closer to the edge on a daily basis, and it's beginning to get under their skin.

Quantum's features flatten out into what I think he must assume is a neutral expression, but it only makes him appear as calculating as I know him to be. Not really what you look for in a diplomat.

"Think about it," he says. "Bogotan has a manufacturing plant, a functioning city power grid with municipal water, and an untold number of experts in everything we lack. Right now, we fight nature just to keep the desal plant running. If we lose that, we are done. The time to form alliances is before time runs out, not when we are desperate."

"Dr. Kittinger keeps the desal plant running fine," Vitruzzi cuts in from where she stands next to Brady.

Quantum shifts his gaze to her, the same calculating expression still fixed. This isn't going well for him at all. Much as I don't like the man, though, I see his point.

Covering a yawn that threatens to split my skull in two, I start inching toward the exit. I already know this is going to end in another stalemate, and I'm too tired to give it more than a minimum of my attention. This is the third town hall in as many weeks, a brainchild of Brady's to help bring order to the colony's slowly expanding population. Obviously, he's well suited to the task after leading Agate Beach for several years, and his own mining crew somewhere on the Spectras before that. Despite few resolutions or social ordinances getting past the discussion stage, I have to admit that the spiking curve of disorder and dis-ease that's been growing among the settlers has at least leveled off because of Brady's lead-taking. Or it seemed to have, but part of me wonders if tonight's meeting portends an about-face in the relative calm of things.

Dusk is falling and some of the air's constant humid saturation is easing off. My shift in the *Andromeda*'s med-bay starts in a few minutes. We have only a few sick and wounded at the moment, so I'm hoping I'll be able to convince whoever I'm partnered with tonight to trade sleep rotations with me.

Karl and David have been out for three weeks on a salvage run—which always makes my nerves sizzle like a slow-burning fuse until I know they're safe again—and are expected back any day now. I didn't go with them this time thanks to a flare-up of what best might be termed *acute gastrointestinal distress*—of the extreme variety. A lovely side effect of using myself as a testing ground for some of the questionable salvage we find. Once that "passed" I reverted to my constant focus on staying busy, despite difficulty sleeping, just to keep my mind off all the possible things that could happen to them. Regardless, I'm about ready to fall into a walking coma, and tonight's shift is just the chance I need to catch up on sleep after the last two days on the platform doing maintenance.

Bidding an unfond adieu to the bickering, I drop to the back of the crowd, catching a suggestive wink from Desto, and start the short walk to the *Andromeda*, surprising myself with the realization that even I'm undecided about whether or not Quantum should get what he's asking for.

THREE

The War, seven months earlier

T
he Corps Loyalist cruiser is down and the last of their air forces are neutralized."

The voice belongs to Lieutenant Steward, the OIC of this operation. At first glance you wouldn't think much of the slight, pale at-one-time career Corps officer, but his mind for strategy has led to the decimation of at least half the enemy we've come across since the war started. Between him and Medina calling the shots, and strong fighters like my brother and most of the rest of the crew of our cruiser, the *Celestial*, I don't see how this war could go on much longer.

The enclave of Corps soldiers we're here on Iso Umm, a moon off Spectra 5, to mop up has dug into a substantial weapon cache hidden in an old Admin mine. It had taken almost a week to neutralize their air defenses, and another three days of constant assault on the ground to breach their bunker. David and I are here with the other 247 fighters from Ground Squadron 8, 90 percent of us former Corps.

Steward continues, "The only thing left is to deal with are the remaining Loyalists at your location. Can your unit handle that?"

The question is rhetorical. He means he'll send a transport to bring us back to the *Celestial* after, and only after, we've handled it.

David gives the affirmative, clicks off his satcom channeler, and leans his back against a black, smooth boulder, the same as the kind that makes up almost the entire surface of Iso Umm. "Fuck," he says.

"No more than another day, tops," I try to reassure him and dig through the remaining containers of liquids our platoon has piled behind our frontline berm. Pulling out one labeled PASSION FRUIT, I squash the urge to celebrate like I'd just won the lottery. Everyone loves this flavor and the passion fruit always disappears first. Sure, it may taste a little like someone tried to mask the flavor of sulfur with asbestos dipped in sugar, but that's just the vitamins (they tell us). Besides, the flavor is better than the rest, which taste more like toxic waste dipped in monkey piss, and I can't believe one got overlooked. I pull off the cap and take a swig, then wave it toward David. "Want a drink?"

He nods and I pass it over. Tilting his head back, he takes several deep swallows. Before he can finish the whole container, I swipe it back with a disgusted "Yeah, you're welcome. Don't mention it," then drain it and go back for a second. Monkey piss it is.

After settling down against the boulder beside him and finishing the drink, I start to nod off when he says, "Christ, what's that stench, Aly?"

"Dunno," I mumble without opening my eyes. "You'll get used to it." He's referring to the cloud of cheap-smelling cologne wafting from my body armor. Some practical joker made me their target. And they will pay.

I hear him scooting across the loose gravel to get some distance from me, then nothing for a few blissful minutes.

But that's all I'm going to get. Being a soldier in a war whose outcome matters to oneself makes sleep both a commodity and a distraction. My eyes jump open again soon, almost as if they're linked to some internal timer. The rest of our platoon, fifty or so dirty, dust-covered troops, encircle us, leaning against boulders of their own with their eyes closed, also trying to get something approximating sleep. It's the first break we've had in forty-eight hours of pushing the last of these Corps Loyalists underground. Third and Fourth Platoons group together nearby, inside perimeters of their own. David took charge of the whole company twelve hours into the ground assault after our CO, a guy from Obal 8 whom I'd liked and respected, got himself incinerated trying to take some of their fighters as captives. All of us now are just waiting for David to give us the final green light to end this operation.

"We could just starve them out," David says, his voice low enough that I can tell he's talking to himself. "They'll come out eventually if they know they're not going to get any reinforcements or supplies."

"Sure," I comment. The thing I don't mention is we're not getting any help either if we don't finish the job. But he's right, and that's the hell of it. It would really be that easy. "What do you think Medina's pushing us to attack for?"

"She wants the weapons."

"And if we leave them in there too long, they could start to sabotage them."

"Exactly." He clicks on his com and links to the other platoon leaders. "Henderliter, Joy, what's your status?"

Henderliter: "We're all green. Ready for go. Over."

Joy: "Ready on your mark, Erikson. Over."

David stands, runs his eyes and hands over his gear in a routine check that's been practiced hundreds of times, and calls out, "Second Platoon, at the ready!"

Fifty-plus soldiers get up with no hesitation. I follow, running my hands over my helmet, body armor, utility vest, ammo belt, and weapons in the same obsessive check, ensuring all straps are secure, all connections are closed.

He clicks on the com and gives the attack command. In a perfect military maneuver, our three platoons infiltrate the remaining thirty Loyalists' bunker and neutralize them in one hour-long push.

Sometimes a firefight is just that. Other times, it's a massacre.

· · ·

Scraping the crust of dried blood and dust off my face and arms and out of my hair is going to be a full-time job tonight. By my estimate, about two hundred of us came back. But none of the Admin Loyalist soldiers are going anywhere except back into the dust—and down the drains aboard the *Celestial*.

"Hey Erikson!" someone yells, and both David and I halt our trudge toward the showers and turn. Potts, a dark-haired ex-citizen, one of the few aboard, continues, "Uh, you, David—Medina wants you on the bridge."

"Can it wait?"

"Guess you have to ask her," he says and hustles past us on some other task.

"Must be something important," David mocks.

I nod. One thing about these ex-citizens working aboard a fighting vessel, they seem to always elevate whatever task or duty they're on into some kind of overdramatic life-or-death status. As if Command General Medina would entrust anything more essential than cataloguing gear or indexing data to these militarily clueless pinheads. Sometimes we get a laugh at their self-created grandeur. Other times, like when we're covered in gore and haven't slept more than a few hours in days, we have a hard time not strangling them.

"Come on," I offer, "I'll go with you."

It's strange to be walking these pristine, gleaming passageways, which are the hallmark of a fleet cruiser. There's no dust in space, and ship environments are as hermetic as they come. Before the Soldier's Rebellion of 2719 and our subsequent desertion, when David and I had still been in the Corps, every reentry of a fleet craft after a planet-side chit included twenty-four hours of quarantine to examine soldiers for new or infectious pathogens we may have picked up. This was after the full-body scrub down, of course. For a soldier, privacy is a myth, and being turned into the focal point of multilevel tissue and cell scopes was never really a big deal—even our bones and guts got more attention from ship doctors and medical analysts than most children get from their parents. We'd been held inside a decontamination airlock until every last speck was scrubbed, sucked, or sponged from our bodies and gear—and the truth is, soldiers looked forward to the observation period simply for the time it gave us to rest.

But because reentry processing took a squad, a platoon, or sometimes a full company out of rotation for so much time, our tours planet-side tended to be as long as, and often longer than, needed. I'd gone from periods of days to months stuck on scattered rocks throughout the system, with nothing better to do than learn new ways to gamble and lose my pay, or collect new recipes from the population for cooking up whatever edible local flora and fauna were around. Populations that were friendly, that was. Which weren't all of them.

We didn't spend time patrolling backwater planets for nothing. We were there with a purpose, usually to quell potential rebellions or uprisings. Someone in the Corps monitoring stations would read suspect satellite message packets or overhear key terms while listening to planet radio coms that would send up alarms. Or an analyst would simply do math on variables such as age spectrum, resource and equipment quality or lack thereof, mortality rates of the population, and a number of other factors, and come up with a higher-than-average probability of rebellious activity, and in we'd go. Mission: keep the locals in line.

In line. There was a term of such extreme vagueness that even the most unimaginative soldier in the system—and that's saying something—could come up with some kind of plan of action or mission goal. I'd seen the words come to mean everything from helping to restore derelict factories to shooting on sight any person or group that was considered a threat.

And what exactly had we considered a threat? That all depended on who would be filtering and evaluating the after-action report. If it was an officer known for their hostility toward non-cits, a threat could be as simple as a fist shaken in anger or a warning to soldiers to leave them alone "or else." If it was an officer with a conscience, our platoon leaders had to keep it civil. We were, after all, the Capital Military Corps of the Advanced Worlds.

Advanced. The word is almost a punch line.

But the situation now is a little different. Medina hasn't quite been able to reconstruct all the prewar protocols that used to be in effect, and David and I reach the bridge without even a second glance from the onboard protocol monitors.

Activity on the bridge isn't as frenetic as I'd expect after such a large-scale assault—the annihilation of a Corps Loyalist fleet cruiser is the biggest success, and biggest operation, in our strategy—but that's how Medina commands. Order and efficiency rule everything she touches, and there are rarely any moving pieces that aren't comparable to precision clockwork. Sometimes I try to imagine what she would look like panicked, but my mind can't seem to dredge up anything that fits. The closest I get is an image of a cartoon caricature of a freaked-out cat, with its back arched, fangs bared, and fur bristling.

"Commander," David says, approaching the bridge's command booth where Medina stands in discussion with her first lieutenant.

She turns around gracefully, her face alert and slightly predatory. David's quiet approach must have surprised her. I'm again reminded of a cat. One that's about to pounce. Then her features smooth out and she says, "Erikson, thanks for coming. I know you must be ready to take a few hours off, so I'll get right to the point."

I can hear her just fine from where I linger, waiting at the rear of the bridge, another indication of how orderly and smoothly everything on the fleet ship *Celestial* runs. The fact that I'm on the bridge at all is something that would have been completely unheard of in my days in the Corps. I'd been an enlisted navigator for surface-to-orbit troop ships, but never on these cruiser-class ships. And only officers worked the bridge.

Medina runs things with more transparency, a quality that seems to have endeared her to more than an expected number of followers and fighters. The Admin's underhanded duplicity and lying is what led to the war in the first place, and I assume Medina wants to make sure no one thinks that way of operating will continue. She's fond of the phrase "unity through trust," which has been a necessary philosophy for helping blur the dividing lines between the citizens, non-citizens, and now ex-Corps soldiers who have been fighting together on the anti-Admin side. Since before people began inhabiting the Algol system, a classist mentality had typically set these three groups at odds, theoretically if not physically. Even the Capital Military Terrestrial Corps and Capital Military Stellar Corps had maintained a vibrant sense of competitive contempt for each other before this war changed everything. The Terrestrial Corps ranks, as David and I had been, called ourselves the "Fight" soldiers and the Stellar Corps the "Flight" soldiers to differentiate ourselves, taking pride in the fact that we spilled our blood in ground combat and didn't have the opportunity (or, presumably, desire) to fly away when things got sticky.

Medina's doing what she can to erase that dividedness and listens to what David has to say about our mission on Iso Umm without a hint of rank bias. As the equivalent of a company commander, and having spent a good share of his time outside the Corps participating in non-cit life and using real-world fighting tactics as a deserter, David's experience and leadership are qualities Medina highly values. His utility to her, and by extension mine, is uncomfortably reminiscent of the reasons Rajcik had hired us on after we deserted the Corps during the Soldier's Rebellion. But I don't let it keep me up nights. Given that every other week since the war began has seen fighting conditions similar to the last few days, I've continually been too overworked to let *anything* keep me up at night when I'm back in garrison.

"How did things look out there?" she asks.

David leans against the control bench. "Same as things always look on these moons. Like God bleached the color out of everything and decided it would be fun to litter the ground with rocks that rip through your clothes like razors."

That's my brother. A poet at heart.

"Did you capture any Loyalists for interrogation this time?"

"None of them seemed willing to live long enough to be taken prisoner."

She scowls at him. Intel has been the hardest commodity to get since the Admin had the Corps wipe out communications system-wide by destroying all of their satellites. *System assets have permanently lost telemetry,* as the saying goes. With the latest mission's success, we know of ten fleet cruisers that have been knocked out of the game, and, last we heard, our side still had four others working with us. But that leaves eleven unaccounted for, and of those, six Admin and Corps Loyalist fleet cruisers remain the biggest threat we face.

"David, you're one of the most experienced ground soldiers I have. Which means you know that anything you can do to get us more information will help us win this war. The sooner we win it, the sooner we can start putting the pieces back together."

"Roger."

From where I stand, Medina's scowl almost looks like it's hardening into stone. David's lack of military decorum has to be like sticking hot needles into her eyeballs, but what can she do? We're not an army, this isn't the Corps anymore, and there's no such thing as a code of military order and discipline. What chain of command we have exists because there's no other way we could keep the ship in the sky, or even survive, without some kind of functioning system. But Medina learned quickly how to toe the line with those of us who deserted after the Rebellion. We lost a taste for taking orders long before she came into the picture. And it doesn't matter that the Admin is a common enemy; David and I, and others like us, will never willingly accept a reversion to old Corps standards.

"Anything else, Medina?"

Her scowl gives way to her regularly composed, yet stern, expression. "Just a heads-up that one of our scouts has reported activity near Broon, off Spectra 6. We'll be moving in to investigate in a few hours."

Bleeding Christ, another operation in just a few hours, a day at the most? David's tone mirrors my thoughts. "Commander, my unit is wiped out. We need a few days to stitch ourselves together before another ground incursion."

"Oh, you misunderstand—of course, Erikson. I don't mean to send your company back in. I'm letting you know that you'll be staying ship-side for a few missions. You, all of you"—she turns her head toward me and dips her chin in acknowledgment—"have shown incredible aptitude and achieved fine successes out there. I know how hard it is to be fighting *against* people you once fought side by side with, and I can't promise you the worlds will ever recognize your sacrifices and courage. That being said, I want to give you some time to rest. It's the best I can do. We'll rotate your company into onboard duties in a couple of days. Until then, consider yourselves to be on R&R, for what it's worth. You'll let your people know?"

"Roger," David repeats, keeping his own face stoic, and I wonder what's going on behind his light-green eyes.

"For freedom," she finishes and turns back to Lieutenant Steward, who still waits quietly in the booth.

David skulks down the corridor to our unit's berth, and I follow along, fighting to undo a dirt-encrusted buckle on my armor's torso plate. When we reach our bay, he slams his hand into the hatch code box hard enough to make its backlights flicker briefly.

"Whoa, big brother, it's zed-zero-zed-five, not *wham!*, FYI."

"Sacrifices and courage? Aptitude and achievements? Who does she think she's talking to? This war isn't about freedom any more than she's still a Corps officer. Maybe before, but not now. If I'm going to be condescended to, she should at least stop pretending she's some kind of leader of a new-and-improved master society. She's just repeating the same fucking bullshit jackboot game that got us here."

The hatch opens and La Mer and Desto come through it. "Hey, Erikson His and Hers! You're back," La Mer quips. "You look like shit."

"And damn, Aly, what's that smell? You visit a brothel while you were playing soldier?" Desto and La Mer both break up at my body armor's odor, still front-and-center, even after the three-day-long incursion.

"This was you?" I ask, finally identifying the prankster behind this nauseating practical joke. "I can barely breathe!"

"Don't worry, Twig. Despite your stench and filthy mouth, your overwhelming beauty and charisma still have the power to turn every man into your personal twat-bot."

La Mer looks aghast. "Jesus, you guys. Gross."

"It's the language of love, baby. Aly and I have an understanding." Desto winks at me.

Rolling my eyes, I reply, "You're going to pay for this. And I told you not to call me Twig."

With a last chuckle, he calms down, and his face grows serious. "How'd it go?"

David pulls his torso piece over his head. Sand and black rock dust filter down around his feet. Pushing his matted hair out of his eyes, he replies, "Brother, all things being equal, I'm starting to wonder if we're even fighting for anything anymore."

FOUR

Another one died last night. He had an unexpected and unquenchable fever and then . . . gone. Like a magazine running dry and the world going silent with your last trigger pull. It's things like this that make me wonder if David had been right. Had we been fighting for anything?

At least it was natural causes this time, not suicide, like the last one. Thank Christ. I don't think the doc could take another one of those. Still, how natural is a death that could so easily be avoided if we had the right medical supplies? I just wish I wasn't the one who will have to tell Vitruzzi.

I step through the cruiser's pedestrian exit to get some fresh air before doing the deed. I don't like to spread news like this on the radio; it feels so—uncaring. Like someone's death doesn't rank any higher than reporting on supplies and ammunition. That's too much like combat, where a casualty count really is nothing more than a number. I'd known commanders who would curse the dead for having the gall to die midfight and leave a battle undermanned. But the fighting is over, and civilized people dignify death with a little more . . . I don't know . . . compassion? Besides, she's usually here early to make morning rounds. I'll tell her then.

This fleet cruiser, once the PCA *Andromeda*, is nothing but a five-city-block-sized steel derelict that's been planted in the midst of vines, trees, and scrubby brush outside Keum Libre's colony like a monolithic statue of a past age. It came down sometime during the war, and the crew who hadn't abandoned have assimilated smoothly into KL's colony. The thing it really is, though, is our last connection to civilization. The technology inside its structure is the only thing that sets us apart from the nomadic tribes of old Earth. One half is an armory with enough weapons and armaments to lay waste to a city, and the other half serves as a hospital for the sick, the feeble, the broken, and the dying. And the supreme god—goddess, really—that haunts its alloy and polymer halls is none other than our good doctor and former *Sphynx* captain, Eleanor Vitruzzi.

Without access to the vast energy sources required for these types of cruiser-class fleet ships to stay in the air, and with the easiest interior to keep clean and sterile, it wasn't hard to decide it should serve as the hospital for wounded fighters who somehow managed not to get turned into carbon sludge during the war. Karl and I, Vitruzzi and Brady, Desto and my brother David, Venus and Jeremy La Mer, and most of the other surviving settlers from Agate Beach put our roots down on Keum Libre as soon as the main fighting was over. Even if the outcome wasn't clear, the one thing that even the dimmest bulb knew by then was that everything was irrevocably changed. After the war, there would be no picking up the pieces and rebuilding the system based on the old model. Even the pieces were in pieces. Knowing the kind of chaos that would be coming, settling on KL was an easy decision. With the desalination plant, the mostly unsettled expanse of the planet, and limited takeoff and landing points, it's ideal for hunkering down and staying out of the line of fire.

And we're doing okay here. We're already growing produce crops—La Mer and Brady's facility with cultivation coming as a surprise to more than just me—and have a small fleet of watercraft that tap the sea to keep us fed. But another purpose of our happy little home has been to provide what aid and shelter we can to the wounded we come across. Becoming an impromptu medic for the colony is never something I anticipated. But V needed help, so we all found ways to do it. I've had my hands in more wounds than I ever thought I could stomach in the last few months, and it never gets any easier. It just gets to where you can shut off your mind and treat it like a science experiment. A science experiment that sometimes screams. I know more about tying off a spurting artery and stitching up a layer of torn muscle than most third-year residents, but at least we're doing more than just waiting for starvation and infection to pick us off slowly. And these days, it seems to be the only thing Vitruzzi can stay focused on.

Haggard isn't even the right word to describe her; she's grown almost too gaunt to find clothes that fit, and frequently I've had to repeat her name three or four times before getting her attention. It's like she's not even present in her own body anymore, and it's worrying everyone. The bad news I have for her today just seems that much worse because I'm no longer sure she's stable enough to handle it. At least she has Brady.

Sunlight reflecting off the windscreen of an approaching hover-runner draws me out of my thoughts. It pulls into the widened-out area beside the cruiser and powers down, settling against the earth with a dull thud. The screen retracts, and I feel an instant sense of relief at the sight of David stepping out of the cab.

Rushing over, I reach him in time to catch his pack as he tosses it over the side. "No one told me you were back!"

He smiles, looking a little tired but happier than usual. "Yeah, we got in about twenty minutes ago. The colony's satellite seems to be on the fritz again, so we couldn't call in."

"Did it go okay? Find anything we can use?"

"Only"—he reaches into the cab and grabs a sealed metal cylinder that rattles slightly—"the jackpot. I'll tell you about it—"

The sound of the colony's heavier track vehicle drowns him out as it pulls in beside the runner. Two of the colonists jump off the back as it powers down and slide open the bars holding the cargo-bed door closed. Then Karl swings out of the cab.

Tripping over my feet with excitement—and more relief than

even seeing David had elicited, which I'd never admit to my brother —I rush over and grab Karl, holding tight. "Missed you, lover," I whisper against his neck.

"Me too," he says, and we stay this way, in each other's arms.

"Don't let the rest of us disturb you," David says eventually.

Letting go of Karl, I wave my hand toward the cargo bed. "Is that the jackpot?"

David smiles at me. "Nope, that's just the first card."

Curious, I walk over and see what's inside. Hard plastic bins about the size of an ammo crate fill half the cargo space, and the remaining space contains boxes stamped with caducei and the names of hospitals or clinics that had once been on Obal 8. The extra medical supplies alone, something we rarely come across even on the longer scavenging missions, make this score better than good.

"So what's in those bins?"

David responds, "Help us unload and I'll tell you."

"It's absolutely beautiful, Karl. But I'm going to have to agree with V on this one. This is less than useless out here," Desto says, clenching his entire body to keep himself from breaking into hysterical laughter.

Vitruzzi had arrived for her morning rounds just a few minutes after David. Her subdued excitement at seeing the med supplies quickly gave way to the same curiosity I had about what the rest of the cargo contained. Because of Desto's ability to identify and defuse anything that might be rigged for bigger surprises, we'd called him up before opening anything. Once he'd inspected everything and given the all clear, we popped the bins.

No doubt, the disappointment and confusion on my face reflect the rest of theirs. A good portion of the cargo bins are full of contraband liquor, something that smells like it had probably been part engine degreaser and part something you'd find at the bottom of a rubbish bin. The stench is suspiciously close to the crud I'd drunk just before my guts jumped ship through the back door and kept me off David and Karl's last run. The rest of the containers hold a mix of more medical supplies and a strange array of sealed chemical elements. Carbon, nitrogen, sulfur, hydrogen, oxygen, and various others.

"I guess now we know why they left it out there. This stuff will make you blind faster than a sledgehammer to the brain stem," Karl responds, chuckling despite himself. "Want to run it past your more refined taste buds, Aly?"

I throw him a scowl loaded with a promise to make him pay later, and he returns it with a half-lifted eyebrow that promises to enjoy it.

Glancing at Vitruzzi, I realize her eyes haven't left the contents of the final bin since we'd broken the locks. The tendons in her neck stand out like barbed wire strained close to the breaking point. It didn't help that I'd had to tell her about the newly shipped-to-oblivion colonist. She'd taken the news with as much silent composure as always, but she didn't try to hide the sag of her shoulders or the tension that had further deepened the lines around her eyes and across her forehead. I understand her disappointment about losing someone, but now, looking at the usual cargo, she looks as if she's about ready to kill someone.

Unsettled by her expression, I try to calm her down. "We're still good, V. We have plenty of bandages in storage, and the antibiotics are lasting longer than we expected."

She snorts, and her expression goes from rage to disgust. She's like an ever-shifting storm front these days. Sometimes I want to tell her she needs to take a vacation, but I value the current arrangement of my facial features too much. Besides, she's Doc V; she's the reason so many in our colony are even still alive. If her job has caused her to lose her sense of humor, I'm sure there's no one here who doesn't think the trade-off was worth it.

"I have work to do," she says, and leaves.

The rest of us stand around the crates, feeling like a group of incompetents.

Finally, David remarks, "So the takeaway is to open the salvage before getting back to KL, next time."

"Don't worry about it," I say. "You know you don't hang around a derelict and take your time looking through everything. That's just a good way of advertising yourself as a mark."

"I think what David means is, he could have spent the last couple weeks en route getting sauced, pickled, and otherwise drunker than Cooter Brown. Missed opportunity if I ever saw one, bro," Desto says, slapping David good-naturedly on the shoulder. Then, more seriously: "Don't worry about it, man. We all know it isn't easy out there."

After a pause David tries smiling and replies, "Pickled? That shit would have turned me into something you'd put in a jar next to a two-headed calf."

"And you'd finally be with your own kind," Desto says, making us all laugh.

"Anyway," Karl puts in, "what the hell should we do with this?"

"Let's see if Venus wants it," I say. "Could be good for cleaning parts."

Everyone nods in agreement, and we spend the next half hour loading the bins back on the tracker to take over to the dock and out to Venus on the platform.

IT'S ALREADY LATE EVENING before Karl and I finally get some alone time.

"Yeah," he says after I ask about the salvage op Venus's new degreaser came from. "It was easier than we expected. The ship was just an Admin derelict hanging free outside of anyone's orbit. We got lucky. I mean it was purely random to find it out there."

Karl hands me his Kaldor 75 sidearm and starts stripping out of his equipment vest. I watch closely, hoping to get a chance to help him with the shirt and pants soon. "We took that route through the Spectras specifically to avoid coming into contact with any other ships. The number of scavs is getting worse again, just like it was right after the war started. I guess . . . I don't know. People are either getting more organized or more desperate."

"Could you tell what happened to the derelict?"

"We didn't have time to do much searching, but it looked to me like it was out of power. The hull, everything we saw, was still intact. The crew must have jet on landing skiffs and probably intended to come back for the goods." He shrugs, his features arranged in disturbed contemplation. "Guess they got sidetracked."

Out of power—same story for most of the bigger ships that are still in one piece, and the same reason the *Andromeda* will stay permanently parked on KL, even if we could repair it. We were lucky that the *Sphynx* had a solid supply of solar seeds when we hit the deck right before Rajcik went off the deep end. That surplus has kept our three scout ships in the sky for the last six months.

Speaking of sidetracked, Karl's not doing anything to stop my hands as they embark on an exploration of the lines of his abdomen and over the lower shelf of his pecs, my fingers running through his chest hair on a safari that feels weeks overdue.

"Next time you go, I'm coming with you," I inform him as I lightly tease one of his nipples.

"Like I'm going to argue," he answers, then pulls me hard against his body in a way that lets me know we're done talking.

THE RISING DAWN SLIPS through our window box, and I reach over Karl to tug the improvised sunscreen over it. There isn't much to scavenge on Keum Libre, but everything that can be stripped from the *Andromeda* has been, and enterprising builders like Karl and me have begun constructing our own private dwellings outside the main colony area. I don't sleep here when he's not around, though—too much quiet for me to be able to relax. For years in the Corps I craved privacy. But now that I have it, I can't help but get a little spooked. And then, of course, there's the coffee-cup-sized arthropods clicking around outside. A face-to-face moment with one of those one morning as I left for work was all I needed to assassinate chivalry for good. When Karl and I stay out here, I always hold the door for *him* to go out first.

"So was there anything else worth another trip on the derelict?" I ask, picking up the thread we promptly forgot about last night.

He pauses before answering, brushing his fingertips along the inside of my arm. "Yeah. I mean, maybe."

"Maybe?"

"It looked like some sort of data-storage unit, but bigger than any I've ever seen. There was a mechanical component to it too. It's hard to explain. Almost like a matter printer—you know the kind I mean?"

I nod.

"We didn't locate the ship's manifest, and it didn't look like something that had any immediate benefit to the colony, so we left it there. In any case, I'm curious. David was too."

"Even a solid-matter printer could come in handy, if we can get the right drivers and materials for it. Are you planning to talk to Brady about taking the *Orika* again?"

"It's probably a good idea. But I'm in no hurry to leave. I just got back and our love shack needs some work."

I roll my eyes at him, and he gives me a sexy half grin. "I know. Venus and Jer are working on the portable com-boxes for all the outlying dwellings that are getting put up. And they're already running an ion net for everyone to tap into power."

"All that has happened in the three weeks since I left? Wow. Those two don't sleep, do they?"

"As if you have to ask . . ."

"C'mon, lover. Let's go get some breakfast," he says and hands me my shirt.

FIVE

Being part of a good crew can get you a lot of places, but one place it will never get you is out of your own head. Mornings on Keum Libre bring that home to me more than anything else. At least, the mornings when I'm not dealing with the tragedy of another colonist's death or some other kind of emergency. In one sense, I guess we're all fortunate that those hectic and troubling mornings are growing more and more rare, but in another sense, waking up and having the time to realize—to fully comprehend—that civilization as we knew it will never exist again can really throw off a person's equilibrium. And discovering how okay with that I am, well, that's the most unbalancing thing of all.

Which explains the spike of excitement I feel when Vitruzzi walks up to our table as Karl and I eat in the *Andromeda*'s main chow hall and says, "You're leaving in thirty-six hours."

Karl splutters into his coffee. "What?"

"You said there are more med supplies on the derelict you and David found, right? It's imperative that we have them, sooner rather than later. The drug stock here is too thin already." She places a cup of coffee on the table and sits down beside me. Drops of the pounding rain, so common in KL's jungles, bead off the tips of her lank hair, emphasizing how worn down she looks.

Inwardly, I heave a sigh of relief. I'm better in the air. All this staying put makes me restless, and the constant arguing among the colonists makes anywhere else sound like paradise. Life's hard enough—without *people* making it harder.

Karl gets over the surprise quickly. Whether he admits it or not, the same jet-setter traits that made him join the Corps all those years ago in the first place still exist. "You know, V," he says, "maybe you should come with us. Jade and Sánchez can handle the infirmary for a few weeks, and we could use you on the ship to help identify things we need."

The Millar triplets of about twelve years old run up to our table, giggling and fighting at the same time, and interrupt Karl. "Mr. Strahan," the silken-black-haired girl says, putting her arm into the chest of her trailing brother to stop him, "can you take us up in one of the scouts? You promised you would when you got back."

Karl smiles at them, then glances around the mess hall, probably looking for their parents, Jennifer and Ivan. "Looks like I can't this time, kids."

"Aw, when?" one of the boys, Jens, I think, asks. Before Karl can answer, the kid stands up straighter and nods at me somberly, like a meter-and-a-half-tall CEO. "Hi, Miz Erikson. How are you?"

His sister and brother start giggling again, and he withers them with his violet glare. Or rather, he *tries* to wither them, but coming from a twelve-year-old it's about as intimidating as a puppy chewing on a sock. The giggling continues until I answer, "Good, thanks, um, Jens? Where's your folks?"

"They're still asleep," the other boy answers.

Shouldn't you be too, then? I want to ask. My facility with children is about the same as it is with kitchen or gardening tools—essentially nonexistent. I've been to dozens of planets and encountered all types of creatures and germs that make sleeping anywhere but inside a sealed room a bad idea, but children are by far the most alien.

"Look, we're heading out again on another scout run in a couple of days," Karl interjects. As their expressions begin to wilt, he goes on, "It's an exciting mission! We're rendezvousing with a mid-class transporter that's full of supplies and who knows what. If we find anything you'd like, I will definitely bring it back. Maybe we'll find some hover-skis or bikes."

"Hey kids," Vitruzzi breaks in. "We have a lot of planning to do, okay?"

"Okay, Dr. Vitruzzi," they chime in unison and take off at full throttle again, as if they'd never even slowed down.

Karl's eyes track them across the chow hall, a strangely bemused glint in them. When he looks back, he's serious again. "So what do you say, V? We could use you to pick out the necessities. I don't want to haul in a bunch of aspirin if there's something more important right there."

"No, that's not—"

"You should go. Get away for a while." Brady comes up behind us with his own tray, apparently overhearing the discussion.

"Patrick, I'm the only doctor this colony has," Vitruzzi protests, as he grabs the stool across from her and sits.

"Yeah, but you're also only human. You *need* to go. Karl is right, and you're killing yourself right now."

As if it's any less hazardous for her health to be flying through airspace that's infested with scavengers, and worse—the desperate. The rumors about what's happening in some of the more remote outposts, the lengths settlements have gone to for the sake of survival, get worse with every salvaging op we run. Some people who were only marginally civilized before the war have become outright animals, and pirates, slavers, and marauding raiders are now just part of daily life beyond KL. I don't mention this, though. Karl and Brady are both right. Vitruzzi *is* killing herself, and she's the best judge of the colony's medical needs.

She sighs, warring with her sense of duty and her sense of reality. She can't keep up the pace she's going, and if there's something else going on in her head, maybe a change of scenery will help her work it out. That's always been my best fix. And I'm completely well-adjusted.

She seems to decide and asks, "How much more cargo is there?"

"A lot more than we can take on one ship," Karl responds. "We'll probably need two. The Orika and the Nebula have the most capacity, but the *Teibo* is in the best condition. And there's this other thing we found—some kind of materials processor, but small. Pretty interesting. It may be worth hauling back and having Kittinger look over."

It hits me. "Materials," I blurt.

Brady stares at me curiously until I go on. "Like all those sealed-up chemicals that were in the haul you brought back yesterday," I tell Karl. "Maybe this thing you're talking about uses those."

"For what?" Karl asks.

I shrug, then Vitruzzi says, "I want Quantum with us."

"Why?" I ask, clamping down on a stronger protest lodged right behind my teeth. I guess you just never stop disliking someone who once kidnapped you. Unless they become your crew, that is.

"I don't want him near the soil compound."

"Look, V," I reason. "Let's just drop him off at Obal 6 like he's asking. You don't trust him, I don't like *or* trust him, and he doesn't want to be here."

"We've offered, Aly," Brady says and takes a swallow of his coffee. "But he doesn't want to go without 'assets,' as he puts it."

"Last time I looked, no one here signed a socialist charter," I respond. "Life's tough. He can either take the offer of a ride, or he can shut up, right?" If Karl were an eye roller, he'd be rolling them at me. When no one answers, I sigh. "Fine. Then I'd like Desto to come too."

"With Zeta pregnant? He's not going anywhere," Brady remarks.

"She's a good pilot; she can fly the *Teibo*. Besides, they've been wanting a honeymoon." My joke falls flat. Tough crowd.

Brady continues to argue. "She was a *commercial* pilot. Tactical flying is a different matter. I don't want to put anyone in harm's way, but especially not someone in her condition."

"Condition?" Vitruzzi asks. "Pat, she's pregnant, not dying of cancer. There's nothing stopping her from flying."

Awkward silence. Outside myself and Karl, I've never met two more stubborn people. Vitruzzi and Brady never fight, at least not that I've heard, but they *disagree* at a level that makes anyone in their orbit feel like they're being tractor beamed into a volcano.

Eventually, Karl says, "Aly, why don't we run it by them before I head out to the platform today. Thirty-six hours?" He raises an eyebrow at Vitruzzi, who nods. "Then I guess I don't need to unpack."

SIX

Spinning slowly in a vertical position, like a carousel with a dying engine, the Admin supply transporter seems to have been pinned to its section of empty space and left there to dry up and wither away. The name—PCA GALATEA—hovers into view for a moment before disappearing with the ship's next rotation. The funny thing about out here, though, is that a hundred, two hundred, even a thousand years from now, as long as nothing barrels into the derelict or knocks it out of its orbit, it will still look pretty much the same.

Our sensors pick up no trace of electrical or other energy fields, and just as David and Karl had said in the pre-mission briefing, there's no one on board answering our hails. It's just as dead in the air as it looks.

While Venus maneuvers us onto a wide, flat surface and engages the magnetic clingers, Karl, Vitruzzi, Hoogs, and I get suited up. Vitruzzi contacts the *Teibo* and directs Desto, David, and Mason to do the same and then join us on the derelict. We'll be able to scour the transport quickly with every able body available to help. That leaves Zeta, who hadn't needed to be asked twice to join the excursion, alone on the *'Bo* with Quantum. If he's wondering why Vitruzzi wanted him along, he hasn't said anything. I wonder how he likes being left out of the search, then realize he's probably more than happy not to be floating around in space aboard a ship that could be home to hundreds of potential hazards. Quantum is not a fool.

The rest of us on the other hand . . .

After we're all gathered and tethered together at the outer man-door that served as Karl and David's entrance on their pass a couple weeks back, V tells Zeta to hang back and keep the *'Bo* on low power with cloaks on until we've had some time to get a look inside the *Galatea*, and Venus keeps the *Orika* attached and waiting. Now we just have to hope that David and Karl's luck held on and no other salvagers have come through.

We drift in one by one, but my scavenger's sense is already telling me what I need to know, and I exchange a glance with Karl. The expression on his face says exactly what I'm thinking: nobody's home, or if they are, they gave up the habit of breathing long before we arrived.

No pressure, no gravity, no air, and no lights. We flip on the high-beam LEDs attached to our face shields, then split up to start a search. Karl and I head toward the lower deck, David and Vitruzzi take a right-hand corridor, and Hoogs, Desto, and Mason go left. Usually, the need to hurry in salvage jobs like this is paramount, but today is different. We have two ships and a lot of personal firepower, which should serve as a buffer to let us take our time going through every room. Vitruzzi's made clear that our main needs are medical supplies and, as always, weapons and food, but with the limited capacity for salvage and cargo aboard our two scout ships, we have no choice but to be selective. Still, an Admin supply ship this size out in Spectra territory is unusual; maybe we can find something on board that will explain why it was here. And just maybe it will be something we can use.

After about an hour, Hoogs contacts us. They've reached the engine room and found severe damage to the flight controls from an electrical fire. By all appearances, the original crew had managed to get the meltdown under control, but not before it had moved into the central grid for the life support systems. Since we've found no bodies or signs of a struggle, the working theory is that, once their systems went offline, they'd been forced to take their landing craft down to Eruo Pium, a moon orbiting Spectra 3, in search of parts and aid to get the ship back together. The theory is further supported when we find no landing craft in the hangar or cargo bay. We know they've already been gone for at least four weeks—between the time it took for David and Karl's scout team to return to KL after finding it and then turn around and come back—so whatever is keeping the original crew away may well be permanent. Bad for them; good for us.

There hasn't been a peep on board, and Vitruzzi lets everyone know she and David are heading toward the bridge, leaving Karl and me to go down the last corridor to where the crew quarters probably are.

"Bingo," I whisper after my first glance down the hallway. Three rooms labeled MEDICAL are lined up in a row. I know how excited this will make Vitruzzi.

I get Karl's attention and gesture toward the first. Inside, it appears that the room has never been touched. Aside from sundry items floating around, the wall cabinets are all closed and locked, and the equipment that's strapped to the ground is in pristine condition. If the other two infirmaries are this mint, we'll be able to gather enough med supplies to stock the settlement for at least six months. Maybe it'll help get Vitruzzi out of whatever funk she's in.

Karl hovers in behind me and shoots me a gleeful grin after getting a look around. "We're in business. Vitruzzi," he says into the com's open channel, "we hit pay dirt. Looks like the medical stations are all intact and still stocked." He puts a gloved hand on the arm of my suit and nods toward the doorway. "There could be more storage nearby where they keep the extra supplies, drugs, what have you. I'll get a look down the corridor and also see what I can find in the way of containers or boxes. Get to work on these cabinet locks until the rest get here to help."

I nod affirmatively and he pulls himself back outside, then lets the others know where we are while I start dismantling the first row of cabinets, hoping to find a healthy supply of antibiotics. Infections stemming from wounds are the primary problem back on KL and cause us to use up antibiotics faster than anything else.

Both scout teams arrive and we pick the place bleached-bone clean. While the antibiotic supply isn't as big as I'd hoped for, a major bonus comes in the form of a data-mesh that lists the contents of a bunch of unlabeled boxes we'd found in the cargo hold: a holographic surgical scanner that will assist Vitruzzi with diagnosing and potentially performing surgery on the more serious patients, as well as several more containers with lab-testing assays and equipment. The manifest doesn't list where any of this stuff was to be delivered, or why the ship was way out here near the Spectras, but with this excellent haul and the good it will do for the colony on KL, it hardly matters.

We direct all of the supplies to the main hangar and stage them with the cargo bins we want to take, along with the machine Karl spoke of—the matter printer, or whatever it is. Small containers can be pushed through the hull breach Karl and David's crew created last time, and someone on the outside will be able to walk them to the *Orika*. It's going to be a different matter to get the bigger containers out.

"If we can link them all together with a rope or a chain, we can secure them to a sturdy wall, then cut a larger opening through the main cargo hatch and the airlock to haul everything out," Karl suggests.

"If we destroy the airlock," Hoogs says, "this bird's never leaving orbit again."

No one says anything. While it may be true, the likelihood anyone will ever be around to try and fix it is, among other things, not our problem.

The comment goes unanswered, and Hoogs seems inclined to drop it. I'm standing next to him, the magnetic grippers of our boots making us and the rest of the boarding crew the only things touching the floor in the hangar. "Then just have the *Teibo* move into range, open the hull, and we can each grab a box and use our suit jump-thrusters to push us out through the airlock and into the *'Bo*."

The group agrees on it being the best idea and we relay the plan to Zeta. Vitruzzi and I start moving the smaller cargo to the *Orika* while the rest tether everything together in preparation. In another forty-five minutes, we're all ready for the *Teibo.*

"What the . . .?" Venus's incredulous query comes through our radio, followed by several seconds of silence. I'm about to decide she forgot she was broadcasting, when: "That's just not right!"

"Venus, what's your status?" Vitruzzi asks, her eyes fixed on the expanse of space outside the breach we created.

"Cap'n, I'd say we have at least one visitor. I'm reading another ship moving toward us."

"Zeta, are you picking anything up?" V asks.

"Yeah, oh yeah," she replies. "Sure am."

"No, dammit," Karl cries. "Not a chance! This boat's been out here for weeks. No way another ship randomly shows up now."

"How long until they arrive, can you tell?" Vitruzzi asks.

"Soon," both pilots respond simultaneously.

Karl and I exchange a glance. "V," he says, "maybe Venus should unlink. She's a sitting duck if they're hostile."

Vitruzzi nods and passes on the order.

"Guys, what about you?" Venus asks. "What happens if they board?"

"I think we'll be able to handle them," Vitruzzi answers. "You two need to put some distance between this boat and yourselves—right now. Keep eyes on and transceiver links up. If you don't hear anything, come back in two hours and do a sweep. Most importantly, keep yourselves clear of engagement. The colony can't afford to lose you or those scouts."

She turns to the rest of us. "The only people with rights to this salvage are the people who own the ship. If it's them, and they can prove it, we'll leave in peace. Otherwise . . ." The statement hangs, but we all know what it means.

I quickly unharness the T-Max laser I carry for outer-atmosphere jobs, everyone else copying the action with their own choice of firearm. We could open a black-market dealership with the range of weapons among this crew. "We don't want to give away our numbers," I remark. "Looks like good vantages from along that wall, up there on the catwalk, and . . ." I gesture at several potential cover positions.

"I'll stay put. Talk to them," Vitruzzi says.

"V, do you want—?" David starts.

"Yes," she answers before he can finish.

"Okay"—he nods—"we'll cover you."

The crew moves out to wait. Karl and I take the uppermost story, while Hoogs, a stringy marvel with chameleonlike powers, finds an out-of-sight niche to occupy on the main deck, and David digs in near the hull's primary hatch. Desto and Mason stand beside Vitruzzi. It's most likely whoever is out there will see our hatch demolition on their own scout pass. They won't see our ships, so they won't expect anyone else to be on board, which gives them every reason to take advantage of the invitation of an already open door. It's possible that they could even decide to go on by once they've seen another salvage crew has already come through. But if they don't, and they enter through some other means, we'll have plenty of time to regroup and confront them from new positions.

Twenty minutes later we hear them make contact. Judging by the lack of possible landing zones we'd observed on our own pass, they've chosen the same spot to cling on that Venus had. Time seems to pass at the rate of ice freezing in hell before the first three come through the opening. My weapon's sight locks on the instant the leading helmeted head becomes visible.

They immediately see Vitruzzi and company holding weapons at the ready. The visiting trio pause, taking in the rest of the bay, then wisely show their empty hands. Vitruzzi gestures for them to approach. There's no mistaking their disgust at getting to the ship too late to claim the salvage—not to mention having guns pointed at them.

When they're closer to Vitruzzi, she signals to them to turn on their coms, then says, "Sorry to say it isn't your lucky day, folks. This ship is ours."

The one in the middle tries to negotiate. "We've come a long way, lady. Any chance we could split some of the take?"

And there we have it. Admission that this isn't their ship to begin with. All that's left is a peaceful resolution to the situation—or whatever kind of resolution they'll take—and Vitruzzi can send them on their way.

A subtle flicker in my peripheral vision distracts me from their conversation, and I look around in time to catch another stranger coming through the upper bay hatchway. He doesn't see me nestled between hull reinforcement struts and moves to a flanking position near the rail, drawing a weapon of his own.

Dumbass.

He's just a kid, about twentyish. Old enough to be brave but not old enough to be smart. I don't want to kill someone who really doesn't have to be, so I give him a chance. Sneaking up and placing my gun barrel on the back of his helmet—where I apply just the right amount of pressure to grab his undivided attention—I lean near enough for him to hear me through the helmet and say, "That's a very clever idea. Exactly what I would do, in fact—find the high ground and get the drop on us."

I can see Karl across the bay with his hand in the air, asking for a status update. I raise a gloved thumb, then take a step around the kid so that he can see my face. But I don't lighten the pressure of the barrel against his head. "Now ask yourself this question. Are you ready to be remembered as a clever *dead* guy that *used* to be on their crew?"

I see the shock in his face, but he doesn't stall when putting his weapon out in front of him and releasing it. It floats there, unconcerned with the reasons why it's become suddenly weightless. I take a swipe and gently nudge it behind us and out of reach. "We're just going to stand by until they figure it out, roger?"

He nods. Not so dumb after all.

"So you just want the cargo? We get anything else on the ship?" one of the guys below is saying.

"That's right," Vitruzzi answers.

The three of them appear to confer while taking not-quite-surreptitious glances at the upper walkway. I pull my new friend to his feet and we wave down at them. "Deal," says the first, finally convinced to see things our way.

They regroup and start scouring the rest of the derelict while we linger in the hold, waiting for the *Orika* and *Teibo*. My O2 meter has dropped uncomfortably close to red by the time they arrive and we've filled them in on what had gone down. The other salvaging crew doesn't bother us, and we make quick work out of getting the cargo lines set up and the equipment moved aboard the *'Bo*.

Vitruzzi and I are still in the hold, just getting ready to jump out with the last large cargo bin. She's untying the line from the deck as I prepare to hail Karl to get ready for us when my feet suddenly begin to feel funny. Not funny exactly, more as if they're vibrating. As if, in fact, the derelict's engines are being cycled for flight. The other salvagers can't be trying to initiate flight operations. Can they?

SEVEN

I turn to Vitruzzi in alarm, about to warn her that we need to get out of here posthaste, but the next second I'm lifted to the top of the bay, shot from the floor like a cannonball. Vitruzzi gets pushed up against the ceiling next to me, and the cargo tether, bin still attached, zings out of the hold like a harpoon. There's a rumbling explosion from the direction of the engines, and I realize, somehow, *impossibly*, the ship is moving.

Frantically, I yell, "What the hell, V? Are we diving? Don't they realize this boat has no flight controls? Or airlock?"

Realize it or not, the fact of the matter is that we've been blown out of stasis. What had I said about them not being dumb? Scratch that. I don't know which direction we're going, but I do know we have to get off this beast before it disintegrates. The foredeck beyond the cargo bay had evac pods, and I grab Vitruzzi's suit, pointing in that direction.

"Come on! We'll be able to set up a transponder when we're outside so the crew can find us." If we're lucky.

At least one engine is online, but the ship's not moving too fast for us to pull ourselves through to the foredeck. The evac pods are two-seaters, and Vitruzzi and I shove ourselves into one. It's like putting sausage into a sausage casing, our bulky suits making the fit, already claustrophobic, worse than my worst nightmare shoved inside a coffin. But there's no other choice.

We're fumbling with the safety harnesses like idiot orangutans when the ship is suddenly hit by what feels like a planet. The hull absorbs most of the impact, and the e-pod's close confines protect us, but the jolt isn't what I'd call pleasant.

"Shit," V says. "We just broke through atmosphere."

We're on a one-way trip to Eruo Pium—not my first choice for an impromptu vacation—with maybe four minutes until impact. Her harness is latched and she reaches over to slam mine closed, then pulls the manual lever that releases us from the ship's belly, gambling that there's still enough time to escape before gravity smears us over the moon's face.

The velocity of our launch is instant and brutal. I feel as if I've swallowed my teeth, and the pressure on my chest makes breathing impossible until the pod's auxiliary pressure stabilizes. Slowly, the speed reduces to within the range of what human bodies can tolerate, and the light outside our pod window port grows brighter.

I'm just about to relax and start pondering what our next step is going to be when something slams into us, jarring both Vitruzzi and me hard enough to make my jaw clack, and knocking us into a new trajectory. A few red lights blink on the small control console, letting us know that things are going—or have already gone—awry. The only thing left to do is hang on and hope the speed dampeners still work.

A minute later another jolt pulls our descent up short, then we're drifting. The e-pod's base thunks to earth, and we slowly tilt over. My stomach lurches as my last meal threatens to evacuate. Then it relaxes, letting me off with a warning.

The impact is far less jarring than I'd expected. For just a second, we both remain motionless, taking in the newfound stillness and silence, the contrast almost unbelievable after the chaos of the last . . . Jesus, has it only been ten minutes?

Yanking my helmet off, I take a greedy gulp of air. At the moment,

I don't feel much pain, but I know that's going to change later. The torque on the emergency pod and our helplessly suspended bodies, caused by whatever had hit us just after crashing into Eruo Pium's atmosphere, hammered my muscles and joints hard, but it hadn't killed us. That's something at least. Still, the minute I have a chance to do a full assessment, I have no doubt I'm going to be sorer than I care to imagine. I might even cry.

"Aly, we're down. Can you move?"

"That sucked," I groan.

"Are you hurt?"

"No, don't think so. You?"

"I'm all right."

She tries getting the coms up and running to see if either of our shuttles is near while I crank at the harness to get it off. They'll know we went down, but the likelihood they'll be within com range is narrower than my firing group. As for the other salvagers, they may be down here somewhere too, but there's no telling. If I remember my Corps training well enough, the type of bug-out we'd just had could sometimes result in as much as a 50 percent casualty rate. V and I made it, so the math isn't in their favor.

She curses and gives up on the com when the control console's last light goes dark. "Dammit. Come on, let's get out of here."

My gloved fingers fumble clumsily at the harness lock, but depressing the release button results in stubborn resistance. It feels jammed, probably from playing bumper ships. As I struggle with the straps, the feeling of being buried alive starts to settle over me like so much stale grave dirt. My throat begins to close up and my hands tug frantically, not doing any good, but there's no stopping them. I can't handle small spaces, and the present small space is getting more stifling by the second thanks to this goddamn harness.

"Hey, hey, Aly, calm down. Let me help." Vitruzzi reaches for the buckle over my chest and deftly cuts me free with the blade she keeps in the space suit. The straps holding me in loosen, but it barely helps. We're inside what amounts to a bullet casing for humans. The only way I'll ever be okay in a capsule this small is when they put me in my burn box for cremation. Even that thought makes cold sweat ooze from my armpits.

"Open the hatch, V," I whisper through a throat that feels stuffed with sand. "I gotta get out of here *now*."

She unbuckles and searches for the hatch handle. We were lucky; the pod fell over with the hatch faceup to the sky. Vitruzzi pulls on the release and nothing happens. She yanks harder, then resorts to kicking at the base of it, trying to jar it free. Whatever had struck us must have jammed the release mechanism; the thought makes the muscles in my jaw clench painfully. Did we survive the destruction of the cruiser just to die trapped inside this metal coffin?

Need to get out, need to escape before it's too late. Need some air. Need—

My focus starts to collapse into tiny pinpoints of light as the volume of panic inside my head goes up another few decibels. Without thinking, I reach for the T-Max I'd tucked between my knees and point it at the release mechanism, ready to shoot my way free if that's what it's going to take.

Before I pull the trigger, Vitruzzi shouts, "No!" and yanks it from my grip. "The frame's buckled. If you do that, you're just going to waste your charge. Take a deep breath and let me think, Aly."

Easy for her to say. *I need some—Calm down, Aly—I need some air —Just cool it, okay. You're going to be okay—NO! I need some fucking air!* This mantra continues, my brains heating to a boil, about to spill over.

Putting one knee into the seat, Vitruzzi turns around and gets into a half-standing, half-squatting position in order to reach into the containment bin overhead. *Need some air—Chill out.* While I tightly grip the material of my pants just above my kneepads and think about breathing in, breathing out, she searches inside. *Hurry up, V. Hurry up. HurryuphurryuphurryUP!*

"Got it," she says, then gets back into her seat. "Put your oxygen back on. I'm going to burn through the hatch."

"What?" I'm barely holding myself together and she wants me to put something even more constricting over my face?

"You have to. The fumes will make you sick. Here . . ." She reaches over to help me with the helmet, and I grip her wrist.

"No. I'll . . . I'll do it. Just be quick."

There must have been a toolkit or emergency prep box in the bin because she has about two fistfuls of E-10 wax that she quickly rolls into long strips and sticks to the shell in a circle big enough for us to crawl through. While I stare at the circle of wax hard enough to ignite it with pure freak-out urgency, she pulls her own helmet on and shocks the wax with the igniter. As it eats through the layers of metal, insulation, and thermal tiling, acrid blue smoke fills the cabin, and my heartbeat finally starts to slow. Surviving spacecraft explosions, firefights, atmospheric reentry in a tin can, and near-fatal midair collisions are all child's play compared to being turned into a human sardine. I keep telling myself it's all in my head. It doesn't help, but when daylight starts to shine through the circumference of Vitruzzi's homemade hatch, my throat begins to loosen up and let more oxygen actually reach my brain. *Sweet Jesus, air!*

Before the burn-through stops, she pushes herself almost into my lap—the hatch is on her side—and kicks the disconnected metal outwards. It gives after three good punts, and I have to stop myself from wrestling her to get outside first.

Where apparently the fun is just beginning.

We've barely put our feet on the ground when dirt kicks up in an abrupt flurry just a couple of meters away. At first, I think I must be suffering from aftereffects of the claustrophobia, but then more dirt swirls into the air and I don't need a lessons-from-the-war manual to know what it is. We're being shot at.

We both dive down beside the pod, but I catch a quick glimpse of who's firing. An open-topped hover-runner is about fifty meters away, closing the gap between us at its top speed. My brain does an automatic calculation, and I take a knee and bring my T-Max up for a shot in one fluid motion. I'd seen two people in the cab, a man driving and a woman standing up and firing at us from above the front dust shield. My first shot hits home, and she flies backward into the HR's cargo area.

My second shot goes into the vehicle's body. It apparently takes out the steering electronics board because the thing keeps moving at top speed—right over the top of us. Just before I duck, I see the driver working frantically to get the vehicle turned, but it doesn't happen. The base of it clips the pod's shell and the whole thing first gains a couple more meters of lift, then tilts over sideways. Its magnetic power mechanism blows and the HR crashes down just past us.

Vitruzzi closes on the driver and puts a bullet between his eyes before he has a chance to apologize.

And I thought the Admin was hostile.

I walk up to the HR and look inside. Both occupants are dead, their blood splattered about the cab. The woman looks to be in her early to mid-forties and the driver just a touch more. Neither wears any kind of uniform, and they're both emaciated, so it's probable they're just settlers or scavengers; the system is full of them now. Without a second thought, I strip them of their weapons. The woman had a carbine AK-80 like mine, which I lament is still on the *'Bo*. The activator that limits its users to only soldiers is disabled, shedding a ray of light on an otherwise gloomy situation. The man had only a laser-firing sidearm, which is out of charge and useless.

Stepping away from the disabled vehicle, I comment, "What a mess. Let's get the transponder up. I'll stand watch if you want to work on it."

She doesn't say anything, and I turn to see if she'd heard me. She's kneeling by the dead man, staring into his face intensely.

"V?" I try again. "We need to let them know where we are. There's no telling how long it will take them to find us, and there could be more scavs around."

I catch a sound and jerk my head up to scan the area. We're in a relatively flat plain, most of the ground around us dry but covered in a stunted, crackly grass. The landscape rises into a line of foothills about a kilometer to the north, and with the dampness in the air, I'm betting Eruo Pium's ocean lies on the other side. Sparse signs of people are evident, mostly just crisscrossing vehicle tracks that extend east–west. These, and the way the hover-runner had arrived so quickly, tell me that we must be close to some sort of outpost or settlement. Another glance at the dead couple is all it takes to hammer a nail of dread deep in my gut.

Then I see the source of the sound; a track vehicle lumbers toward us from the northeast. They can't go faster than a few kilometers per hour, but they're coming from the same direction as the HR. They'll be here within a couple of minutes. There's nowhere within a reachable distance for us to run, and our only cover is the pod and the overturned HR. Track vehicles usually have thick steel bodies and are very, very hard to penetrate with regular arms. Dammit, I did not plan to spend my day in multiple firefights. I should never have left Keum Libre.

"More company. Get ready," I tell Vitruzzi as I crouch with her behind the HR and dig in to wait. The newly acquired carbine has an almost full energy clip, so I should have enough rounds between it and my T-Max to keep the tracker crew occupied. For a while.

The tracker grows noisier, then suddenly quieter as the engine cuts to an idle. I look around the rear of the HR and see the passenger door of the cab swing open.

"You all okay?" a man shouts from the opened door. "We saw you coming down. Anyone hurt?"

So their angle is to check us out and see if we need help. I'm touched. I nudge Vitruzzi's shoulder—she still hasn't said anything—to indicate she should follow my lead, and keep my eye on the tracker. If we stay quiet, we should be able to draw at least one of them out and reduce their numbers.

"We have a medkit if you need it. Don't be afraid. Our settlement's just a little way from here. Food, water, aid, whatever you need. Hello?"

No one climbs out of the tracker, so I try to entice them. "My friend's injured. Looks like a broken ankle. Do you have a splint?"

"Yeah. Yeah! We have that. Come on over and I'll get it for you."

"No. I can't leave her here; please bring it."

No one moves or says anything. Then, to my utter surprise, a man jumps down from the cab and starts walking toward us with a splint in one hand. I don't see any weapons on him. Despite the tracker and the med supplies, the man looks like he could recently have been napping in a pile of dirt. He's filthy and ragged and as thin as the other two we'd shot.

He stops about five meters away and says, "Here," while holding the splint out.

Before I realize what's happening, Vitruzzi stands and moves past me toward him. She holds her pistol limply in one hand, and she's walking as if she's about to shake hands with the man. Has she lost her mind?

I jump forward and grab her by the shoulder, intending to pull her back behind cover. As soon as we're both in the open, someone else in the tracker opens up with a rifle, the shots low and aimed at our legs. Fortunately, the man approaching us ruins their field of fire and they miss, but I shove Vitruzzi as hard as I can back behind the HR and dive for the cover of the e-pod with the rest of my momentum. Hitting the rocky soil with my knees—and sending a silent thanks to the god of combat for my kneepads—I get into a good firing position in anticipation of V hammering them with cover fire from her own T-Max. I wait. And nothing.

Risking a quick look over the pod, I see her still crouched behind the overturned hover-runner. She's dropped the pistol beside her in the dirt and is hugging her knees like a child that's seen something scary in the dark. I don't see any blood or wounds anywhere.

Mystified, I shout, "V, you okay?"

I take the opportunity to get a couple more rounds at the tracker, which do no good, but she still doesn't respond. Dammit! She's freezing on me. I've seen it before, but she's the last human on the planet I would have expected it from. From here, I can't try and shock her to her senses. All I can do is yell at her and hope for the best.

"Vitruzzi! Pick up that pistol and cover me. I'm coming to you. Do you hear me?"

No. Goddamn. Response.

Pushing my back into the pod, I take a second to analyze the situation. Options, options. There are always at least two, but a lot of the time one of them is dying. The tracker crew isn't doing any firing. Just waiting us out. They know we have nowhere to run, and they'll have a clear shot if and when we break cover again. So *that's* not an option.

There was a time when I never left my rack without explosives. What happened to the good old days? As I look around, all I have at my disposal are rocks, sand, dead-looking grass, and broken shards of atmo-shield from the pod. Nothing that goes boom.

Another quick peek shows V hasn't moved. A round flies uncomfortably close to me, but I have enough time to see she's adopted the look that every person in the system knows at this point after the war: the thousand-yard stare. The only thing she's seeing right now are the horrors inside her own mind, both the real ones she's witnessed and the ones she's imagining on her own. Fuck. It's worse than I expected. And from Vitruzzi, one of the most level-headed and stalwart women I know. My day just went from bad to absolutely drowning in used toilet water.

Except . . . maybe there's some fuel left in the pod's tank. It uses combustible fluid in its reverse thrusters for slowing down when it gets near earth. Vitruzzi and I hadn't used up all the supplemental oxygen either. I might, just might, have what I need for an old-fashioned package of fuck-you. If the hull is as damaged as it looks, there's a chance I can get the O2 tank off and roll it under the tracker.

The one piece of luck I have is the fact that the pod's hatch is on my side. Pulling out my bolo, I lean inside and start attacking the upholstery of the seats. Soon nothing's left but the frame. It's fused to the steel cabinet that houses the O2 tank, but that's okay. The small toolkit from the overhead bin gives up its screwdriver, and I'm able to disassemble the interior of the seat enough to get to the steel cabinet's door.

It's been quiet for too long, and I pop out of the pod to see what might be sneaking up on me. Vitruzzi—same. Tracker—still quiet. Diving back in, I'm inside the cabinet in seconds, but discover that the pressurized O2 tank is bigger than the cabinet's opening. It's made to be refilled but not removed. Goddammit!

"Aly."

I jump back out and the sweat pours off my forehead, momentarily blinding me. "Aly," Vitruzzi says again, and to my relief, when I blink the sweat away, I see her looking at me. But the expression on her face is about as close to panic as I've ever seen. "It's over."

"No, we'll make it, V." Trying to make the most of her lucidity—who can guess how long it'll last?—I prompt, "Look inside the hover-runner. Is there anything in there like a grenade? Something we can toss at those cocksuckers?"

She stares at me like I'm from another planet for a minute, then turns her head to look inside the damaged vehicle.

"Give it up, ladies! You come out, we promise you won't get hurt."

Fantastic. We've arrived at the deal-brokering stage. I take a short second of pleasure knowing that their *not* knowing what we're up to is making them more edgy than we are. That second ends quickly, though, because I also know they'll get sick of waiting soon. That tracker could start up any minute and roll right over us.

"V! You have to hurry. Is there anything in there?"

She doesn't answer and appears to be going catatonic again, so I give up thinking and just start doing whatever my instincts suggest. After I crank the refuel cap and interior valve off the side of the pod with my screwdriver, my nostrils are hit by the tank's heavy, oily fumes in a nauseating wave. Next, I yank my utility vest off, followed by my jacket, and finally my shirt, tying the latter around the end of one of the internal support bars from the seat and shoving it down into the fuel tank. It comes back out dripping thick amber gel, which I light up with my portable torch. Black smoke immediately fills the air, the lack of a breeze making it hang around me in a gag-inducing cloud. Not that it matters. Hucking a nearby rock over the top of the pod and squeezing off a pair of rounds as a diversion, I take a quick—possibly final—breath and stand up with my flaming torch.

One solid swing of the carbine launches the blazing shirt onto the tracker's window screen. It hits with a satisfying splat that shoots burning fingers of flame across the screen and down the front. The fuel gel isn't going to burn itself out soon. With my momentary advantage, I streak to the hover-runner. Vitruzzi gives me a look so dark and full of despair that I can hardly believe she's the same woman. What happened? What sent her over the edge?

Not that I have time for worrying about it now. Yanking my jacket back on, I can see from my original vantage point that the guy who'd come out has retreated back into the cab. Time is short; they're not going to wait much longer. Scrambling through the meager entrails of the hover-runner and the former occupants' clothes gets me nowhere. Turns out that's okay, though. Before I have time to get more than averagely frustrated, another voice comes from the tracker.

"Friend of yours?"

People always describe it as a sinking feeling in your guts when you realize you're totally screwed, but right now, what I'm experiencing feels much more like a gas ball of rage exploding in my guts.

"Say something, scav!" This is followed by the sound of someone grunting in pain.

Then a new voice says, "Are you survivors from the *Galatea*?"

Goddammit. It's that kid I'd let go. The one who didn't want to be a clever dead guy.

"We have more of your buddies in the back of the tracker," says the tracker guy. "If you don't come out, you'll get to listen to them die."

Buddies? That isn't exactly the word I'd use to describe the other salvage crew. But . . . still, they could have survived. Or the scavenger could be lying. It could just be the one kid. I'd let him go once; is it my fault he wasn't capable of making it on his own?

But that's not me, not anymore. I can't let them die for us.

Leaving the carbine and T-Max in the dirt, I grip Vitruzzi's shoulder once again and pull her up beside me, our hands holding up the sky.

EIGHT

Of the approximately fifteen thousand soldiers originally occupying the PCA *Celestial*, more than half are foot soldiers —the ones with boots on the ground. And that's all it takes, combined with the might of a fleet cruiser and all of the ordnance and weaponry at its disposal, to take control of a moon or a planet with a population of more than a hundred times this. Corps training, Corps strategies, but most of all, Corps resources, are that good.

But we're down to about ten thousand now, after Medina's command early in the war to "restructure" the Admin-loyal troop faction. I'll say this about Medina, she's thorough. Her effectiveness scores as a fleet commander must have been among the highest in the prewar Corps. I still have a hard time believing she was central to the anti-Admin pockets of resistance ever getting off the ground and organizing. Someone this good at being a soldier is rarely anything but.

Still, she's clearly as shrewd and politically competent as any Admin Director. It took more than polished lockstepping and persuasive order-barking to become the commander of one of the Corps's twenty-five fleet cruisers. In her position, she'd have been a regular attendee of Capital Strategic Planning Summits, and would have had the ear of most of the leading Ministry advisors. Which is how she had everything she needed to raze their entire bastion to the ground.

I'm on the bridge rotation of my navigation team when Medina enters, ready for her new shift SITREP. I should be on the R&R we'd been offered, but the one constant truth about being ship-side for R&R is that boredom is a hundred times more insidious and soul crushing than nearly any human enemy. For that reason, I'd reentered my name on the duty logs. It's better to be on flight-deck duty than sitting around waiting to get called into battle or hanging back when a company returns from combat and watching them pick the grit out of their skin.

We've remained in orbit around Broon, one of Spectra 6's satellite moons, for the last forty or so hours, hiding on the moon's dark side with all the *Celestial*'s cloaking systems running to keep the settlement and incoming and outgoing ships we're surveilling from knowing we're here. Another reason I've kept myself busy is because we're just a few hours' flight time from our old home, Agate Beach. The knowledge that we're so close to what was the only place I had ever truly felt was home tugs at me, making me restless and more than a little dismal. I know I'm not the only one. Karl and Vitruzzi have had hair-trigger tempers since we got here. It must be so much worse for them. Agate Beach was their settlement, their life, for several years, before it was all ripped away. Ultimately, the Admin's decision to arrest the Beachers and make us all outlaws had resulted in this war—though, knowing what I now know about the organized resistance Medina, Quantum, and many others had been planning since the Soldier's Rebellion, it's clear the war was coming no matter what. Destroying Agate Beach was the ignition, but the fires had already been set to burn.

But I try not to think about it—Rob Cross's betrayal, Rajcik's mad mission to destroy the Admin, Bodie's death. None of it can be changed now. If there's a future, we have to target it, because there's nothing left in the past worth holding on to now.

Lieutenant Steward salutes Medina out of habit, then prepares to brief her on the last six hours that have passed since her off-duty rotation.

"Commander, they don't appear to be any stronger than we initially assessed from our drone passes. Heat signatures and visuals suggest no more than three thousand bodies, and our mission analysts report an estimate of about eighty percent active combatants."

"What do we know about their fighting force resources and equipment pool?"

"We cross-checked the data from both our drones and scouts and calculate their air forces to consist of only three active armed craft, forty unarmed craft, and fifty to sixty land craft. They have no detectable surface-to-air or surface-to-orbit weapons. The analysts predict the usual number of personal weapons."

"No, they wouldn't have surface-to-air ordnances. This is a makeshift settlement. Probably an outpost they erected hastily to refit damaged ships," Medina says.

"That could be the case, Commander," Steward agrees. "We've noted a number of troop transports, mostly former Corps but a few civilian, coming into and out of the settlement. Their behavior indicates supply transfer, but we haven't been able to get close enough to get a solid fix on what they're doing."

"How much time is elapsing between takeoffs and landings?"

"Minimal. Between twenty minutes and an hour. A few remain overnight, but none have stayed for more than a day or two."

"That kind of quick turnaround isn't the behavior of damaged ships coming in for fixes," Vitruzzi cuts in. "It's possible they've set up a casualty collection point. They may be bringing wounded in for treatment."

Vitruzzi showing up on the bridge out of nowhere is nothing new. Since the war started, she's made it a point to be involved in most of the major operations' planning, in one way or another. I haven't missed that her visits usually coincide closely with Medina's debriefings—particularly if any heavy actions have been predicted. Vitruzzi's lack of trust in the war commander may not be explicit, but it's definitely implied. So much so that tension between the two has become a topic of discussion among all of us who've crewed with Vitruzzi since Agate Beach.

Medina cuts her eyes in Vitruzzi's direction, then turns to face her. "You have a good point, Doctor. Steward"—she turns back to her LT—"is that population count steady, or does it fluctuate?"

Steward spends a few seconds manipulating information from his console, then pulls up a series of graphs on the holoreader. The three of them look it over for a few seconds before Steward speaks. "This output plots the ship traffic patterns," he says, pointing, "and this one, the population approximations based on different calculation variables. The pop counts lag behind by about thirty hours. We don't have enough intel readers in the area to keep a steady flow of data, so we recalculate new baselines every six hours, then build a new population count data set from that, which accounts for the three-hour lapse. Numbers show a slight rise when new ships arrive, and intermittent larger drops, but without being able to do an actual person-by-person head count, we can't tell who's coming or going."

"So the information here is three hours old?" Vitruzzi asks.

Steward hesitates before responding, and his eyes remain on Medina until the CO nods slightly. "That is correct."

Vitruzzi says nothing, studying the graphs. From where I'm sitting in the navigator's bench, I have to turn away from my controls halfway to watch them. Medina's gray eyes land on mine, holding them, knowing that I'm eavesdropping. "Anything else, Lieutenant?" she asks, still staring at me.

Steward continues, "No, Comm—"

"Have you sent any scouts to follow the outbound ships?" Vitruzzi interrupts.

"Our primary objective has been to surveil this post. We don't have the resources to send long-distance scouts," Steward responds.

"So you're saying you don't know who's down there, what they're doing, where they're coming from, or where they're going."

Steward's carefully controlled neutral expression cracks for a moment, but his silence is the answer Vitruzzi expected. She addresses Medina, "Commander, it doesn't appear to me that we're doing any good by sitting up here making wild guesses. They could be doing anything down there. I think we need to put someone on the ground to take a closer look before we decide on any action."

Ever calm, Medina's eyes remain steady and clear as she nods her head. If she resents Vitruzzi's unsolicited advising, she doesn't let on. "I agree. Lieutenant, muster a force of thirty bodies, armed, and six battle-ready troop transports."

"Medina, I think you misunderstood me," Vitruzzi says. "Going in there hot isn't what I had in mind. If we want intel, we can certainly get that without inviting—or instigating—a firefight."

"As always, I appreciate your feedback, Doctor. I'm sure we can avoid bloodshed if this colony is nonthreatening. As you said, we need to get closer first to assess that."

"Of course, but we can get close enough with one ship and a crew disguised as refugees or freelancers. We can see they're mostly nonmilitary from the intel Steward has. There's no point in—"

"Vitruzzi, this is my call. And it's been made." Medina's voice is like a steel trap that's been sprung. There's no arguing. "Since you're here, would you like to update me on our overall medical and casualty status for the day? If you need to get back to the med-deck, I understand. I can make my rounds down there per usual later. So . . .?" Medina lets the question hang, very much done discussing anything to do with Broon with Vitruzzi present.

NINE

The crash of the *Galatea* is like the old-Earth fairy tale of manna from heaven for these scavengers, but cleaning up after it seems to be just another day on the job for them. Two other survivors from the salvage crew and a handful of other people—settlers maybe —had been brought back to their camp on the track vehicle and locked inside this crudely built shack V and I now inhabit, the pieces comprising it scavenged from a hundred different derelicts and other debris. Despite its haphazard-looking construction, the walls are strong and unyielding to our efforts at breaking out.

When I say *manna from heaven*, it isn't irony. This group looks like they've been here awhile, probably from the early days of the war, and in a camp this far from any food sources it's obvious from the start that they're willing to eat whatever falls into their laps. I've heard about gangs of people going this far over the edge. I would have been more than happy to never witness it firsthand.

After a short trip in the tracker, I'd spotted at least two more shacks like ours when we arrived just under an hour ago, and that unmistakable stench of burned bodies clings to the camp like mustard gas in a trench. Most of the shack's occupants, like Vitruzzi and me, are basically uninjured, but everyone isn't so lucky. A woman with one side of her head badly swollen has been in and out of consciousness since we were rounded up.

All the captives have been tossed together and I scan the filthy room, trying to assess who may be the best assets in case an opportunity for escape appears.

"Hey, kid," I whisper to the survivor from the other salvaging crew who'd boarded the *Galatea*, "mind telling me what the hell your crew was thinking when they cycled up that derelict's engines? Because, I don't know about you, but I would have preferred dying of old age to being made mincemeat by a bunch of half-lunatic cannibals."

He looks up at me from where he sits with his chin on his knees across the shack. The dirt covering his face and the wide-eyed, almost guileless, expression on his face make him really look like a kid barely old enough to join the Academy. For someone like me, adapting to a war wasn't that hard—I've always been a soldier of one kind or another. But his life now must be one-eighty from what it had been two years ago. I'm too busy figuring out how we're going to survive this to spare much sympathy at the moment.

"Hurley, my boss, wanted to know if it had enough power to bother trying to salvage it," he finally says after giving the question time to sink through his undeniable shock. "We couldn't get the feed-back gauges to work, so he thought he could force output from the engines, which should have back-fed their specs to the flight deck." He pauses. "I guess he got his wires crossed . . . or maybe the ship's systems weren't working right."

"You think? Maybe you should have assessed the damage before . . ." I stop myself. This kid isn't the reason I'm pissed. He's just a convenient scapegoat for my frustrations. "Anyway, did either of the other crew with you make it?"

"I don't know," he says simply.

"You two want to cut the chitchat?" another one of the captives says. "We don't want to draw attention."

I turn my head to glare at the speaker, the shed's dim interior light vaguely illuminating a medium-sized man with blond hair and thick limbs resting against the wall farthest from the door. He doesn't hold my eyes.

"Kid." I get his attention again after a second. "Want to help me with something?"

Luckily, he's still aware enough that I'm able to recruit him to help me find structural weaknesses in the shack, at least somewhere we can punch out an opening to try getting some fresh air and hopefully a visual of what awaits us on the outside. Keeping busy helps me do two things: take my mind off the small, crowded space, and hold off the muscle soreness the crash caused that lies in ambush just at the edge of my nerves.

The *Teibo* and *Orika* crews know we went down; there's no doubt of that. But the low chance of them being able to locate us easily doesn't leave me with much hope. Even if we weren't in hot water at the moment, Eruo Pium is a reasonably big moon, and our e-pod's trajectory lost some of its predictability thanks to whatever we'd hit that knocked us out of our dive. V and I are going to have to get out of this mess on our own.

The sound of metal sliding against metal freezes me from trying to work free the edge of one of the thinner steel sheets welded to the wall, then a shaft of light comes through the doorway at head height.

"Everyone back up." The short barrel of a carbine appears in the peephole to help us make the right decision. Almost everyone moves toward the rear wall, but the two men with Blondie linger near the door, planning to attack anyone who opens it.

"I see nine bodies and I know there's eleven in there." The small space erupts with the carom of a shot being fired, and one of the prisoners at the back falls to his knees, grasping his shoulder. The rest of us hit the deck in a panicked knot of limbs.

"Get over here!" someone cries, and the two hiding out of the peephole's sight back into the throng carefully.

"Good." The door is pulled open. A group of three, all armed, stand outside with their weapons pointed. One of them enters and trains his rifle barrel at me where I half squat against the wall. "Come."

Why me? Do I just have a face that begs to be interrogated? I certainly can't look that appetizing, having barely more meat on my bones than the locals. Vitruzzi and I exchange a glance, her eyes looking dead, and I step outside.

They walk me to a gazebolike structure, the journey enough to let me take a good, long look around the camp. In truth, it's more of a semisquare compound, about two hundred meters end to end. With the exception of the prisoner confines—only three total—most of the structures are barely standing, and the ones constructed out of primarily steel components are badly rusted, making the place a tetanus incubation hot spot. However, they've used this to their advantage and built a shambling, shoulder-high barricade around the area that's clogged with spikes and sharp corners. Getting out could be just as hard as getting in.

We pass by a lander discarded against the barrier, displaying the same eight-digit ship ID as the *Galatea* derelict. The hull is battered with small-arms fire, and it looks like one of the engines flared out, incapacitating it. I guess now I know why the transporter's crew didn't make it back.

One of the scavs notices me looking around and backhands me across the mouth. The skin of my top lip splits and bleeds, then I'm pushed onto a stool and surrounded by gun-toting savages on three sides.

The biggest of the three stands in front of me, looking me over. His face and the backs of his hands poking out of his ragged sleeves are badly scarred, an obvious indication of having once been, but most likely no longer, a sun-head. Given the lack of civilization on this planet, I doubt there's much of the drug to be found anymore. The real surprise is he'd survived the detox.

He asks, "Who are you?"

"Your fairy godmother."

This is followed by a protracted silence that allows me enough time to think up a brief will and testament, then he begins to laugh in short, choppy grunts that quickly prove whatever mind he has left is missing a few important bits. Just as quickly, he stops, and says seriously, "You must be Corps."

I give him a short, disgusted chuckle. "Don't you get it? There is no Corps anymore."

Since the end of the major fighting, the Spectras have been left to themselves, and what's happening right now is the reason why. Anyone who lands in a Corps ship or wearing Corps uniforms is attacked. The Spectres don't trust anyone who used to be part of the Admin, and who can blame them? Problem is, the only long-range ships that are still operational and have energy are either overtaken or abandoned Corps ships. Consequently, since no one likes their search-and-rescue or salvaging op to turn into a suicide mission, the Spectres have been left to fend for themselves. Enclaves of scavs that have turned to cannibalism, like this one, are the result.

"No one is Corps, or Admin, or a soldier. We're all just survivors, like you," I go on, not expecting any sympathy.

"We saw the ship—" Another pause, this time punctuated by a massive twitch in his right cheek, as if the skin is trying to jump off his face in a gruesome rebellion. I can't help but be a little horrified. After a second, he slaps that side of his face, then grips the flesh with his hand, apparently trying to get it under control. Oh, yeah, he's a poster child for the delights of being a solar stoner. "—go down. Straight into the ocean," he finally finishes, pointing with his free hand out toward the west. "A big one, like a fleet transport."

Interesting. The ship had gone down at sea, and Eruo Pium only has one. Whatever previous crew owned the *Galatea* are lucky they weren't still on it. If not treated, the water on this moon is toxic to humans. Even too much water vapor from waves or wind can be harmful. This fact also explains a little about why the scavs here have turned to cannibalism; they can't eat the sea life, and I didn't notice any Mr. and Mrs. Pioneer–type vegetable gardens.

"Yeah, so? Like I said, the Corps is history. If you're worried about anyone coming in and threatening your, uh, settlement, don't. There's no one else up there, and Eruo Pium isn't exactly anyone's idea of a fun getaway."

His un-twitchy eye glares at me ferociously for a few seconds. One of the other abductors—a hunched, squat man with enough loose skin, dirt caked into its jiggling folds, that it is clear he'd once been on the fat side of corpulent—encircles one of my wrists with his own hand. The skin around his fingertips looks gnawed and infected, like maybe they've become his new favorite after-dinner snack. Yanking my wrist free earns me a snarl, and he raises his fist, ready to strike.

"Bulgaç, hands off," Twitch says. "This one knows something. She just needs some incentive to tell us."

Relaxing more and getting comfortable—I could be here awhile —I say, "What could I know? You saw what happened. My crew was in the ship that went down. You picked us up. I've never been to Eruo Pium"—*and hope to Christ I never have to come back*—"and don't know a goddamn thing about the planet except the sea's poisonous to humans. Besides wanting to get the hell off this rock, I don't know a single. Other. Thing."

"Wrong!" His breath assaults my face like a rancid acid bath as he leans over me. "We picked up chatter. There are other ships, and they're coming. We want to know where you're meeting them."

Picked up chatter? "You mean a transmission? Is there a satellite in your orbit?"

That broken laugh again, like he's gagging with every breathy expulsion. I know *I'm* gagging on his every breath. "Ha-ha. I like this one. She thinks like a scav."

Without a hint of what's coming, his broad hand is at my throat, lifting me off the seat, and hurling me to the ground like a sack of shredded meat. My knees and elbows groan in protest. "Take her back to the shed and bring me the other one. The one we picked her up with. The juicy one."

As I roll over, a boot connects with my diaphragm, sending every molecule of air spewing from my lungs in one giant spasm. Clenching my guts with my hands, I writhe in the dirt for a second, black spots doing the cha-cha-cha in front of my eyes. " . . . f'n bas . . . tard."

Someone wrenches my arms up behind me and drags me to my feet. "Walk."

Forcing my legs into a shamble, I do as he says, encouraged by an occasional shove. As soon as my abdomen unlocks and air starts to flow back into my system, my vision clears. Vitruzzi is in no shape to be interrogated. She hasn't said a word since she came apart at the crash site. If they get their hands on her, she's as good as lunch for them.

Twitch follows behind. Too busy calculating the odds of getting to either his or Fingernails's sidearms before getting myself turned into the appetizer, I almost miss the sound of a tracker engine approaching. It isn't until a voice coming from the cab yells, "Ferenzi," and a hand on my shoulder stops my progress that I notice it.

The tracker—the same one they'd picked all of us up in—stops at an idle about ten meters away, and a woman jumps out.

"Hold her," Twitch tells the two men with us and skulks over to the truck.

An animated conversation takes place between him and the driver, her hands waving frantically at the rusted barrier between us and the sea beyond. I'd smelled its somewhat fetid odor as soon as Vitruzzi and I landed, and the occasional flurry of a breeze confirms we're just southeast of it.

"Close the barrier!" Twitch suddenly cries, turning to us. Neither of my other two captors does anything for a moment, so Twitch pulls out his sidearm—a modified Bowker O9, it looks like—and points it at them. "MOVE IT, YOU FUCKWITS!"

Dumping me like last night's stale beer, they start running to an opening in the barrier, waving their arms to advise what few other scavs are in the area. The tracker's driver follows them, leaving the vehicle where it sits. Twitch spears me in the back with the Bowker's barrel, directly on top of the scar left by Rajcik, and propels me toward the shed. Whatever's going on has him spooked, which, despite the situation, gives me a tiny spark of hope. Enjoyment even. Survivor of the war or not, this is one vile scav who's just wasting oxygen.

We reach the shed. Trying to save myself another cheap shot in the kidneys, I fall to my knees and cower, giving him a comfort zone to fish for the keys to the heavy chain and lock holding the door closed. That and the noise of the barrier gate clanking shut and being fortified with a backfill of whatever junk they can find distract Twitch enough for me to suddenly shift around, sweep my fist up to nail him in the crotch, and follow through by gripping the butt of the Bowker he's reholstered.

TEN

Smashing in his surprised grill with the stock turns out all his lights, and he crumples next to me. None of the scavs notices, and I crouch to retrieve the key Twitch has dropped to the dirt. Quickly unlocking the chain, I swing the door wide and whisper-shout inside, "Everyone, get out and find cover. We're taking over the camp."

Shock peeks through the grime streaking most of their faces, and I hold up the Bowker, pointed skyward, to help them grasp the situation. "This is it, people. Time to run!"

Vitruzzi is the first up, slipping through the opened door with all the stealth and reflexes I've come to expect from her. She spots the downed scav and quickly rifles through his filthy jacket and pants cargo pockets, coming up with a folding knife. Opened, it's about the length of a butter-knife blade, but looks sharp enough to carve up much tougher material. It'll have to do.

I steal another look at the group of scavs working on the barrier—

And my heart goes into a tailspin.

"Aly, what in the name of bloody Christ are those things?" Vitruzzi gasps, but my brain is barely able to interpret what my bulging eyes are seeing.

A torrent of some kind of multilegged crustaceans, like crabs but with long, scorpionlike bodies complete with hooked tails, pours over the wall en masse. It looks like a waterfall of ocean vermin, except their bodies are the size of German shepherds. They have four eyestalks that seem to retract until the eyes wave only centimeters above a hard-shelled, thick forebody, and two sets of hand-sized gripper claws extending from their flanks about half a meter to either side. As gross as they are, and as many as there are, they still don't look all that capable of doing much damage.

Then why are all the scavs screaming?

The first wave, at least a dozen of them, has hit the dirt inside the compound before I unfreeze. And I finally see it. One of them seems to rear up, almost like a Sufi doing a backbend, and long, wickedly jagged plated pincers unfold from its thorax, grabbing ahold of a scav with each and sawing through the unlucky bastard's leg and neck with the ease of a surgical knife.

Ah, *that's* why the screams.

The things move faster than I could have dreamed possible, almost floating over the ground on who knows how many centipede legs. The twenty or so scavs begin to scatter like terrified rabbits, the monsters in pursuit.

"Get to the tracker!" I manage to yell, and bolt.

A meter and a half from the tracker's still-open door, a creepy-crawly darts at me. My first shot blows off at least two eyestalks but doesn't penetrate the shell. At least it slows down—just enough for it to do its bizarre rearing thing. Those pincers start to reach out, and I shoot straight below the plates they're connected to. As I do, a hole, maybe a mouth, opens near the top of its underbelly and spits at me.

A cloud of tiny white darts emits, and I spin sideways to try and avoid them, feeling, nonetheless, a few of them sink into my side. The pain is like white-hot needles being rammed into my ribs and the back of my firing arm. But my shot hit a soft spot and the thing tumbles forward, greenish-red ichor beginning to saturate the ground beneath it.

The shot draws the attention of the scavs, and when they realize

I'm not one of them, three begin running toward the tracker. Vitruzzi jumps into the cab and I pull myself in behind her, closing the door and leaning from the side window to aim at the scavs. I don't need to fire, however, as their sprint is easily overtaken by the local fauna.

Vitruzzi is hammering on the control console, and I risk a glance behind me.

"There," she says as the whine of the opening rear cargo doors drifts into the cab. "Get us closer to the shed."

The engine is still running and I follow her directions, hearing the satisfying crunch of a crushed crab shell as I drive over the one that came at me. The rest of the creatures have spread out, following anything that's running, but haven't keyed in on the tracker yet. I get the vehicle as close to the open shed as I can, and V shouts, "Get in the back! Hurry!"

Once the other abductees start to come out, telling them to hurry is wasting breath. One look at the crab-things and they rush into the back, three of them carrying the unconscious woman.

"Go to the other sheds," V says. "We have to help."

"We have to get the hell out of here!"

"Just do it!"

The tiny crab darts stuck in my side make my skin feel as if it's being slowly peeled from my body, and I'm grateful the tracker has a steering ball instead of a wheel as I spin toward the next shack. V jumps out and gets lucky with the key from our cell's shed on the lock while I cover her with the Bowker. But there are nothing but bodies inside. Inside the third shed, we find . . .

Four kids. Jesus. Vitruzzi and another of the prisoners haul the kids inside the back of the tracker, then V jumps into the cab and closes the rear door. Her face has gone intensely pale and slightly greenish, like sea foam.

"Go."

My tour of camp had given me the impression that the barrier's thinnest spot is its northeast wall, so I maneuver the steering ball toward it and press it down for acceleration. It isn't a fast vehicle, but the heavy steel body keeps out the monstrosities teeming through camp—both kinds. The scav with an appetite for his own fingers breaks from his cover as we pass, grabs the rear bumper, and uses the cargo door's hinges to pull himself up. As I'm watching through the rearview screen, a crab grips one of his legs and climbs him before he can get all the way aboard. Severed bits of him leave a trail behind, and what's left finally comes free and drops to the ground as I push the tracker into the barrier. Drooping skin folds or not, the guy had had a hell of a grip.

The barrier's rusting plates of metal and discarded junk give way easily under the tracker's relentless pressure, and we hit the grassy plain outside, slowly gaining speed until we max out at the vehicle's limit, forty kilometers per hour. The earth is bumpy and uneven, and a long, slow whine clanks from the tracker's undercarriage after we've gone a few klicks.

"Looks like this is as far as we go for now," I tell Vitruzzi.

She barely dips her head in acknowledgment and continues staring through the window at the scrubby hills beyond.

Pulling to a standstill, I leave the engine running. "Look." I have to speak with more force than I normally would just to get her attention. "V. We're out of the woods. Those crab-things aren't going to get this far, and I highly doubt there're any more scavs in the area. And the best news . . ." I pause, hoping for a reaction, but get none. Sighing, I finish, "Is that they have a receiver, maybe even a transmitter. They said they heard chatter after we went down. Which means there's a working satellite up there somewhere. I propose running a recon back to the camp later on and see if we can find their unit. We have a better chance of getting rescued if we can send a message. Are you reading me?"

She nods.

For a second, I just stare at her, trying to assess what had put her in this wicked state of mind and what I can do to change that. She's just sitting there like a zombie, and finally, I snap. "I don't know what the fuck your deal is, Vitruzzi, but you need to get your head back in the game. We're in some serious shit—"

She slaps me so hard my opposite temple whacks into the back of the cab with a dull thunk. Fury and boggled disbelief paralyze me, and I stare at her with my hand pressed against my burning cheek and reopened split upper lip. Almost immediately, her face relaxes from the mask of rage that had slipped over it to genuine regret.

"I'm so sorry, Aly. I don't know . . ."

I finally find my voice. "What the hell was that for?"

"I don't know," she repeats, sounding completely believable. She really doesn't know what she's doing, or why. Vitruzzi, for all her stalwart and controlled composure, has cracked.

A knock at the window behind me draws my attention. It's the kid.

"You think we're in the clear?" he says, his voice muffled through the window's composite material.

Shooting him a thumbs-up, I return my attention to Vitruzzi, a hundred different thoughts about what to say to her tumbling against each other in my head like sand on a stormy beach. She's leaning forward with her elbows on her knees and her head in her hands, her hair coming loose from the braid it's normally held back in and sticking to her damp and salty cheeks. My stomach does an uncomfortable flip-flop at the sight.

Unable to conceal my anger, I say, "Let's check on our passengers."

ELEVEN

"God, what a fucking mess," one of the refugees, a youngish, dark-haired woman named Cari, says as she looks over the cannibal camp. "I don't think we have to worry about the scavs anymore." She tosses a disgusted look in my direction.

The tracker's night beams wash over the inner courtyard, glistening off puddles of viscous fluid that look like oil, but which we all know are blood. A few mangled bits and pieces of the scavs dot the area. And that's it. The crabs must have dragged off the bulk of their victims. I shudder, not at the gore, but at the memory of the creatures. If the critters back on KL give me the creeps, those crustaceans were enough to make my blood freeze. I'm just hoping they stay gone until we get gone.

When we'd made our escape I'd hardly been worried anyone from the camp would chase us. It seemed the whole entourage had been out trying to fight back the crabs. If any had survived, they had more to worry about than trying to hunt down us escapees. Regardless, with the extra two weapons I'd found in the tracker's cab, a pistol and another carbine, and help from the passengers, we'd stayed put and set up a watch until dark, keeping our six covered.

The kid from the other *Galatea* salvagers—I finally got his name,

Ryan—turned out to be a big help with the tracker. The engine was fine, but its fuel cell was low on water. He told me we could use seawater if we needed to. Lucky for us, we'd only been a klick from the high-tide line. After a discussion with the rest of the refugees, some who'd seen the Admin ship drop into the ocean, our best guess is that the disturbance caused by the crash may have been what sent the crab-things onto land. Apparently the cannibals weren't the only predators in the area with a taste for human flesh. The most important thing is that it looks as if they'd returned to their normal hunting grounds before we came back.

We'd lost the unconscious woman just before dark. With no medical supplies, there was nothing Vitruzzi could do for her, and the swelling on her brain went critical. The two men with her explained that they'd been abducted by the cannibals while out on a long-range search for resources, downed ships, scraps from orbit, things like that. Vitruzzi bandaged the arm of the man who'd been shot by the guard—a superficial wound, fortunately for him—while they described their own settlement that lies over six hundred klicks to the northeast. Others from their group had run into the cannibal enclave months earlier but escaped without being detected. These three had been desperate and foolish enough to travel on their own without sufficient firepower and been hijacked. The price could have been all three of their lives instead of just the one woman, but I hadn't needed to offer my opinion on it. They already knew.

"Ryan—you stay on my ass and hold that Max at the ready. Cari, keep that 'bine tracking along the edge of our light. Anything that moves gets a bullet. Copy?"

Ryan nods, and Cari waves the affirmative from the tracker's roof. I glance back inside the cab, where one of the dead woman's friends is driving, and give him a nod. We push forward, walking slowly while the vehicle follows in our rear. Our destination is the main building—or rusted shack—where I'm hoping the former inhabitants' communications equipment is kept.

The camp is eerily quiet, the air heavy with mist. Despite that, the disquieting stench of dead bodies lingers lightly, as if the back of my nasal passages have been permanently stained by the smell. The tracker makes the only noise. I have to admit that I admire how quietly the kid walks over the packed sand and rock. Nothing moves in my periphery, and I keep us moving forward. Only twenty meters to the shack.

A carbine being fired explodes through my focus. A blossom of dirt spikes up about eight meters to my left and lingers in the thick air and light of the tracker's beams.

"Cari?!" I yell, needing to know what she's firing at.

"I thought I saw movement," she replies as the tracker halts.

"Thought or did? Now is not the time for guesswork." Keeping the irritation out of my voice takes more energy than I can spare. I'm tired, hurt, hungry, and at my limit. The fact that everyone else is too doesn't reduce my frustration. At all.

"Uh . . . thought."

"And now?"

"It's, uh, clear."

Swallowing my suggestions for what she can do with the next round of guesses she may have, I wave my free hand at the kid and start moving to the shed again.

Before we reach it, I note that the door hangs ajar on slightly bent hinges. It looks deserted, the inside blacker than the barrel of the pistol I carry. There's no way I'm walking in there without light. No way.

"Kid, go to the back of the tracker and ask Vitruzzi for her VDU."

He hurries around the vehicle, and I keep pressing forward until the tracker's front end is only a couple of meters outside the doorway. Movement is limited to a few shadows bouncing around the interior, which only increases my nervousness. Shadows? Or men with guns? Or worse—critters with pincers the size of my forearm?

Ryan comes back and hands V's wrist communication unit to me. Turning the display on and setting the screen to full bright, I press up against the shed's exterior wall, crouch, and flick the VDU inside. It comes to rest near the shack's center, throwing a strong white glow up to the ceiling. Nothing moves. This could go well, after all.

The kid tries to move past me, apparently judging the lack of movement to mean all clear, but I grab his arm and pull him up beside me. Pressing my fingers against my lips, I stare hard at him, making sure he stays put. I cup my hand behind my ear to indicate he needs to wait and listen, and we hang tight for three full minutes before moving again.

Finally, I pick up a nearby pebble and toss it in, waiting for any response. Still nothing. After turning the display on my own VDU up and cautiously moving inside, I strain my eyes to catch any surprises.

The place is trashed. Consoles lie scrapped on the floor, toppled from makeshift workbenches, their wires jutting in every direction.

"Sonofabitch," I whisper, dropping my arm, still holding the pistol, to my side. Our chances for contacting the scouts just dropped to zero, and I don't have the most positive outlook about spending what could amount to weeks on this rock waiting for them to find us.

The kid steps over to a cracked screen and picks it up, eyeing it critically. He puts it back down and looks over the heap, then moves toward the back wall behind the workbench. "Huh," he grunts.

"Jubels," I shout at the driver of the idling tracker. "Back up. There's nothing in here."

Could the day get any worse?

"There never was."

Turning back to the kid, my expression makes him flinch. "What?"

"There never was anything in here. This"—he sweeps an arm over the broken equipment—"is all just junk. There's no power coming in."

"You're saying there may be another com setup somewhere?"

"Well, yeah. If they were telling the truth about picking up a transmission, there has to be. Right?"

Right. But where? Everything in this camp looks as stripped and bare boned as their recent meal du jour. Before I open my mouth, he says, "What about that wrecked lander? It has to have a comsys. Could be what the scavs were using."

Where did I find this kid? Once more, he could be right. This camp looks like no more than a junkyard where even the junk is too run-down to be considered refuse. Besides the tracker, the only other thing that isn't totally derelict is that landing craft.

Waving him forward, I reply, "Let's check it out."

I KNOW I'M NOT the only one that feels a monumental sense of relief as the landing lights of not only the *Orika* but also the *Teibo* descend out of the sky like twin dei ex machina.

The kid was clever, just as I'd originally thought. The lander's receiver worked just fine, but the transmitter had required some TLC and very ingenious jury-rigging of the tracker's fuel cell to feed power to the lander before we'd been able to send a signal. My electronics skills are enough to help me arm an explosive device or short out a lockpad, but Ryan turns out to be a jack-of-all-trades. He figured out what the transmitter needed and how to get it done within minutes, and now that his shock has worn off he hasn't shown any signs of fading in the twenty or so hours since we'd met aboard the *Galatea*. I grow happier with every passing hour that I hadn't shot him. His kind of handiness is the mark of a true survivor, someone who'd made it through the war by being adaptable, smart, and quick on his feet. Just the kind of asset—and person—we could use on KL. Depending on what kind of provisions are left on the scouts, and whether or not this kid has anywhere else to call home, I may make a case for bringing in another stray.

Our ships locked on to our signal within a couple hours of Ryan's magical fix-it skills. The junction box kept overloading, so we couldn't maintain a conversation with Zeta on the *Teibo,* but we had managed to give them our coordinates. We've rotated standing watch, two per shift, since then. This isn't the first all-nighter I've pulled, and I'm still on watch while the suns' glow begins tracing the scouts' hulls as they drift onto a flat landing area just outside the compound.

David and Karl are the first ones to come through the main gate, where we'd cleared away the hastily piled-up obstructions.

"I can't even tell you how glad I . . . *ooph.*" This is all I get out before Karl has me in a hug so tight I think he might dislocate my ribs.

"Dammit, Aly," he says. "Don't do that to me again."

My right arm is pinned against the spikes still embedded there, and I suck in a breath as he squeezes me tighter.

"Shit, are you hurt? Let me see your lip." He pulls back and stares squinting into my face. His hand comes up and gently cradles my cheek as he glares at my upper lip. "Where else?"

"Nowhere. Just these . . . I don't know . . . crabby, spikey things in my side. I'm okay. Really."

David's face rearranges into that frustrated-at-having-been-freaked-out older-brother smirk, and he steps up. "I'm glad you're safe, Twig. You said V isn't doing well? Where is she?"

Indicating the tracker with my chin, I answer, "She's back there. Been sleeping all night. She's not hurt, didn't take a hit or anything, but she's just . . . off. You know, the twenty-meter stare in a ten-meter room type of off."

"What the hell happened down here?" Karl asks, finally looking around and taking in the scenery.

TWELVE

"Whoa! Hey, get a room." As I walk inside the *Orika*'s main cargo bay, Zeta and Desto have themselves entwined in an amorous embrace so flamboyant it could make a *kagema* blush. "There's a kid present for God's sake!"

Desto lets his hands fall from Zeta's ass, and she turns to smirk at me. "Kid here? C'mon, Aly, I know you're not that puritanical. This kid"—she pats the small bloom of her three-months-pregnant belly—"isn't going to grow up with any illusions about where she came from, anyway."

"And what's wrong with the room we're in?" Desto adds. "Plenty of space for everyone in here. What do you say, sweets?" He winks at me.

Zeta laughs and gives him a playful slap on the cheek. "You're going to embarrass her, Bomani."

"I swear, *Bomani*, I can't believe you're breeding, especially since every other ex-Corpsmember in the galaxy still shoots blanks."

"Ha!" He snorts, gently taking one of Zeta's hands in a gesture I find surprisingly sweet and protective. Desto may be a letch, but there's no doubt of their love for each other, or that he would do anything for her. "The Corps should have known better than to think they could drown the power of my epic swimmers."

I pass by, shaking my head. "A soldier can't even walk through her own scout without feeling like she was just violated when you're around."

"Aly, you quit being a soldier the first time you saved someone's life," Desto says, and his deep laughter follows me through the inner hallway as I make for the locker room.

I've just finished filling the two crews in on everything that had gone down during these last few hours for V and me. No one was surprised; we've all seen or heard the stories about camps like this one. After I introduced them to Ryan, Karl woke Vitruzzi, and Desto and Zeta came back aboard to start the preflight routine, freeing up the rest of the crew to begin attending to the mostly low-priority wounds, mild dehydration, and extreme hunger of the remaining fugees. We are all exhausted, even the crew that had been searching for us. The word *relaxation* doesn't exist when your friends are in trouble and you're not sure where they are or how to help them. It had all turned out for the best—this time. The scariest part, and the one we all work hard to ignore, is that if anything were to happen to us out here, no one on KL would ever know.

Once in the locker room, I drench a towel in hot water from the reserve tank and grab the hem of my shirt, already gritting my teeth against the pain I know is coming when it brushes over the embedded crab spikes.

"When we're ready to launch, it may not be easy to keep them off the ships."

I spin around and find Quantum standing in the doorway, his unreadable gaze assaulting me. His comment catches me totally off guard. "What?"

He moves to the window port that gives a view of the exterior and flicks his hand at the group of eight adults and four kids still milling around the tracker outside. "The fugees. We don't have provisions, or room, to bring them all with us. We'll run out of food and water at least a week before we arrive at KL."

I take a seat on one of the benches. Fatigue is beginning to make my limbs heavy. "Have you said anything to V or Karl?" I look back through the port, where my view settles on Ryan helping one of the children with the lid of a water bottle.

Quantum's right, and he knows I know it. However grudging and hostile our understanding of each other is, Quantum and I are similar in our pragmatism. In a world that has come to rely on fact over feeling to survive, this shared quality has made us ideological, if not actual, allies.

"Erikson, Vitruzzi is not capable of being trusted with the kind of decision that has to be made about them. She's—"

"Hold it, Quantum. You watch what you say about her."

His eyes flash with anger, but intelligent anger. The man is genius, and not just intellectually. He's clever and cunning. "Look," he continues, "you know I'm right. She needs a . . . vacation. Some time away from the pressure she's under from running her personal little fiefdom."

"She doesn't need a vacation. She needs a shrink. But that doesn't matter. She's the leader on KL, her and Brady. They call the shots, that's how it is, and this conversation isn't happening without her. Come on."

Fucking stingers aren't going anywhere for a while, it looks like.

Once outside, I lean against one of the *Orika*'s ramp struts and catch David's and Karl's attention, waving them over. When they get close to us, I say quietly, "Quantum just brought something up. I want to get your opinions on it."

"What's up?" Desto asks, emerging from inside and wiping sweat from his forehead.

Quantum stands beside me and sighs as if it pains him to have to repeat himself, then says, "You've thought about the next steps? We used up a lot of resources looking for Erikson and Vitruzzi. We'll have just enough to get back to KL, *maybe*. And then, there's them." Without even attempting to conceal the gesture, he waves a hand toward the group.

David gets it immediately and bites his lower lip, clearly unhappy with the implications.

"Hmmm . . . we can't leave them here," Desto says matter-of-factly.

"We can't take them with us," Quantum replies.

"Shh!" I warn. "David, will you get Vitruzzi and Venus? There's no need to freak any of the fugees out. Not with a bunch of kids."

"I think Mason and Hoogs are doing a perimeter sweep," he says. "I'll get them too."

"No," Desto says. "Aly is right. We don't want to freak everyone out by having a huddle behind their backs. Lets talk this over nice and quiet."

After Venus and Vitruzzi join the rest of us and Zeta in the *Orika*'s galley, the debate starts heating up.

"The majority aren't even from Eruo Pium. They're settlers who crash-landed on their way to Obal 6," Vitruzzi says tonelessly. "And they need our help getting off this rock, where they have a chance."

"Vitruzzi, *you* may be in the search-and-rescue business, but the rest of us are concerned with our *own* survival," Quantum says.

"Yeah, we know what you're concerned with," Vitruzzi responds angrily, the first spark I've seen in her in what seems like weeks.

"Does it matter?" Quantum continues, looking around at the rest of us from where he stands by the freezer. "The reality we're facing is simple: limited food, limited time, and limited risk avoidance. If anyone else sees where aiding a group of refugees fits into that equation, now's a good time to explain it."

It's hard to meet the rest of the crew's eyes, but I know where I stand on this one. *Sorry, Ryan.*

Finally, David says, "A few of them are from the settlement they mentioned, somewhere east of here, at least. We can take them back and drop off the rest with them. Give them something from the salvage to barter with."

"David's right," Karl says. "We can't just abandon them out here. You agree, Quantum?" His face is a mask of neutrality as he turns to the wire-rat, but I know what's going on behind his eyes. *You started the war that caused this, you bastard.*

Karl and I have had many late-night conversations about the events that had brought us into this situation and started the war between the Admin-Corps and the vast numbers of non-cits that were taking the brunt of the Admin's "policies." Policies that included a lot of people dying. Ultimately, the only one to blame is the Admin. They brought the fight to themselves when they started treating people like petri dishes. Despite that, however, Quantum was the one who unleashed the first salvo, so to speak. He helped organize the anti-Admin-Corps forces and pushed the button that set everything that's happened in the last eighteen months in motion. I'm not saying what he did was right or wrong, but if he hadn't, David and I would be either dead or still running black-market smuggling deals on the fringes of the system. Which may as well be dead. And Vitruzzi and Karl and the rest of the Agate Beachers would be fugitives or dead, too. Wasting time hand-wringing and judging all the scenarios as good or bad doesn't do any good; they just *are.*

At least, that's where I stand on the issues. But something happened in that war that hit others deeper, more in the heart than in the guts, and Karl is one of them. He's not as used to the darkness people have within them. Seeing the cold and methodical ferocity the Corps adopted in dealing with the uprising took even world-wise people like him by surprise. The way the humanity of Admin-controlled Corps soldiers bled away in the face of battle, turning them into conscienceless automatons instead of people—it took a toll, on almost everyone. The result is that now survivors are looking for answers and searching for reasons to explain what had happened and why. Finding someone to blame is part of, if not the healing process, at least the reconciliation process. Being able to blame one person makes it easier to ignore the ugly possibility that it's really *every* person that is to blame.

So Karl harbors an unspoken resentment for Quantum. The only thing that keeps him from acting on it is the fact that he knows, deep down, that Quantum is too small for that much blame, and Karl would waste the rest of his life trying to dole out the remainder of it.

Quantum's fixed gaze doesn't waver from his. "If that's the group's vote."

After another minute, it's settled. Desto and David volunteer to apprise the fugees of what we can offer them, and I, hopefully, can take care of my own thorny issue.

"Aly, can you help me prep the *'Bo* for takeoff?" Zeta asks. "Venus is helping Karl sort some of the salvage."

Sure, why not? These spines aren't going anywhere.

ONCE WE GET AIRBORNE, I finally get the moment I've been waiting for.

Standing next to the full-length wall mirror, I slowly begin pulling the synthetic fabric of my less-than-optimal-smelling shirt first away from my torso, then over my head. When the rag grazes my skin, I grit my teeth. It feels as if tiny needles are stabbing into my lats and rib cage, and the material tries to snag on them as it comes up. Dammit, what had those crabs been made of? If I didn't already hate multilegged, crawling and clacking minimonsters, this experience would be the defining moment.

Dropping the shirt to the floor with a sigh of relief, I crane my head around to try and see what the hell I'm up against. Three of the fugees stand around the benches, doing their best to clean the grit of their own captivity off. I'm not sure if what they're doing would be called ogling or gawking, but they aren't even pretending they're not watching me.

"You want to take a picture, boys? Or would you prefer an ass-kicking to remember me by?"

The blond one reminds me of a schoolyard bully whose body has outgrown his brains. He'd been the most vocal and angry when we'd told them they couldn't come with us, but none of the fugees could argue that we had any responsibility to take them. They know the deal out here. Everyone looks out for themselves first.

He snickers and says, "Sweetheart, with an attitude like that, you're just asking for someone like me to set you straight on some things."

Can this be happening right now? I'm half-naked, bleeding from at least three places, my torso is a chaotic tableau of unattractive yellows, greens, and blues, and this guy wants to first drool over me like a poodle with a puppy treat, then threaten me for not appreciating it? After I'd saved his ass? I momentarily entertain the wish that the Admin had started a weapons research program to develop bombs that only killed stupid people.

Muttering, "And if you had the capacity for complex thought, I'm sure you'd be the man for the job," I dismiss him and return my attention back to examining my side.

"What did you say?" he asks, but I ignore him.

With my arm in the air and my head twisted almost into my own armpit, I catch a glimpse of the small, spiny projectiles, about a quarter- to half-centimeter long, running in a line just at the base of my rib cage and up. I reach around with my right hand and gently feel for them. It stings like crazy when my fingers brush over their tops, but the searing pain that happened when I was first struck has at least dulled. The things feel brittle and a little flexible, not quite as stiff as fine wire.

"I said, what the hell did you say, girlie?" Blondie has come over beside me and leans over me, his breath hitting my face and making me flinch a little. "You got something to say, you go right ahead."

I ponder it for a minute and flip a glance toward his friends still by the benches. They're all part of the five-person crew that had crashed on the way to Obal 6, these three, the woman named Cari, and another older woman. Neither of the other two men will look at me. Blondie catches my glance and grins obnoxiously, assuming he's scared me.

Finally, my voice giving away my utter disinterest in him or anything he has to say, I advise, "If you value anything down here for any reason, you'd best find someplace else to stand. Someplace where I don't have to look at your ugly fucking mug."

The surprise on his face when he realizes I have a modest but laser-torch-sharp bolo knife pressed against his nuts should be entertaining, but I realize with resignation that I've seen this kind of idiot wake-up call too often to be moved one way or another by it anymore. The goal is simply to send his stupid ass on its way so I can start pulling these damn spikes out of me. They're making me cranky.

"Erikson, is there anything I can help you with?"

Blondie turns his attention to the locker-room entrance. Quantum has come through and is holding the pocket of his jacket as if to reach for something inside. A quick glance lets him know I'm all set.

Blondie's hands go up in a warding-off motion, and he takes a slow step back. Before he thinks of trying anything else, I reach down into my boot without looking away from him and withdraw a Sub-Oss, just for some added incentive. Without another word, he spins around and joins his mates, the three of them hurrying out past Quantum like they're late for lunch. Good fucking riddance.

But at least it was a distraction from these damn stingers. I should be grateful, actually. Now I'll feel much less bad about stranding them in some far-flung, sketchy colony that probably hasn't seen running water or electricity in a year.

As if reading my mind, Quantum walks toward the sink, then says, "Now you understand my reasons."

"Quantum, if you keep showing up while I'm in the locker room, I may have to interpret your behavior as a threat."

Ignoring the comment, he continues, "You're just holding on to a broken idea. The old system no longer applies. Now it's every person—"

"For themselves," I finish for him. "Thanks for the sociology lesson. Now, do you mind? As you can see . . ." I wave the knife at my blemished flank before resheathing it and the Oss.

"I want to talk to you about something." He pulls off his jacket and rolls up his sleeves before turning on the wash powder dispenser.

"Can it wait?"

"No." Facing me, he says, "I know what that machine is."

"You mean the thing we have in the hull? What is it?"

"A seed sequencer."

My expression must show my confusion, so he continues, "A generator, of sorts. It takes raw materials and creates new seeds for crops, for food crops. Do you see what that means?"

"Yeah, it means we're going to be better off than ever at the colony. We can produce whatever we need. But how do you know?"

"Hoogs accessed the *Galatea* commander's drive and found his directives. That Admin ship was in the Spectras to drop off the seed sequencer. What we have in the hull was the only thing on the transport that fits the description. I looked it over, and I believe I can operate it."

I'm still hung up on the first thing he said. "Why would they drop something that produces crop seeds in the Spectras? There's hardly enough viable soil in most places to grow anything worthwhile."

"Not on the other side of this moon."

"Huh? It's barely . . ." He's looking at me expectantly, waiting for me to understand. And then, I do. "They used the soil compound, didn't they?"

His lips thin out as he presses them together in a look that reminds me of a dead snake. "The recorded directives clearly outlined the fecundity and success of their soil enhancement project. The Admin intended to begin planting synthetically generated seeds within the year. The year before the war, that is."

How many people had lived on Eruo Pium? How many had the Admin snuffed to test their poisonous compound?

Feeling my guts go hollow with disgust, I ask, "So what does any of that have to do with me?"

"KL is too small, too disorganized—and most of its settlers are war casualties with too many injuries—to be able to fully deploy the capacity of the seed sequencer. In other words, the colony isn't capable of sustaining itself. I want your help to convince Vitruzzi to let me take the soil compound and the sequencer to Obal 6."

I laugh, assuming he's joking.

His stare grows cold. "We can't expect to live on salvaged food stores and canned vegetables forever. We have to begin working toward a long-term solution."

Cutting the laugh off like a gangrenous limb, I ask, "How does the soil compound count as a long-term solution, Quantum? It's poison. You know that. It kills everything—for years—before it becomes inert. Where would you even use it?"

"Obal 6 is a big planet. They may be willing to deploy it to help provide for their remaining population, and to plan for more growth."

"No. That's crazy. We don't fully understand it. You can't just let this stuff loose out there. People could get killed."

"Why do you care about a few hundred people? How many did we just see killed in the war?"

"Exactly, there's been enough death." I know he's an opportunist, but I never thought he had it in him to be so incredibly callous. "We don't need to increase the body count. It's time to put the system back together, not add to its decay."

"You have to under—"

"No! You have to understand—this conversation is over." I turn back to the mirror, keeping an eye on him in the reflection.

After a pause, he says, "Don't make the mistake of believing the war is over, Aly." Rubbing his hands against his pants to dry them, he finally leaves.

What the hell does that mean? The war *is* over. That's why every-thing has taken on these wonderful new dimensions of fucked up. What war is he still fighting?

Clicking on my VDU, I scroll to Karl's channel.

"What's up, lover?" he says.

"I'm in the troop locker room. Do you think you could swing by and help me with something?"

"Yeah, be there in a minute."

Trying to shake off the conversation, I pick up a pair of splinter forceps I'd snagged from the med-bay and clamp onto the first spine. Something tells me I'll be finding myself in the midst of Quantum's war sooner or later. No reason to start with my flesh looking like a porcupine's hide.

THIRTEEN

After sleeping the sleep of a war veteran on farm animal tranqs for a couple of hours, during which time the two scouts take flight to Eruo Pium's remaining settled colony, I wake up to the sound of running feet outside the berth Karl and I share. My guts go on a roller-coaster panic drop, but my mind quickly registers the giggling shrieks that trail behind the footsteps. Those kids we'd picked up must have slept less than I just did. But I thought children were supposed to need to recharge?

Karl's leg is draped over mine, and he snorts, still asleep, as the last of the laughter fades down the corridor outside. Like me, this is the first chance to rest he's had since before we boarded the *Galatea*, and I take a second to just enjoy being next to him. From being a soldier, to deserting and becoming a criminal, then to fighting a war, and now scratching out existence as a scavenger (which is an ugly word for it, but I promised myself no more lies, not even to myself, when Rob Cross had come back into my life and nearly wrecked it) in a system full of equally desperate scavs, I have a habit of living every breath like it will be my last. And no one can blame me for stealing a few minutes of peace to appreciate this man who had saved more than my life; he'd saved my soul.

My stomach rumbles and reality penetrates through my tranquility. Trying not to wake Karl, I reach inside the gear loft over our bunk and retrieve my VDU to tap out a message asking Venus how much time till we arrive at the colony. She responds with less than an hour to go.

Deciding that it will be better to be awake and alert than still be horizontal when we get there, I gently nudge Karl until his sepia eyes open, and he smiles up at me.

"We there?" he asks.

"Not for an hour or so. Thought we'd grab a snack and get ready."

His arms wrap around me and he pulls me on top of him, then starts nuzzling my neck. "Delicious," he whispers through his exploring lips.

Giggling, I play-fight him off. "Not that kind of snack."

"But it's the only thing that sounds appetizing."

We're interrupted by the children's laughter and echoing feet running down the corridor again, this time in the opposite direction. "I thought I'd dreamed that sound," Karl says.

"Nope, they've been playing around out there for a while. They barely slept. It's like they're not even human."

He rolls onto an elbow and looks at me with a bemused expression. "Have you ever thought about it?"

"About what?" Then I realize what he's asking. "Having kids? Didn't joining the Corps pretty much ensure that wasn't something either of us ever *had* to think about?"

"Come on, Aly. The Corps doesn't even matter anymore. Nothing is the same as it used to be. There're tons of kids like them in the system, ones who need homes, safety, people to look out for them." He pauses. "So, have you?"

The concept is so foreign to me that my next words come directly from instinct, not contemplation. "What's there to think about? They eat, sleep, cry, and want things. Basically the same as every adult in the worlds. That's not really much enticement, if you know what I mean." His face closes off in frustration, but he doesn't say anything. "Besides, can you imagine me as a muh"—I can't quite get the word out—"guardian, some kind of role model? I could teach a kid to shoot from prone and reload faster than average, but—"

"I know, lover. I get it. It was just a thought. Come on, let's get some grub."

After dressing, we walk to the mess and find Mason and Hoogs already there and occupied with teaching the children how to unload and reload a weapon in combat time. I give Karl a meaningful look, *See?*, which he emphatically ignores. The oldest girl looks only about eight, and the youngest boy maybe six, but it's hard to tell beneath their rags and malnourishment what their real ages are. I'd joined the Capital Military Corps Academy when I was fourteen, the youngest age you could enter, but the grim awareness in these kids' faces shows an intensity of understanding and wisdom that is years beyond where I'd been at their ages. Eight-year-olds with guns. The oldest girl points the pistol Hoogs hands her directly at me before he pulls the barrel aside and warns her not to, and I quickly decide to keep my distance from the children. Looking into her eyes—even for an instant—had been like looking into a ghost's.

"Are you cold?" Karl says.

Before I can ask him why he'd think that, I glimpse the gooseflesh that has sprung up on both of my arms, wrists to shoulders. "Nah." I shake my head. "Just..."

He stares at me, waiting for me to finish my sentence, but I don't know what to tell him. That I had a sense that, even though we'd rescued these kids from a gruesome end, I still feel like they're doomed? That I felt a sudden certainty that the last war was the final war humanity would ever fight, because we're *all* doomed?

Stepping over to the rations cabinets, I enter the code only the KL crew has and grab him and me ready-to-eats. Handing one over, I let him know I'm heading to the bridge. I don't want to eat in front of those hungry kids, with their shining eyes crawling over me like grave beetles.

When we'd divided up for the flight to the colony, I'd been relieved that the only ones coming with us were the kids and Mason. The rest of the refugees stayed with the *Teibo* after we'd transferred all the essential salvage aboard the *Orika*. None of them had seen the kids before, and the children who weren't too traumatized to tell us their story said they hadn't seen their parents since their transport ship had been attacked, less than a week prior. Before those cannibals had been eaten alive by the swarm of crab-things, they must have bragged to each other about their good week of "salvage."

Trying to shake the creeping feeling thinking about those children and their parents' fate has given me, I join Venus in the cockpit.

She's at the pilot's console, spinning a small object around like a top on one of the flat displays.

"Hungry?" I ask, dropping a nutrition bar on the console between displays.

"Thanks! All clear in the rear?" She chuckles at her pet joke and picks up the object, which I can now see is a ring made of some kind of matte-textured metal.

Nodding, I bite into my own bar and perch on the edge of the navigator's seat. Trying not to be obtrusive, but curious nonetheless, I comment, "Pretty baubley, what is it?"

"Molybdenum and titanium alloy. It's a piece off the *Sphynx* that Jer welded into a ring for me."

"A . . . ring? Like, are you engaged or something?"

"Yeah." She says it with the gushing joy of a kid getting her first magbike, her happiness nearly too big to be contained in the small cockpit.

And it suddenly hits me—in spite of all the losses, deaths, uncertainties, and just the way almost everything in life has become so *hard*, there will never be a total loss of hope, never be a total loss of what it means to be human. When the scale of everything is out of proportion, happiness and enduring optimism adjust accordingly, but they do not disappear. The realization is a weird contrast to the gloomy feeling I'd just had about the kids, and the competing extremes give me a moment of cerebral vertigo.

I take another bite and chew it, clearing my head. "I'm really happy for you, Venus. He's a good guy. Actually, he's a great guy."

"I know," she states as a matter of fact, then chomps into her nutrition bar.

I lean forward and start cycling through feeds and data to get a sense of our landscape. "Older satellite images show that it was a fairly good-sized mining colony," I mention. "Wonder how many people are left?"

"We'll know in about three minutes. It's just on the other side of this range. Snap in, Aly." After confirming by radio the distance and a good landing area with Zeta on the *'Bo*, she makes a general announcement to our crew over the com that we'll be landing shortly.

As we crest the peak of a barren, snow-dusted, twenty-five-hundred-meter mountain, light from two of the suns breaks into weird shadows through our viewscreens, draining the cockpit of any real color, turning everything a simmering sepia brown, like rust. For a few seconds, Venus's hair appears to be aflame in the glow, and I realize mine must look just as fiery to her. It will be night again soon, or at least nightlike for a few hours. This side of the mountains looks like it will be colder than the cannibals' side.

She pushes the engines harder, expertly taking advantage of the thermal currents coming down the back side of the mountain range, and the mining colony comes into sight within moments. The *Orika*, like all ships based on its model, is sleek, solid, and built to take a beating. Mostly interplanetary, they have a range of a few hundred thousand kilometers on a full nuclear-core load and the capacity to carry 750 cubic tons. Mostly, they were commissioned by traders and shippers for local jobs. Nearly one of every five non-Corps vessels in the air were ASHTs—Admin Starclass Hypermaneuver Transport Craft—prior to the war, and being one of the most resilient hull designs ever made, more of them survived it than any other model.

Despite the *Orika*'s notable carrying capacity, room for personnel is spartan at best. A central shower, a galley that carries up to fifty days' supply of meals and beverages, a rudimentary med-bay, a private captain's bunk, which Karl and I are sharing on this run, and a separate general sleeping bunkroom for up to six crewmembers make up the living quarters. Only three people are needed to fly it at once, but backup mechanics and cargo handlers are usually included on the manifest. If something happens in space and you need to keep flying, someone has to staff the engine ports to keep it going. Fortunately, most of the shipping lanes were well trafficked enough before the war that a broken-down vessel was rarely left in the lurch for long.

After the war, these shipping lanes provided the easiest pickings for scavengers and salvagers (though, in reality, I'm not sure there is any difference). We picked up both the *Teibo* and the *Orika* herself from one of these orbital highways. The Beachers may have been backwater-planet dwellers, but their combined mechanical ingenuity and engineering moxie are among the best I've seen outside of the Obals. Something about living tangential to the "civilized" world brings out qualities in people that seem to be dormant within those whose lives were a clear path of steady and consistent submission from the cradle to the grave.

Sometimes those qualities are extraordinary. Other times—horrifying.

We start a circle around the mining settlement, giving me time to take it in, though we plan to land a few klicks away—just to be safe. It must have still been functioning before the war. Scattered mining equipment and drill pieces dot the area and line the southern edge of a pit in the earth that could easily swallow both the *Orika* and the *'Bo* and still have room for every building within the community. It's as if the moon were hit by an asteroid, the crater almost too deep to see down to the bottom, particularly in the spreading twilight.

Both scouts come to rest north of the colony. We don't want to invite trouble or give them an easy target if they're primed to fight. The fugees will have to walk the rest of the distance, but they shouldn't complain. They're getting a couple of bins of water and some food, a couple more bins of medical supplies—even precious antibiotics, at Vitruzzi's insistence—and everyone gets a weapon and a couple of clips of ammunition. It's a lot to carry, but they'll find a way. After we're prepped to leave, that is. Vitruzzi's one other requirement is that the orphaned kids come back to Keum Libre. It'll make rations tight for the trip home, but without someone to look out for them, their fates out here are easy to guess. After Karl's and my earlier conversation, I'm wondering if he's thinking we should be part of those someones.

None of the refugees had been happy about our plans to leave them behind, even the ones from the mining colony. I can't blame them. Regardless, postwar fact number one: altruism is as dead as the Admin. What had Quantum said? We're not in the search-and-rescue business? That's the absolute truth. They should be able to make the best of things here, maybe acquire enough salvage of their own to barter for a ride off and a better chance next time a ship comes through. And if Quantum had been right, only a couple thousand klicks from here, there's a planet ripe for growing all the food they can eat.

I don't let myself think too much about the extremely high likelihood that not one of them knows a hoe from a combine.

With no reason to leave the *Orika*—Desto, David, and Zeta can handle any trouble—I dig into a food bar and watch through the viewscreens as we wait for the *'Bo*'s cargo hatch to retract.

And wait.

Venus stands up and stretches, then turns as if she's planning to leave the cockpit.

"Hold it," I say.

The strain in my voice stops her. "Something bugging you?"

That cold feeling I'd had earlier when looking at the ragamuffin kids comes back, but this time it moves into my spine, making my body feel rigid and brittle, ready to crack. It's the same instinct that's kept me alive for this long. Without answering Venus, I click on the com. "Anyone back there? Is the ramp on the *'Bo* open?"

After a second Hoogs gets back to me. "I'm in the cargo bay, Aly. The ramp is still closed. Can you ask them what the holdup is?"

I activate our transmitter. "Zeta, it's Aly. Need any help over there?" Venus stands behind me. We wait for almost a minute—no response.

I switch back to the com: "Everyone, the 'Bo's crew is in trouble. We need to get—" Before I finish the sentence, an engineering hatch on the other scout's underside bangs open, and five limp bodies fall to the earth. None of them moves, and they hit one by one, first stacking on top of each other and then tumbling into a disorganized heap, devoured by the ship's shadow. My heartbeat suddenly fills my ears, the blood roaring through my body and brain like a supernova. I'm outside the cockpit and sprinting for the cargo bay door before the last body has settled. Dimly, I hear Venus's voice over the intercom, telling the others what we've seen.

Skidding to a stop in front of the cargo bin where we keep the larger weapons inside the bay—the carbines, Dragunovs, and Brownings—I enter the code and scoop up my AK-80 as Hoogs lowers the cargo ramp. With everyone closing in behind him and me as fast as they can, we burst outside. But before we can reach the bodies, the *Teibo*'s jets accelerate to launch torque and force Hoogs and me to our knees, shielding our faces with our arms.

And like that, the ship is screaming forward, gaining momentum before exiting the atmosphere. Leaving a pile of corpses in its wake.

FOURTEEN

"David!" My voice rips out of my throat hard enough to hurt. I'm pulling him over onto his back while Mason and Karl untangle Desto and the others. "No, no, fuck, David, no."

"There are no injuries, no wounds. No . . ." Vitruzzi says, kneeling down and patting their bodies intently, checking their eyes, their pulses. "No, wait!"

Frantically, she yanks open her medkit and withdraws a breath scanner, which she holds over Desto's mouth for a few seconds, staring intently at the readout screen. Her body visibly sags when the device finishes its job. "Just drugged. They've just been drugged. Jesus Christ." She does the same with everyone else—Ryan and the two survivors from the mining colony—then sits hard on her ass, looking shell-shocked.

The nausea that I hadn't realized I was feeling suddenly wins, and I stagger a few feet away, retching out everything I'd just eaten in a ropy puddle of orangish goo. But it makes me feel better. Walking back to David's prone form—though now my brain recognizes the movement of his chest rising and falling with breath—I take off my jacket and cradle it beneath his head.

"What the fuck . . .?" Karl begins, but none of us has the answers.

"Let's get them inside, get some fluid in them," Vitruzzi says. "It was a GABA. They should be conscious within a couple of hours."

The six of us carry them inside. After a short wait, just as Vitruzzi predicted, they begin to regain consciousness, and David is the first to awaken. The twilight outside has darkened to an inky blanket, though the air is thin and cold. We've buttoned up the *Orika* to keep out both the chill and any settlers that could wander out this far to see who we are.

The scout ship's infirmary isn't big enough for all five of the patients, so we laid the two fugees and Ryan out on the extra crew bunks we'd screwed into place in the storage room for salvage runs, and keep watch over David and Desto in the crew's berth. Eleven adults and four children is nearly triple the ship's normal crew size, making things much, much tighter than they ever should be.

"What do you remember?" I ask David. "What happened after we left the scav camp?"

Vitruzzi monitors his vitals and vision as he blinks confusedly. I glance toward her nervously, my query written on my face: *All clear?*

"It's wearing off fine. Nothing permanent to worry about," she says, then moves over to Desto's bunk to check on him.

At first David is groggy and seems unclear about what had happened. "Are we home?" He scratches the back of his neck, then finally focuses on me. "We still on Eruo Pium, Twig?" Then: "Jesus, I'm thirsty."

Vitruzzi had thought of that too and hands him a container of water as I answer, "Yeah. You and the rest of the crew were drugged, knocked out. Do you remember anything?"

After a long drink that seems to bring him back to the here and now, he says, "Desto and I were sitting in the mess having some food. Quantum and one of the fugees came in, and Quantum . . . he asked me if I wanted anything from the ration locker. I remember hearing it open behind me, seeing the fugee walk by Desto, something sharp in my . . ." He reaches behind his head and scratches again.

"David, look toward the wall," I say, then study the skin on the back of his neck when he turns. A tiny scab, the size of a needle prick, shows faintly just to the left of his spine. "Bastards. You said Quantum was be—"

"HAAARRUAH!" Desto shouts and grabs Vitruzzi's wrist so hard I'm afraid he's going to snap it off.

"Desto! Relax, it's me!" she yells, putting her other hand to his chest to try and calm him. Just like David, he starts to blink, trying to focus, then lets go of her.

"What the fuck!" he hollers. "What the . . .?"

Vitruzzi quickly explains what David described as I pass him the water container. Venus comes and leans through the doorway, her face tight with concern. As Vitruzzi wraps up the story, she says, "The two colonists are awake too. And him." She points and Ryan steps into the doorway beside her, looking dazed and close to falling over. Beyond him, I catch a glimpse of two of the fugee kids standing in the corridor, their somber eyes wide and questioning.

"Have they said anything?" Karl asks. Then, looking suspiciously toward Ryan, he follows up: "Is Hoogs on the flight deck?"

Venus nods. "Yeah, he's still trying to hail the 'Bo, but . . ." She shrugs, the corners of her mouth drooping in frustration. "They told me variations of someone grabbed them from behind, then they woke up here."

"You think Quantum had something to do with this?" Mason asks from where he leans against the wall next to Desto's bunk.

David swings his legs onto the floor, ignoring my comment to take it easy, then sits up slowly, gripping the bunk support bar with one hand. "Maybe, unless there was someone else in the room. I only saw the one fugee, the big, blond one who looks a little like—"

"Where's Zeta?" Desto cuts in.

Vitruzzi looks hard into his face, silent, but I drop my own eyes to the floor.

"Where is she, V? Where the fuck is she?"

"We don't know. We think she's still aboard the *Teibo*."

His face flushes an alarming shade of purple as he jumps out of the bunk, nearly busting his melon on the sleeper above him.

"Wait, just slow down. You're not ready to—" I start, but he's not listening, already pushing past Karl and heading toward the doorway.

"Why isn't this thing in the air, Venus? What the hell is everyone standing around for?"

The fury in his voice is frightening, and I see the kid Ryan stumble back to get away from what he must think will be an onslaught. It might take the whole crew working together to bring Desto under control—I don't want it to come to that. Before he can start barreling toward the cockpit, Karl jumps forward and grips one of his wrists, pulling him to a standstill. Karl puts his other hand on the back of Desto's neck and brings their faces close enough to stare eye to eye. "Calm down, brother." His voice is rock solid but compassionate, almost serene. "You gotta smooth out, get still, think this through. You're not going to help her by losing your shit. We will figure this out. But first you need to get it together."

Desto licks his lips, his eyes fused to Karl's, then slowly backs away, relaxed enough for Karl to release his grip.

"Uh." The voice comes from Ryan. Everyone turns to him, surprised, like they'd forgotten he was there. He swallows and reaches out to the wall as if needing support. "I walked in on them while they were planning it."

"Planning what?" Desto growls.

The kid's face is pale, but he soldiers on. "The big one, the blond guy, and your crewmember . . . Quantum? They were talking about hijacking the ship. Said they could use the cargo to barter for something. I didn't, uh, I didn't get what they were talking about. But when they saw me, the blond one grabbed me and then, um"—he looks helplessly at Venus—"then I was here."

"That sonofabitch," David sneers.

The conversation between Quantum and me in the locker room bubbles to the surface of my thoughts. "I think I know where they're going."

FIFTEEN

I just came off my last rotation at the nav bench in the latest six-hour on-duty–off-duty cycle and head for the squad's utility closet. First order of business: get even with Desto for the nauseating stench he doused my body armor in. I've sprayed at least a bathtub full of degreaser and caustic cleaners on the plates, yet the odor of cheap cologne still hits my olfactory bulb like a haymaker when I take a deep breath, but now with the added infusion of cancer-in-a-bottle chemicals. My turn. He'll know exactly what I mean the next time he puts on his combat suit liner and has to suck in lungful after lungful of the cleanser they use in the galley ovens. Nothing like spending a few days trapped inside a bubble of odor that smells exactly like singed hair and burned grease. Unoriginal as the plan may be, the beauty of it is that Desto's size will make it hard for him to find a replacement at the last minute before going out on an operation. I shake the bottle of liquid with glee just thinking about it.

On the way back to my unit's berthing area, I decide to pass through the med-deck to check on Dan Hoogs, who I've become quick friends with since being on the *Celestial*. He took one in the shoulder on our last excursion, but it's healing fine. In a few years the ghost of that impact will sink into his bones deeper and deeper until, in his old age, he'll feel like the bullet took up permanent residence. My own shoulders ache in sympathy. I've hit the deck enough times in my life—in firefights, escapes, life-and-death two-steps—using my hands and knees to break my fall, that pain and my joints are on a first-name basis. The likelihood of either of us living to be old enough for it to matter, small as it is, serves as a tiny—scratch that, *nano*—comfort.

While I pass by the chief medical officer's station, the sound of familiar voices raised in an exchange best described as *heated* stops me short.

"It was a goddamn massacre, Medina." No doubt that's Vitruzzi, and she is clearly pissed. "And you intended it to be from the start. They were nothing but civilian and military casualties, not an organized fighting force."

I hadn't heard the outcome of the operation on Broon, but I'm sure it's what they're discussing. Last I knew from the discussion I'd overheard on the bridge it was supposed to be a surveillance mission to establish the outpost's status.

Medina: "They were potential combatants. This *is* a war. Do I have to remind you?"

Vitruzzi: "That's bullshit! They were *noncombatants*. What you did was murder wounded people and take their supplies."

Medina: "They were Admin Loyalists and sympathizers, which makes them enemies. We give no quarter to enemies."

There's a long pause, then Vitruzzi continues: "No. I am a doctor. I won't allow you to do this. Not again."

Medina: "Dr. Vitruzzi, what you are is an asset. When you stop being an asset, you become expendable. Have I made myself clear?" There's an extremely loaded pause, then Medina continues, "One more thing. Before you and your previous crew decided to blackmail the director of the Ministry of S&E, we had a plan for hollowing out the Admin from the inside. An organized rebellion under my command might have been able to accomplish the goal of a newly formed system peacefully. But you chose an arrogant and absurd vigilante approach, and this war is the result. Maybe you don't like it, but you can't deny that we are in this situation because of you, and someone has to finish it."

I don't have time to get the hell out of there before Medina walks through the doorway, nearly coming nose to nose with me.

"Erikson," she says, her face unreadable.

What is there to say? She pushes by me, and I swing aside to let her pass without a word. As I turn back, Vitruzzi is already on her way out.

"Aly." She stops, the heavy vein that descends from her hairline to between her brows prominent, and seems to consider something deeply before continuing. "Do me a favor, get Karl, Desto, Venus, everyone from the old crew and meet me in Brady's and my bunk in twenty minutes. We're leaving."

THE DISCUSSION WAS BRIEF. Not one of us had the stomach to continue fighting Medina's style of warfare. Brady recommended we bail and join the group of original Agate Beach colonists who'd stayed put at Keum Libre when the war broke out. Others from the Beach had joined the scattered anti-Admin fighting forces or tried to make it back to Spectra 6, their home. We didn't hold out much hope of seeing many of them again, but we'd all had to make our own choice.

By that week's end (six months ago), the plan was in full swing. Medina hadn't so much been consulted as informed of our imminent departure. Vitruzzi, Desto, Brady, Doug Mason, Karl, David, Venus, Jeremy La Mer, and I were splitting off with a few months' worth of supplies and materials and going our own way. No one who knew the plan—though we'd tried to keep it as quiet as possible—had dared to stop us. Not even Medina had tried, but then, how does the unelected commander of a no-longer-military vessel declare a mutiny? Allegiances in any war only run as deep as the fighting force's beliefs; and this war, this large-scale slaughter of the very foundations of our system and civilization, hadn't left much to believe in beyond survival. Medina knew it. And she'd known the second she tried to curtail the rights of anyone on that ship who had fought alongside the rest, the slaughter wouldn't be in the air or on the ground. It would be at her feet.

A handful of our closest friends had joined us at the last minute, including Dan Hoogs. To everyone's surprise, Quantum had elected to join us too. My own reservations about bringing him—the guy, after all, had once kidnapped me and threatened to kill me—didn't amount to much. Someone with his wire-rat skills, as well as the ability to pilot many types of crafts, was an asset we couldn't pass up. And so he came with us. And so . . .

SIXTEEN

My disclosure of what Quantum and I had talked about on the 'Bo is met with all the warmth of people being told they've been selected to test a new enema probe. Not surprising, given the already nonexistent feelings of affection for the wire-rat, despite the fact that he'd helped us get the upper hand on the former director of the Ministry of Science and Engineering, before the war.

"So we're going to Obal 6 to get the ground-down piece of shit," Desto states, rubbing the back of his neck and preparing to leave the bunkroom. "And then I'm going to tear him fifteen new assholes."

"It's not that easy," I say, trying to take him by the wrist and slow him down. Though direct action is my usual course as well, the issue isn't as simple as flying in with guns blazing.

"Aly's right," David says. "Our food and water *might* be enough to get us to Obal 6, but then what?"

"Then what? Then we stomp that conniving bastard into bone powder." Desto glares at each of us in turn. "Since when does this crew decide going after one of its own is too difficult?"

I continue, "I'm not saying we don't go after Zeta. I'm just saying we need to think this through. All we know about that colony is that they're buttoned up tighter than the Fortress, they're armed, and they're not friendly to anyone who can't offer them something better than a hungry mouth to feed or another body to protect."

"The big question is what Quantum plans to tell them. Yeah, he has the—what did you call it, Aly? Seed sequencer? They'll see the utility of having it," Karl says. "But what will he tell Obal 6's colony leadership about Zeta?"

I give him a sharp look to warn him that following that train of discussion isn't going to help right now, but it's too late. He's scowling like he's just swallowed a squirming insect and avoids looking in Desto's direction. What would any unscrupulous person who's kidnapped someone and forced her to fly a stolen ship to a potentially neutral, but definitely not co-conspiratorial, colony do to cover up his crime? Easy: kill her and make it look like an accident before she ever gets a chance to out you.

To Desto's credit, he takes it in stride and responds calmly, "That's exactly what I'm saying. We have to get there before he does, or we're writing her off. And my kid."

"I'll get us up," Venus says, turning to head to the cockpit.

She stops when Vitruzzi says, "We have other kids to worry about now."

"What?" Everyone's face shows the same shock as mine. "What are you talking about?"

Vitruzzi slumps against the wall—when had her posture turned into an S with a broken back?—and won't look at anyone. "These four kids only have us. We have an obligation—"

"To help our crew!" Desto nearly yells.

"Yes, Desto"—she straightens and looks him in the eye—"we can go to Obal 6. We can try and convince them we're the good guys and Quantum is the bad guy. Maybe they'll believe us. Then what? We have no more food, no more water, so we give them everything we have in the cargo bay to buy enough to get us back to Keum Libre. And we're back to where we started. Barely holding on, resources dwindling. For all we fucking know, Keum Libre isn't even there anymore. Some other scavs could have gone in there and wiped it out." Her voice starts to shake, and she takes a deep breath. "Don't you get it? We're fucked. The whole goddamn system is crumbling. We might be too stupid to lie down and die with it, but maybe that's exactly what we should do."

Karl scrambles over to her and puts a hand on her shoulder, soothingly, an old friend trying to offer support. She shrugs it off. No one speaks as she looks around at our faces. I've seen people crack before. The dark shadows from being too strung out to even sleep anymore that crowd into the hollows under her eyes, the way her 1.8-meter frame can barely hold the meat that hangs from it, the edge to her voice when she speaks, like the fading scream of a jumper before they hit the sidewalk—Vitruzzi is a walking case of nearing the terminal breaking point.

As if someone's drawing a curtain away, I'm suddenly thinking back to PCA *Thor's Hammer*, a long-range patroller tasked with joining a convoy of gunships sent out to suppress mutiny on the PCA *Frontline* a week after the Soldier's Rebellion broke out in earnest. I remember his eyes the most—my squad's heavy gunner, Enlistee First Class Tollhut—the way they had darted around the bunkroom like a mismanaged marionette. "We can't board her, not a fleet ship! he'd said. We can't fire on our own people!"

I'd been called out of the navigator's seat down to the armory bay to help calm him down. We'd gone through the Academy and boot together and had served in the same company for the prior two years on the *Hammer*. He trusted me, and more importantly to our command, I was the only one who could fit through the narrow opening between the bunks and cargo bins he'd piled around himself like some kind of last-man-standing barricade.

"What's going on, Tollhut? What's with the drama?" I may be good at fitting into small spaces, but I'm no psychologist when it comes to talking someone off the ledge. Which was rammed home that day.

"That's one of our ships, Erikson. They want us to shoot our own brothers." He stood near the back of the bay behind several hanging racks of bugsuits. I caught glimpses of him moving around and heard clicks and bangs while he spoke, but I couldn't tell what he was doing. "You're always talking about it; can't you see? This is where the line is drawn. *This* is what separates the humans from the monsters in Corps uniforms."

Yeah, I'd known exactly what he was talking about. The story they were feeding us was the Rebellion was a bunch of disgruntled soldiers taking over a few scattered ships. But then it became more than a few ships and more than a few soldiers. Fighting was breaking out on several stations, even on the Obals, and despite how hard our COs tried to keep us from knowing all the details, the stories poured in with every transmission we received and every port we docked at. Something big was going down, and the Corps was beginning to fracture like an overstressed viewscreen in deep space. Tollhut wasn't the only one who thought being asked to fire on our own Corps brothers and sisters was insane.

But what could I tell him? I hadn't known then what to say any more than I know now. I'd rattled on about his duty to his comrades and his duty to justice, and he didn't want to hurt anyone, did he? And blah blah blah. All the while, he'd been putting on a bugsuit— or Goldblum Squad Leveller suit—the heavy-fire body weapons we used for urban terrain seek-and-destroy missions.

When I heard Tollhut say "Switch to full-auto," I jumped behind a crate. When he fired a cement-mixer explosive through his barricade, I'd been knocked unconscious. I'd woken up with David screaming into my ear that we had to get off the ship, we were going down. The *Hammer* never fired a shot on the *Frontline*, and besides us, I never knew how many others made it clear of the ship before it blew. And David and I had spent the rest of the Rebellion trying to stay ahead of the Corps.

Vitruzzi's eyes look just like Tollhut's had.

She's as close to the edge as you can get before falling into the abyss, but I don't know what to tell her. The doomsday shiver from just a little while earlier works its way through me again. I know exactly what Vitruzzi is going through, and I have nothing to offer her. What if she's right? Shaking off that thought, I offer in a voice that's barely above a whisper, "Don't say that kind of thing, V. Yeah, shit's hard, life's not all bubble baths and daffodils, but we just have to keep going. Sometimes survival is as good as it gets."

"Right," she answers, almost accusingly.

"Eleanor, come with me. You need some time to get your head straight," Karl says, turning aside and waving a hand toward the doorway to try and convince her to go. The room suddenly feels like it's shrinking around us.

Finally, without looking at anyone, she pushes past Karl and walks down the corridor toward the cargo bay. No one follows her.

Desto glares after her and the rest of us exchange a knowing look. Mason breaks the cold silence with his always practical observations. "We're going to have to dump the two fugees and keep the salvage we were going to give them."

Nodding thoughtfully, Karl says, "This is their colony anyway, so . . ." I know we're all sharing the same relief that we don't have to ditch them somewhere dangerous or unwelcoming. Then again, we have no idea what life is like in this colony. And there's still Ryan from the *Galatea*. Karl is looking at him, no doubt pondering his fate.

Before someone else does, I make a decision and turn to him. "Guess what, kid, this is your lucky day. You get a choice. We can either drop you here, or you can join the crew. What'll it be?"

To his credit, the look on his face is more excitement than abject terror, and he only hesitates for a second before responding, "With you," then adds hurriedly, "and don't worry, I'll pull my weight."

I try on a grin that doesn't get far, but it's better than nothing because he relaxes a little. "You already have."

Nodding his agreement with the addition of a new crewman, Karl says, "Venus, let's move out."

SEVENTEEN

W e can easily outmaneuver that flying brick, Venus. Why not just shake him off?" David comments from the rear of the flight deck.

"Yeah, I could. But the two *escorts* at our six are military-class scouts. They could yo-yo around us like we're standing still."

David pushes up closer and looks at our radar, finally seeing the tiny specks of the ships that have been dogging us since shortly after we broke into Obal 6's atmosphere. The red glowing specks they make on our nav interface are marginally less worrisome than the equally red but much brighter power-diverter malfunction indicator on the main console telling us we can choose to land within the next couple of hours, or the choice will be made for us.

"Fuh . . ." He trails off, realizing what Venus and I already know. These two scouts are equipped to take out a squad of ships our size if they want to.

"Unidentified transport craft, you are in controlled airspace belonging to Bogotan. What are your intentions? Over."

Venus and I look at each other. Finally, contact.

I respond normally, as if anything is normal anymore. "Bogotan, we are a salvage operation from the Alpha Quadrant with an imminent system malfunction. Request your permission for an emergency landing. Over."

There's a delay, presumably while the scout communicates with someone else. Then: "Negative, scavs. You need to keep on moving."

"This got hostile way faster than I expected," I comment, already running my hand along the nav console and pulling up landscape schematics. In case we have to break for it.

"How far from the city are we?" David asks.

"Just under ninety klicks. We could be there in ten if we didn't have to worry about getting turned into missile kabobs."

"So we could potentially force them to fire on us over their settlement if Venus works some of her magic?"

"Yeah, I mean, we could, but . . . the way she'd have to fly, those kids in back might get tossed around too much—"

"You have one minute to divert, scavs, or we will take aggressive action," the scout warns.

"We are in a situation up here, people. Get buckled in as tight as you can. Things are about to get fun," Venus announces to the crew, then clicks on an audio autocounter that plays over the onboard intercom to give the deadline. David hustles from the cabin, slamming and engaging the cockpit hatch.

"Thirty seconds . . . twenty-nine . . . twenty-eight . . . twenty-seven."

"Aly, you just let me take over," Venus says excitedly, like a kid that just heard their shiny new bike doubles as a rocket racer. "I can handle them."

"Sixteen . . . fifteen . . . fourteen."

I give my harness an extra tug to make sure nothing gets pinched by a loose strap when our g-forces suddenly turn me into a five-hundred-kilo rag doll. A pinched-off boob would give an entirely new meaning to the phrase "on my tits."

"Nine . . . eight . . . seven."

"What's your plan?" I ask.

Venus's head tilts slightly sideways in thought, like an attentive pup. "I haven't quite decided yet."

"Venus . . ."

"I could pull an Ivan, but we'd just end up dead in the air with no place to go but down." She taps the control stick pensively. "Nah."

"Venus . . ." A bit more of an edge in my voice this time.

"Maybe cut the engines, pop the air brakes, and let them fly on by?" She glances at me the way somebody asking for an opinion might—but really not. "No, that's way overdone."

"Four . . . three."

"Dammit, Venus! Can we do anything like that with the power diverter on the fritz?"

"Probably not. We're probably going to die in a meteor of fire." With that, she flashes me a quick grin and cocks an eyebrow. "Just playing, Aly-oop. We're golden."

"*One.*"

"Oh, sh—" I begin, but before I know what's happening, g-forces slam me into my seat, cutting off my breath and slapping my head down with force enough I'd have bitten through my tongue if I weren't lucky. *Hope those kids are squared away.* Apprehension—and a spine-crushing amount of g's—make my throat tight.

Venus yanks the stick hard back, firing us into an insanely steep climb straight up. The ship groans and shudders violently in protest but holds together. Venus's hand darts to the throttles and flicks the port engine to idle. The *Orika* slews sideways. Impossibly, the g-forces get worse, and my grip on consciousness starts to slip.

With barely a strain to her voice, she announces, "High-g pitch-back turn." She glances out the port window. "Should put the sun at our backs too. The old ways still work, y'know?"

She flings the ship hard uphill and turns the belly into the wind. Our airspeed drops to nothing, and the other ships shoot by, far underneath us.

The world through the viewscreen spins wildly: ground, sky, cloud, a blinding flash of sunlight, now ground again. Through my diminishing vision, I see a double pulse of light and two streaking vapor trails.

Venus grunts. "That's two missiles we won't have to worry about. Now, the fun part."

She straightens the controls and slams the port throttle forward again. Instantly the g's relax, and I desperately suck in a breath. My vision comes back to normal, and our speed climbs rapidly as we dive back down like a bird of prey.

Venus rolls the ship a few degrees, then pulls hard back on the stick again. The g's hit once more but not quite as strong. Her eyes dart to the radar, then back to the viewscreen. Eyes narrowed in concentration, she calmly says, "Give me the ventral thrusters when I ask for them, please."

I'm already too sick and oxygen deprived to ask why. Then the enemy ships appear in our viewscreen, dead ahead. The thought *suicide run* flashes in my mind, but then she pops the nose of the ship up.

"Ventral thrusters . . . *now*."

She flicks the throttles back with the dexterity of a concert pianist, and we level out barely meters above their ship, with the blast from our thrusters reflecting off their hull and against ours, giving just enough extra cushion to keep us from slamming into them. Even so, I think I felt the slightest impact, like we actually touched.

Almost as if she's in my head and hearing my thoughts, Venus says, "We did. I misjudged it by a couple meters." She shrugs and continues straight on. "One of those scouts is a newer pilot. He wasted his missiles on a wild shot when we did our climb, then he couldn't stick with us. His leader is smarter." She grins her silly, slightly wild grin again. "So he wouldn't fly into the blast of what he thought was a kamikaze run."

She snaps the controls hard over and jams the throttles to their stops. With a rending screech, we slide sideways off the top of the other ship, roll upside down, and pull hard up, down—shit, *whatever* —toward the ground. The world outside does another sickening psychedelic kaleidoscope routine, and I feel my last meal, maybe *literally* my last meal, looking for a way out.

"Yep, here he comes again," she calmly announces. "His angle on us isn't too good, but it's close enough that he'll probably try a—yeah, thought so. Missiles inbound." An earsplitting buzzer nearly drowns out her last few words. "They'll be on us in a few seconds."

We're pointing straight down at the ground with the engines screaming at full thrust. A thin layer of wispy clouds is in the distance, far below us, then all of the sudden it isn't, and the ground is perfectly clear, colorful, and getting more so by the instant.

"The nice thing about the really fast missiles," Venus murmurs, "is that they don't turn well."

I close my eyes, suck in a breath, and grit my teeth, just in time for another assault on my senses as she makes yet another maneuver that smashes all my internal organs into what feels like chunky tomato soup against my pelvis.

Dammit, I wish he'd just shoot us down already.

Through the pain and what I hope is a silent scream on my part, I feel a couple small jolts, like driving over bumps in the road.

Venus says cheerfully, "Missed. I'll bet that lead scout must be getting pretty frustrated by now. We're over the city, by the way."

I open my eyes as the last hills and trees flash by our sides, and we break out over Bogotan, slowing and dropping in altitude enough to make shooting us down here guaranteed to damage the city. "That's the craziest set of flying you've put me through yet," I comment, my voice a reluctant rattle. "I hope everyone's okay back there."

Venus replies, "They'll be fine. I left the gravity compensators on full back in the hold."

"So you just needed to turn it off here in the cockpit?"

"Yep." She climbs to get a little bit more altitude and take the engines back from redline. Then she relaxes a bit more in her seat. "Well, no. I just thought it would be funny. You probably didn't know it, but you can make some really nutty faces." Without missing a beat, she keys the radio. "This is the *Orika* to Bogotan, requesting landing clearance. Or we can just slam into midtown. Thanks for your attention. Over."

Venus looks as relaxed as a cat in a sunbeam. If I could take the cue from her, I would, but my skeleton currently feels like it may have recently been used to support a skyscraper.

"We're on approach," she notifies the crew. "Should be landing in about a minute. The kind people of Bogotan are more likely than not going to be welcoming us in full splendor, so I suggest we do the same. Out."

Our high-speed approach only allows for a limited glimpse of the infrastructure, but our nav scopes record everything and create an instant three-dimensional map. On the two-week trip here, the crew used every hour studying the archival images and prints of Bogotan. As a smaller city with limited manufacturing, it had missed most of the systematic destruction of first the uprising masses, then the Admin when they went through the system and razed all communication satellites.

With a radius of just under five thousand kilometers and a surface of 75 percent water, Obal 6 is the smallest Obal in the system and had the lowest population density of the Admin-ruled planets—now, given its low priority during the war, it may have the highest. To citizens, it had always been thought of as the backwoods Obal, the kind of place an eccentric old aunt or moonshining pappy would have settled down.

On my last trip, just before the war, we'd been brought here by Quantum to take advantage of the vast web of citizen-owned communication satellites, our intent being to blackmail T'Kai, former director of the Ministry of Science and Engineering—though now I think of him simply as the reason the human race just got blasted about a thousand years back toward the Stone Age. This time we'd dropped out of orbit into its atmosphere on the planet's dark side and flown over two of its five major continents. The destruction, even from ten thousand meters, is unreal. Blackened craters mar the landscape where most of the major cities used to stand, and those that weren't annihilated seem to have fallen to ruin through inside fighting, loss of civil structure and leadership, or just abandonment.

Depending on what side people took after the mass-broadcast revelation of the Admin's policy of using citizens and soldiers as biological test subjects, the cities had become too dangerous, especially for citizens who were known to have been former Corps or higher-ups in the Admin echelon. Some say half the system's population died, some say more. What I know is—there's no one left to take a head count.

"Easy. Easy, now. Just cool your jets a little, people. We aren't that scary."

Venus is talking to herself, but her audience could be the scouts now hovering on our wings as we glide to a landing zone on the settlement's edge. Two smaller ships, retrofitted citizen-class compacts, were apparently also scrambled to "welcome" us, and the *Orika* is now covered from four angles, making escape impossible.

The skids hit the earth and the hydraulics settle smoothly. Venus has already unstrapped her harness and heads toward the cockpit exit without a glance back. I unlock too and rise to my feet but have to blindly reach out and grab the back of the navigator's seat to keep myself from pitching headfirst into the console. My legs take a couple of seconds to decide if they're still part of the team, then I'm finally able to follow Venus out.

Karl meets me in the cockpit's antechamber, his face nearly as blanched as my own must be. "You okay?"

"Yeah." I give him a grin. "You?"

"Someday I'll get used to Venus's flying." I raise my eyebrow at him, and we both force a short giggle. "Or maybe not." His face turns serious. "Look, Aly. I'm . . . I don't know how to say this, but I want you to follow my lead on this. Eleanor's not . . . herself, and Desto, well, you know. I don't trust either of them to make sound choices right now, so I'm taking point."

I nod, feeling more relieved about his plan than I'd expected.

"I'll back you up too, bro," David says, joining us from the crew deck below. "And I know Hoogs and Mason are on board. We all heard V . . ."

He doesn't have to elaborate. I'd told Karl about the way Vitruzzi had reacted when we crashed back on Eruo Pium, the way she froze up when the hovercraft attacked us. It's clear the word got around. After her meltdown before leaving the mining colony, the rest of the crew isn't taking chances.

"They'll be knocking on our door soon. Let's get it together," Karl says.

The hold is secure for now, but anyone with the proper motivation and a high-output plasma torch can get inside in no time. The crew gathers, ready to implement part two of the plan.

Which is to say—improvise.

"Desto, I clearly remember you being present when we said we were going to try this with no guns. Did you forget how to count?" Karl says.

The father-to-be stands in the hold next to the manual hatch release, waiting for us, and his body bristles with barrels and blades pointing in every direction.

"You know they outnumber us by a few hundred. We're not going to handle this thing like kamikazes," Karl finishes.

The hard set of Desto's face makes me think this isn't going to end well. The eight of us, nine if we count Ryan—but he strikes me as too smart to jump into this kind of fray—could restrain a man of Desto's size, if we're willing to take a few hits. After all, none of us wants to get shot before we even have a chance to get off the ship, but we're guaranteed to be bruised and bloodied, and—

Desto swings the Thresher over his shoulder and drops it on the deck, his eyes peering at the rest of us like a judge passing sentence on condemned heretics. The rifle clatters loudly in the tight space, and he sends a carbine and TorcherMax to follow it. His hand goes to the Sinbad on his right hip and stops there. No glare ever promised more pain if anyone steps up to challenge him.

Drawing a breath that doesn't quite hide his relief, Karl turns questioningly toward Vitruzzi. She has the four children drawn up around her like a squad of miniature soldiers. Despite their malnutrition, the most hollow set of eyes in the group is Vitruzzi's. She stands near the rear of the hold, letting Karl run the show.

"Why isn't anyone demanding we open up?" I wonder aloud.

"Maybe they're waiting for an invitation," David replies, surreptitiously pulling his jacket tighter around the pistol in his shoulder harness. In this crew, a decision against carrying guns is really a decision against carrying *visible* guns. Some people have lucky rabbits' feet, others have lucky firepower.

As if on cue, Desto depresses the hatch control and the ramp begins to lower.

"Remember, they're not our enemies," Karl says quietly.

Right, I think, *because if they were, they would have fired missiles at us*. But pointing out the obvious would be counterproductive at the moment.

"Wait, where's Venus?" I spin around, searching for her, but don't see her anywhere.

The ramp hits the tarmac outside, and no one says a word. Is she hiding? We hadn't talked about leaving anyone on the ship—too late now.

I shiver, suddenly hit by a blast of dry, cold air. It feels like the planet has been locked inside an icebox for the last year, but anywhere feels that way after Keum Libre's humid sweatbox climate. My muscles clench in protest. Cold muscles slow down reaction time —I'll need to keep moving to stay limber.

From where we stand, the tarmac appears empty. If anyone waits for us, they're holding back until we're clear of the *Orika*'s relative cover.

"Hello?" Karl calls into silence. Nothing. "We're stepping outside. We are nine adults and four kids total. Our intentions are peaceful."

Another blast from the icebox whistles up the *Orika*'s crew deck corridor, but nothing else.

Karl nods to me where I stand on his left, then to Desto and Mason, on his right, and we amble as a group down the ramp, our hands remaining visible. It feels like we're walking off the edge of a cliff.

I sense a movement far to my right and glance over. The older little girl, a blonde-haired one of about seven, has left the bunch circling Vitruzzi and moves up to Doug Mason. She grabs his big, rough hand in one of hers and squeezes it, as if she's trying to reassure him. Doug smiles down at her. When he does, his face opens up in a way I've never seen—never even imagined—and for the first time, I realize that Mason could be someone's kindly uncle, or their dad. He'd had a wife, another soldier, but she died in a friendly-fire accident prior to the Soldier's Rebellion. This is the face of Mason who might have been—if so many things had turned out differently. The girl—was her name Cassandra?—tugs at his hand, then reaches up toward his neck. He squats and scoops her off the ground like she's made of feathers and sets her in the crook of his arm. She leans in to hug him, and he rubs her back.

Shaking off the odd feeling seeing this new, or, not new but *other*, Mason causes, I pull my attention back to the moment. Out on the landing tarmac, nothing stirs. The four ships standing guard on us maintain their hover but don't land.

The curly headed younger girl, with features close enough to Vitruzzi's that she could be the doc's daughter, looks around the empty tarmac. "What happens now?" she asks in a voice teetering between curiosity and fear.

"What the fuck?" Desto says. "Is this some kind of ghost town?"

"If it is, those scouts are some of the liveliest ghosts I've ever seen," David replies. His head swivels as if on bearings, evaluating the locations of the sentry ships.

Mason juts an elbow into Desto's bicep. When Desto glances at him to see what's up, Mason scowls, then glances meaningfully at the top of the girl's head.

"Shih—I mean, damn, sorry, man."

Everyone's attention turns back toward our surroundings. Besides the scouts at our periphery, the place could be abandoned. But the breeze carries the sound of some kind of machinery, possibly the steel plant on the north end that we'd all seen on the town's schematics.

"I'm cold. Can we go back inside?" one of the little boys asks. His dark hair and the gleaming blue of his eyes remind me of Cross.

"We can soon," Vitruzzi promises him. "We just have to find whoever lives here first. They may have . . . a friend of ours may be here, and we need to find out."

The boy's lip wrinkles back in resignation and he looks at the ground. Something about his childlike disappointment tickles my funny bone, and I grin. David gives me a curious glance. Shrugging, I say, "Well, if they're not going to bring us a 'welcome to the neighborhood' fruit basket, we may as well go to them. Desto, you ready?"

He starts to walk forward but stops when David rests a hand on his shoulder. Desto glances back at David, who slowly shakes his head. "It has to be a trap."

"Doesn't matter. We're here, they have all the advantage. We can't just stand here with our thumbs up our asses and wait for them to bring us some nappies." Desto's severe expression communicates a resolve that nothing short of a missile through the middle of him will dampen. He's right. There's no changing our minds now.

My voice sounds tinny in the cold air. "Let's do this."

We've landed on the original docking tarmac. Forty meters ahead is a brick and steel berm, fifteen meters high, designed to protect the dock control buildings from the blasts of exploding engines or skidding out-of-control ships. A heavy steel gate, wide and tall enough to accommodate large track vehicles or trucks, leads through the berm to the town beyond. Both the gate and sections of the berm are marred by dents and gouges, showing the age and heavy use this airfield had seen, at least in the past, if not currently. Bogotan had once been a reasonably busy city, but Desto is right—it feels like a ghost town now.

"Through there, let's go," Karl says, leading the way to the gate.

Standing up close, it towers above us about six meters. There doesn't seem to be a man-door anywhere, the gate the only way through. It remains as closed and sealed as an airlock at our approach, and David steps forward. He knocks. The ridiculousness of his maneuver is enough to burst the tension running through me, and I can't help but chuckle. Shrugging and grinning too, he puts an ear to the door.

"No porch light," he says. "Maybe we're early? They could still be out grocery shopping for the dinner par—"

Before he finishes the quip, the sound of a rattling and ill-kept engine begins somewhere deep in the berm. Involuntarily, I jump a little and reach to my belt—where no weapon hangs. Muttering a curse, I back away a few paces, mirroring what the rest of the crew is also doing.

The seam in the middle of the two gate doors begins to gape as the opening mechanism pulls them apart. I feel utterly naked and exposed. How did we think this was a good idea? How? What they failed to do with the scout is going to be laughably easy with us just standing here like idiots. My breathing starts to feel shallow, as if panic is setting in. *Think of Zeta,* I tell myself. This is about her and about doing what we can to help her. If we didn't try—and Desto didn't mow us all down for being cowards—we wouldn't be human. We're doing what's right, what we have to for the sake of our existence. Survival isn't the only thing.

Convincing myself of this is going to take a lot more than a self-pep talk, however.

The grating sound of the poorly maintained gate reaches into my throat and drags claws across my insides, and my vision begins to narrow. This isn't right; something is about to go terribly, irretrievably wrong. I'm having a hard time breathing, and it's getting worse. Like someone is squeezing my lungs.

"What's wrong with her?" I hear one of the children ask, but his voice sounds far off.

I begin to turn around, ready to sprint back to the *Orika* and pick up the weapons Desto had left lying on the cargo deck, the feeling of dread sinking into my core and making my whole body feel heavy. And then—*Why am I lying on David's feet?*—a shroud covers me.

EIGHTEEN

"Aly. Aly." Karl's voice parts through layers of cobwebs encasing my brain.

My eyes slide open and he's there, leaning over me, concern filling his sepia eyes and his hand cradling my neck.

I'm fine, I try to tell him, but it comes out: "Mfffmmf."

"Can you sit up?"

Wherever we are, there's enough light to see clearly that I'm lying on a military-issue cot, like the one Venus keeps in her maintenance bay on KL's ocean platform. The rest of the crew are scattered around me, sitting on or standing near more cots. I reach out and Karl grabs my hand to steady me as I pull myself into a sitting position.

"Where are we?" I ask.

He shakes his head. "Dunno, exactly. Some kind of school building."

"A school?" It's as if he'd said we're in a cotton candy factory; my mind is too fuzzy to process or make any sense of what he's saying. I remember standing at the landing-field gates, panicking. Had I passed out? The two things don't add up. "Why a school?" is all I can manage.

"Whatever the reason, they want us alive," Mason says from a couple of cots away.

"What happened?"

From the bunk next to mine, David explains. "You forgot to take out your filter. The air is good here and you didn't need it, so you were breathing almost pure oxygen, plus your blood pressure hadn't fully regulated after all the fancy flying Venus did. You blacked out right before our escort arrived." He drops the offending apparatus on the cot next to me, and I stare at it as if it's an alien that had until recently lived in my skull.

I blink a few times and take a couple deep breaths, and the last of the fog starts to clear. "You're saying I fainted?"

"And scared the shit out of all of us," Karl adds.

David nods. "Then colony guards rounded us up and brought us here." He smirks, but not in amusement. "You really missed out on the fun. We've been waiting for about ten minutes for"—he shrugs—"something." He peers at me closely for a couple more seconds, then stands. "You're all right. Now, let's see what we have here."

Everyone has been disarmed, down to our last blades, but the locals left us alone otherwise. So the situation is simply that we're being held inside a school gymnasium, at their mercy until they decide otherwise. So far, our improvising leaves a lot to be desired. We spread out and begin to sweep the room, leaving Vitruzzi seated with the kids while Karl moves up to the main doorway, keeping an eye out for company. Walking along the vista-screen that covers the back wall, I search for the control booth that runs the giant image player schools use to help students train for different sports. The material of the screen is hard but thin, but that doesn't matter because it's probably backed up by either cinder block or something equally solid. I come across the control panel at the far end, but instead of being in another room—where we might get lucky and find an exit—it's just an interface box on the wall for loading and operating new training programs. Frustrated, I turn toward the others, hoping for different results.

"Anything?" I call.

Desto doesn't respond, and I realize I've lost sight of Mason. As I scan the massive rectangular room for him, my eyes catch on a doorway set into the wall on my left—which Mason is coming out of.

Immediately breaking into a jog, I stop short of him when he shakes his head. "Just a bathroom," he says.

"Hey! Company," Karl shouts and starts backing toward the cots, which are all clustered a few meters from the main entryway.

We quickly group around Vitruzzi and the kids, ready for whatever. As ready as you can be, that is, when you're trapped in a high school gymnasium, shipless, weaponless, and until recently, unconscious.

The doors retract smoothly, sliding into the grooves in the walls on either side, revealing three silhouettes. The light outside is much brighter, punctuating the overall dimness surrounding us and nullifying any sense of safety or protection—no matter how false—the dark might have given me.

The three enter, one man slightly in the lead. He's lean and tall, all angles, with sharp elbows and long, thick-jointed fingers, a pointed nose that looks like you could use the ridge of it to cut the heads off small animals, and straight, broad, but almost dainty shoulders. His whole body resembles a delicate but deadly medieval torture instrument. Even the blue of his eyes is piercing, though they are heavily bloodshot.

Despite his thinness, nearly gauntness, his approach is deliberate and stern. He walks like a man who is used to being listened to and who never makes a move without a purpose. He walks like someone no one fucks with, and I'm utterly certain that our foray into Bogotan is not going to be dull. Hasn't been so far, in any case.

This man—obviously the honcho—and his two flanking musclemen plant themselves a meter in front of us. The crew stands in unison, mentally and physically alert and ready for whatever's coming next. Before saying a word, he looks at each of us individually, and as his bloodshot blue eyes look into mine, the intelligence in them bleeds through like a strobe light on a dark night.

Breaking the silence, he asks, "I'm glad to see everyone on their feet. Is anyone suffering from any immediate needs? Injuries, thirst, hunger? Any chronic medical issues that require tending?"

A query about our well-being is about the last thing I had expected, especially with the amount of authentic concern in his voice. I glance at David questioningly. *Did I hear that right?* His raised eyebrow shows the same level of surprise.

"Anyone? No? Okay, that's good news." He turns his head to the man on his left, a brawny, scowling meat sack that oozes militancy and rage like a bad skin infection. "Van Heusen, their meal, please."

The muscleman returns to the door and steps out, and our captor continues, "Please, everyone, let's all sit and discuss the circumstances we find ourselves in."

None of us move, not about to let our guards down, and he and the other bodyguard continue to stare at us—him with calm but detached concern, the meathead with a blank gaze that could belong to a robot.

"I see," is all he says.

A second later, the first guard comes back through the doorway pushing a plastic, four-wheeled cart in front of him. The smell of warm bread nearly knocks me off my feet, the reality of how hungry I am immediate and severe. None of us has eaten a decent meal in a few days, having been worried and diligent about rationing to hopefully make it back to KL. A tsunami of saliva rushes into my mouth.

Without waiting for the go-ahead, the four fugee children swarm the cart, ignoring Vitruzzi's urgent "Hold it!"

The blue-eyed one who reminds me of Cross uncovers a platter, and exclaims, "Cinnamon rolls!" Then looks inside a box: "And comic holos!" He seems more delighted about the live-action comic holographs than the cinnamon rolls. The guard whispers something to their leader.

"We intend to provide for everyone, I assure you," Skinny says. "We wouldn't have fired on your ship if we'd known you had children aboard."

"Why did you fire on us in the first place? Who the hell are you?" Desto asks, the longevity of his patience shorter than my eyelash.

"Desto," Karl says and moves his hand in front of him in a *calm down* gesture, then he regards Skinny. "Look, we don't know who you are, but you have some explaining to do. Firing on an unarmed transport ship without cause? What kind of people do that?"

Vitruzzi and Mason hover over the kids protectively while Skinny takes his time responding. All four of the children have helped themselves to the rolls and dig in with fervor while watching the action holo, which they've set up on one of the cots.

Skinny steps over to the cart the man he'd called Van Heusen brought in and opens up the sliding door on one side. The smell of warm bread gets stronger, and I see plates and carafes inside. He gestures to it. "Help yourselves. We've brought coffee, eggs, toasted bread, and, I believe, some fruit." When none of us move toward the cart—despite what I'm certain is naked longing on our faces—he sighs and continues, "I understand your anger and confusion. That's natural. We fired on your ship with engine phase bots that would disable you and bring you down, but not harm you. Surely you understand our need to keep our population safe?" He gestures at the food again. "Please. You don't need to be concerned. We are all too short on allies in this new world."

A gurgle of hunger twists through my stomach, the noise audible to everyone in the room. Shit, if I'm going to die on this planet, I may as well do it on a full stomach. Stepping up and grabbing the cart by the handle, I pull it closer to the crew and pass them plates and forks. No one hesitates to take one.

After we all dish ourselves up, completely emptying the food platters, Karl says around his first mouthful, "We're here for one reason and have no intent to stay. Two weeks ago, a friend of ours was kidnapped, along with the long-range transport ship she was piloting. We think the kidnappers brought her here, so we came to find out. That's it. Is there anything you can tell us?"

Hanging on Karl's words, I study our captors, hoping to read some good news in their faces. The thugs stay cool, but recognition flits over Skinny's face.

"You know something," Vitruzzi says, seeing the same thing. "Tell us."

"Ms. Zeta Abrams, flying the *Teibo*," he states, and my guts knot up. "She's already on her way to your home. Keum Libre. She's fine. Almost four months pregnant, too."

What? How would he know that?

"What the hell are you talking about?" Desto asks, his tone betraying a confounded and barely harnessed rage.

The guards react. Van Heusen reaches behind his back and withdraws a set of stun sticks. Thug Two does the same. Each stick is good for two loads, but the more important thing their choice of weapons tells me is that they don't want us dead. But why should we believe Zeta had been sent back to KL if they're holding us captive?

The questions keep piling up. "Answers, Skinny," I prompt. "It's time for some goddamn answers."

"Yes, of course." He smirks self-consciously and his eyes blink rapidly in a tic of some kind. Yet their focus on us never wavers. "First off, I am—or was—Port Control Authority Deputy Jim Whitmore. Now I'm just Jim, and I help keep safe and secure the last colony of consequence here on Obal 6. These men are Daimler Van Heusen, who heads Bogotan's security crew, and Jono Zabriskie, another of the colony's important members. I want to assure you that you are not captives here, and that we fired on your transport merely in an attempt to keep you from endangering the city." He clasps his hands together in front of his waist, almost wringing them. "Obviously, we have much to learn."

"Zeta, how did you know she was pregnant?" Desto demands.

Looking surprised, Whitmore responds, "Well, she told me. Over dinner the night before she flew home, which was three days ago. She was quite exhausted after the trip here, being one of only two pilots among the crew she arrived with, and—"

"Quantum and the fugees. Where are they?" I break in.

Whitmore smiles patiently. "I'll come back to that. I think you're all first concerned with the well-being of your friend, as anyone would be." I have to grit my teeth at his not-quite-condescending tone. "As I said, she was quite tired but understandably in a hurry to get back to your home moon. She and the others explained the situation regarding your salvaging operation, which is quite harrowing. We gave her the resources she needed, and she went on her way. After hearing Ms. Abrams's story, we anticipated the possibility of your arrival, but unfortunately, our airspace security team is jumpy—for good and obvious reasons. I can't apologize enough for the way things have developed."

"You sent Zeta back to KL," Desto reiterates, "on the *Teibo*."

"Yes, that's right."

"She's on her way home—alone. On the *Teibo*. A ship that requires a minimum of two to crew. That what you're saying?"

Desto rises from his bunk and looms like a multikilo colonnade about to crumble into them. Van Heusen says, "Easy, scav. Don't give me a reason."

"Desto," Karl says quietly to get him to calm down, then turns back to Whitmore. "Answer him." Then, as an afterthought: "*Please.*"

Whitmore steps up to the cart and casually pours himself a cup of coffee while continuing. "Ms. Abrams's crew—"

"Kidnappers," I cut in.

He glances at me and sips his coffee. "Yes, if you insist. Quantum and the other men did not harm Ms. Abrams, which she was explicit about. The dynamic between them was unfortunate, of course, and this colony doesn't tolerate that kind of aggression"—*unless someone's flying a transport ship you don't recognize*, I think—"but we did listen to their reasoning."

"But didn't you try shooting them down the way you did us?" Desto inquires, reading my mind.

For the first time, Whitmore shows signs of impatience, placing his cup down hard enough to make the coffee splash lightly over the rim and onto the cart. "No, they did not appear to be as threatening. They hailed Bogotan from several kilometers distant and landed, then waited for our security team to reach them."

"You can't expect us to believe a goddamn word you have to say unless—"

"Desto, let the man speak," Vitruzzi cuts him off, an edge in her voice that I haven't heard since the war.

"This is bullshit, Vitruzzi, and you know it! Where is that sonofabitch now? This talking head is just stalling until . . ."

From the corner of my eye, I catch Van Heusen aiming his stun stick at Desto. Things are about to start going much worse for us if he doesn't cool it. For just a second, I consider letting Van Heusen take him out. Then think better of it.

"Hold it, Bomani. Just chill." I turn to Whitmore. "Look, we've been through some rough shit lately. This hemming and hawing isn't going to get us anywhere fast, so let's just cut to the chase, Whitmore. We need to know our friend is safe. What can you do to assure us, and when are we getting out of here?"

Karl gives me a grateful look and his shoulders relax just slightly. Mason has stepped in front of the group of kids, who've stopped watching the holo and stare wide-eyed at the exchange. The thought flits through my mind that their adult selves are going to contribute brand-new colors to the spectrum of psychologically damaged. "So?" I prompt.

Whitmore links his hands behind his back and steps out from behind the cart toward Desto. "You're the father, I presume. Please believe me, I understand what you're going through. I have two of my own. Sons." He steps closer to the group of kids, and Mason tenses for a moment, staring hard at Whitmore. But he drops a shoulder and lets Whitmore by, where he puts a hand on the blue-eyed boy's shoulder in a fatherly gesture. The kid doesn't flinch, but he doesn't smile either. He just looks at the adult emotionlessly. "I wish I knew where they were."

No one speaks for a moment as Whitmore continues to look at the boy, and his eyelids do another series of fast-paced blinks. Finally, he turns to face the rest of us. "I understand your worries, so I'll just give you the details you want. Ms. Abrams went back to your colony with one of our pilots and a third crewmember to assist. We plan to send a team to pick them up within the week. And they're also going to retrieve this soil amendment compound your former colonist Quantum told us about, along with the cache of raw materials other members of your colony previously retrieved on a salvaging run. Quantum is going to assist us in recreating this world."

"I'LL KILL THE BASTARD."

No one responds to Desto's pronouncement. I glance at Vitruzzi to see her reaction to the news that Quantum has bought his place in this colony with the soil amendment compound, and for the first time in what seems like weeks, her expression shifts into the Vitruzzi from before the war.

"You can't do that," she says.

Whitmore looks surprised. "We can't do what?"

"You can't use that compound. You don't know how to, or what it's capable of."

"Miss...?"

"I'm Dr. Eleanor Vitruzzi, previously the head of R&D in the Ministry of Science and Engineering. My expertise is in the field of cyber- and bio-physiology with considerable overlap with virology, immunology, and disease research. So when I tell you that you *can't* use that soil compound, I know exactly what I'm talking about."

"Dr. Vitruzzi, I-I am, I would say, I am *grateful* to meet you." For the first time Whitmore's in-control attitude gives way, revealing a postwar survivor with the same hanging-by-a-thread worries everyone has. "We in Bogotan are doing our best to stay out front of any catastrophes of the nature of which you are so skilled in coping with—"

"I don't want to hear it. You have no idea what you're dealing with in terms of that compound. I don't know what Quantum told you, but it can't be the truth. The man is a calculating opportunist, nothing more. He didn't like the way we run our colony on Keum Libre, so he looked for the easiest out and he took it—without regard to the health of a pregnant woman, I'll add. The fact that you've listened to a single goddamn word he's said to you, knowing what he's done to get here, says all I need to know about your judgment. And I'm telling you, that compound *cannot* be used."

Shit. Vitruzzi's tactician skills must have been another casualty of the war. But none of us disagrees with her approach.

"Doctor, I understand your opinion, but based on Quantum's explanation, it has the potential to become a vital link in replenishing the planet's food supply. It could save thousands, even millions, of lives. We cannot let a useful resource like—"

"No, you're not listening," Vitruzzi cuts in. "This soil compound isn't a resource. It's a poison that we don't fully understand."

David adds, "If it were deployed and you lost control, no one knows exactly what could happen."

"Actually, we *do* know exactly what will happen. The survivors of the KL prison settlement saw the results of the Admin's testing first-hand. An extinction-level event on a scale we haven't seen since the terra-forming disasters of last century." Vitruzzi pauses, then adds, "Or the war. "

Van Heusen speaks up: "Then we don't lose control. It's that simple."

"Simple?" V says. "Have you been paying attention to anything but your own ass for the last twenty-four months? *Simple* doesn't exist, not anymore."

Karl tries to cut in. "Eleanor—"

"No, goddammit! You're talking about—"

"That's quite enough, Doctor. Please." Whitmore's posture is tense, but his voice hasn't lost any of its calm. "This is a necessary and important discussion. My biggest hope is that we can carry it out in an amicable and thoughtful way. But first, let us get our team back with the compound. We can evaluate next steps then. Together." He turns to the man he'd called Zabriskie and says, "Jono, can you ask Korine to bring them coats and hats? It's autumn on Obal 6," he explains, turning back to us, "and I'm assuming you don't have many warmer clothes."

"Does that mean you're not holding us?" Karl asks.

"No, of course not, Mister . . . ?" When Karl doesn't respond, Whitmore blinks rapidly, gets it under control, then continues, "No. This isn't a prison, as I've already explained. We'll afford you the same hospitality I would hope you'd extend us if we came to your settlement. As far as we're concerned, Bogotan and the people of your settlement are not enemies. This is about cooperation, not antagonism. You're free to stay here, in this building, while you're on Obal 6. Come and go as you please. As long as you don't endanger any of our colonists, we will make sure you have what you need until our colonies reach a mutual agreement."

He pauses and reaches for his coffee cup but doesn't pick it up. "My ultimate hope, however, is to integrate. Pool not just our resources, but our people." He returns his blink-free stare to all of us. "We are not factions, we are survivors. We all need each other to ensure a future."

Before Whitmore and his men leave us in the gymnasium, he informs us that his people had attempted to "secure" the *Orika*, but she was locked up tight. Everything they tried to open it had ended up with the hatches either remaining locked or reversing as soon as they started to release. We all know it's Venus, still inside and keeping herself barricaded in as long as she can, but we don't tell him that. Karl lets on that it's the security system and nothing more, and given that it's our vessel, no one's getting aboard but us. Looking dubious, Whitmore makes the decision to drop it—for the time being—and exits.

"I don't care how much Whitmore acts like sweet old Uncle Fred, we have to get the hell out of here and back to KL before—who knows what," David says.

"Yeah, of course, we all agree that's the case. And if we play nice and Desto doesn't step on his dick, we can probably do it without anyone getting hurt." Karl stares hard at Desto as he says this, but his message is loud and clear to all of us. Between Desto's rage and Vitruzzi's bouts of . . . *ineffectiveness*—to put it nicely—we have double the number of loose canons to cope with, which is twice more than we want. "I don't think Whitmore wants any trouble either," he finishes.

Desto cuts in, "What he wants and what he asked for are two different things, Karl. You heard him. He's letting that bag of recycled meat vapor walk around free. And—"

"He's letting us walk around free too—"

"—after what he did to Zeta, he can't be trusted. Hell, V, you said it yourself. The guy has no judgment; he's off the hook and we don't know what's really going on here."

"I'm not saying we have to trust him, but we're in his kitchen. We can't start cooking his food behind his back and hope he doesn't notice." Karl looks at all of us in turn while he speaks, and I roll my eyes at his analogy. He shrugs, knowing how ridiculous it sounded.

"I'm not suggesting we do anything behind his back," Desto continues. "We take our goddamn ship and leave. If anyone tries to stop us, we blow their fucking balls off. *After* I rip Quantum's off with my bare hands."

"What did I just say about not stepping on your dick?" Karl's reasonable tone begins to show strain, but he takes a deep breath before continuing, ignoring Desto's grimace of fury. "If we do that, we'll get shot down, or worse, get stranded midtrip when we run out of fuel. And what about food? And them?" He waves a hand at the kids, then turns and looks off toward the far side of the room, thinking. Turning back, he scrubs his palm over the heavy stubble lining his cheeks and chin, then says, "Look, maybe we need to take a mental time-out. We've been at war for almost two years; our first reaction is to fight. But . . . maybe we're past that. Maybe we have to *let* ourselves be past that. Maybe this is the first chance we have—the first chance *people* have—to start picking up the pieces. If we handle this carefully, calmly, *rationally*, everyone might get what they want."

The crew is quiet for a minute, all of us listening thoughtfully. Impulsively, I grab one of Karl's hands. It's cold inside mine but begins warming up quickly. He turns to look at me, having to tilt his head down because I'm so close. The warmth and gratitude in his eyes make it impossible for me to drop mine.

And I realize—this is it. This is the reason we have to stop fighting, have to stop running, and have to start finding a way to, as Whitmore put it, "recreate this world" together. People helping people. We have to give up the divisions and the factions and the war and the hate because of what I see in Karl's face when he looks at me. There *is* more to our lives than surviving, ticking off the minutes until we're all dead. And he's standing right in front of me.

Turning back to face the group, I say quietly, but firmly, "I'm with Karl. This isn't about shooting our way out of here. It's our opportunity to try something new." My eyes find Desto's. "Think about your kid, Bomani. If you ever want to meet her, you have to be willing to give yourself, and the rest of us, a chance."

The muscles in his face are as tense as a rebar armature. If his stance were any more rigid, he'd be a statue; only his nostrils move, flaring in the anything-goes moment between giving up or blowing up. Finally, he spins around and grips one of the cots, hurling it into the emptiness of the gymnasium with a rage-filled yell. One of the little girls begins to whimper, and Mason pulls her closer to him, letting her squeeze against his leg as he gently strokes her hair. No one says anything. No one dares.

Desto's back stays to us as he glares into the darkness, his shoulders heaving and shuddering and—and . . . is he crying?

I glance toward Karl. His stare rests on Desto's back as he begins to take a step toward him. I reach out and put a hand on his forearm. Turning to me, Karl cocks an eyebrow questioningly. "Let me," I whisper, giving his arm a light squeeze.

"Hey, man." I speak as gently as I can after walking up to Desto. "Zeta's going to be fine, all right? She's tough and she's been through worse. We're going to get home and you'll see that you're worried for no reason. These people seem on the level, you know? They have no reason to hurt anyone."

There are no tears on his face, though his shoulders still quake and his breathing comes in quick gasps. The lack of actual tears doesn't surprise me. I have a hard time imagining he could be capable, but I've been wrong about others—grown men, tougher than titanium plating, breaking down in ways that are usually devastating and never pretty. War does strange things to people. It gets to a point where you have to start expecting it.

"Bomani, you okay?"

He takes a deep breath and finally looks at me, managing a stunted half smile. "Yeah, Aly, I'll be okay."

Reaching up, I put a hand on his shoulder, hoping the contact will be reassuring, followed by a smile of my own, hoping it looks more encouraging than it feels. "All right, then."

Unexpectedly, he wraps a rough and callused palm around my neck and pulls me into a hug. My arms barely reach around his wide, muscular torso as I hug him back. It's a moment of pure, genuine affection, bringing home more than ever how much my crew has come to mean to me. We're all in this together, no matter what. No war, no fighting against gangs of crazy, desperate, or greedy scavengers, and no hardships or scarcities are going to get between us again and break this group up. We stick up for each other, through whatever this chaotic system can throw at us.

Releasing me, he turns fully back to the group. "We need a plan."

NINETEEN

We sketch out something rough and digestible that won't draw anyone's suspicion. The first thing we have to do is ensure Venus knows we're okay and find out if she is, too. Which means a trip to the *Orika*. From there, we hope to have more options and information that will illuminate a long-term solution.

Volunteering, I go to the gymnasium door through which Whitmore and his meatheads had entered. It opens freely, but the one called Zabriskie is outside on guard. He looks at me expressionlessly when I step into the hall.

"So," I begin, very aware of my innately poor negotiation skills, "we're wondering if we can check out our ship. Make sure everything is, uh, being taken care of, and get some of our stuff."

"No."

Okay, this is going to be fun. "Whitmore said we're free to do as we please." God, it's like I'm a child arguing with another child.

"Yeah, you can run around Bogotan. But not together and not without a guide."

"Which is you."

"You got it."

"And our weapons are . . .?"

"Secured."

"Uh-huh. So why can't we get on our ship?"

"Whitmore told you. We're trying to work out a deal with your colony. We don't need more talking heads in the mix making things difficult."

"We're not goddamn talking heads, we're people—wait." I stop myself. Pissing off this guy will get me nowhere. "How does access to our ship make things difficult? We can't communicate with KL anyway. Unless you're telling me you have working satellites." His silence is answer enough. "You do, don't you? So why not just contact KL from here, why send some of your people with Zeta?"

To the cynic—a.k.a. *realist*—in me, it seems obvious. They're going to hit Keum Libre with an attack if Brady doesn't give up the soil compound willingly. They must be using Zeta as a negotiating chip, and Whitmore had probably been lying about sending a ship in a couple of days to pick up the crew he's sent to accompany her. They must already have backup in the air, ready to hammer KL as needed. It's vital that I inform the crew of my suspicions ASAP. This could be the info we need to decide on a game plan. Knowing they have a working satellite is a very, very good piece of information.

But dammit, Whitmore had seemed so reasonable.

"Look," I continue, "we'll stay off the flight deck and out of the com room. Just let us get to our belongings, changes of clothes, et cetera. If we're stuck here, it just makes sense. And it's *polite*."

It will be a risk to let these people near our stores and weapons—not to mention the risk of exposing Venus—but if we can reach out to her, we can covertly establish a communication protocol, as well as give her a sense of what's going on out here. She may not know if we're alive or dead, and Venus could do something to compromise herself if she stays in the dark too long. An ace in the hole is only good for us if she's playable, after all.

"Wait one," Zabriskie says and gets on his com. After talking with whoever's on the other end, he clicks off and says, "You'll have an escort in an hour or so. Until then—" He juts his chin toward the gym door.

"You're a prince," I comment before heading back inside, but inwardly I'm relieved. Besides, being held hostage here beats the shit out of being held hostage by cannibals. I'm a lot more comfortable with the menu, at least.

BEFORE OUR ESCORT—who end up being Van Heusen, Zabriskie, and to everyone's surprise, Whitmore himself—arrive, I quickly sketch out my suspicions to the crew about a potential attack on KL by Bogotan if Brady doesn't do what they want. We don't have any time to fully grasp all the implications of this before the gym door swings open and Van Heusen steps inside. The ambidextrous draw holster sporting two pistols draped over his shoulders captures my attention immediately. What made them switch from stun sticks?

"Which one of you is the pilot?" he asks.

We hadn't discussed what would happen if this question came up, but Karl immediately steps forward.

"Okay. Then, you, you, and you," he says, pointing to me, David, and Ryan. "The rest stay put."

"Only three of us can go aboard?" Hoogs asks.

Van Heusen doesn't bother to answer, just steps to the side so the three of us can get past him.

Sighing with exasperation, I give Karl's hand a quick squeeze as I walk by. "Back soon," I promise.

As I approach the entryway, Desto's weighty shadow follows. *Oh man, don't fuck this up, Desto.* Van Heusen cuts him off before he steps through the door behind me, and I turn on my heels to be ready for whatever happens.

The two men face each other, and Van Heusen, no shrimp, is nearly eye level with him. One of his hands already clutches a pistol grip. "Are you deaf, scav?"

Desto stares at the security chief coolly, but I see murder in his eyes.

Seconds float past in a dream—or nightmare—then Desto smiles at the other man, all of his white teeth bared in mirthful savagery.

"Don't forget my shaving cream, Aly," he says, then abruptly turns around and rejoins the others.

I rein in the sigh of relief wanting to slip from my lips, and head into the corridor. The three of us had wrapped up in the hats and coats the woman named Korine brought us, and I'm grateful for them as soon as we step outside. KL and Spectra 6 are warm year-round, sometimes oppressively so; the only way I'm going to get used to this type of cold is if we're here awhile. I just hope that doesn't happen.

Expecting to walk to the landing zone, I snug my synth-wool hat down tight and recheck the zipper on the coat to make sure none of the penetrating breeze can slice through. Instead we're loaded into a ten-seater land trans. Whitmore drives while Van Heusen takes the backseat and Zabriskie the front. For a moment I wonder if the gym is now guard-free. Not likely. This group hasn't shown a hint of bad strategy yet.

Algol A and B are in full view, the sky perfectly crisp, cloudless, and blue. The city streets and buildings extending in every direction look just as well-maintained and clean as they must have been before the war—possibly even cleaner. With fewer people living here, less garbage and fewer signs of consumption mar the cityscape. The moment takes me back to life before the Corps and before this war, and I remember what it was to be a citizen of the Obals in a society that was orderly and peaceful. Out of nowhere, my emotions suddenly feel ripped in half. On the one hand, I'm hit with a wall of sadness and a sense of loss that makes my chest tight and my eyes hot in their sockets—so much devastation, so much waste. But on the other hand, I'm surprised by a sudden clear-headed sense of hope, almost excitement. This is another chance, a new system with new opportunities to get it right.

But can we this time?

The drive lasts only a few minutes. With ordinary prewar traffic, it would have taken at least triple that in a city this size, and David and I use the time to examine the area's layout and organization. No matter how good your sat-maps and schematics are, things always look different from ground level. Occasional lights pepper the buildings, few of which show signs of battle. The mag-rails and streets all seem to be untouched as well. It's as if the war bypassed Bogotan, and I see why they've made it their home. Yet few people walk the streets. Much like Agate Beach and even KL, I'm sure the city's inhabitants have little free time, occupied with getting and keeping the basics of survival up and running.

Reaching the southern edge, we get our first exposure to the scars of the war. This side of the berm safeguarding the city from the airfield, which I hadn't seen after landing thanks to my fun with the nasal filter, looks like the gateway to the apocalypse. A ten-meter-high wall of earth and steel had been—there's no other way to describe it—*melted* and turned into a standing wave of fused metallic obsidian before it could collapse into a puddle. The damage extends down the length of the berm from one side of the gate about fifty meters before I recognize an impact crater. Odd. Based on the shape and angle of the crater, the missile that had caused it came from inside the city, as if someone was trying to make the berm impenetrable to those coming from the airfield. Was it the city's attempt at self-defense, the occupants trying to turn this wall into a stronghold that would keep attackers out? A large contingent of ground forces would most likely have come from a strike from ships using the airfield to get their teams close. The other option would be to send forces inside using the city's major streets and thoroughfares. I'd bet my favorite carbine those locations are well guarded, maybe even blockaded, too.

In any case, their aim had been off. The giant gate still works, as we'd already seen. Yet it leaves me wondering why a city filled with people who were so worried about outside attackers that they tried to destroy their own points of ingress was never, in fact, attacked.

We approach the cargo hold hatch, Whitmore, Van Heusen, and Zabriskie trailing the three of us. The wind kicks up, rasping against my exposed cheeks with a gritty feel of dust, but it smells clean. The Obals always make you appreciate good air, and the war hadn't damaged O 6's atmosphere significantly if it's still this fresh. I have to admit, KL is starting to look a little Paleolithic by comparison. It's possible to walk around without a breathing filter there, but after a while the thickness and particulates in the air clog your throat and lungs enough to make you feel like you're trying to breathe underwater. Uncomfortable, to say the least, and who knows what the long-term effects would be.

"Just have to enter the opening sequence," David says, approaching the *Orika*'s outer panel, which gives access to the manual entry keypad. If Venus is still inside and saw our approach, she'll be able to override the safeguards that keep anyone else from getting aboard after David keys in his code.

"Nice and easy, scav," Van Heusen warns.

I'm really starting to not like this meat sack, and the dirty look I throw over my shoulder at him must make that obvious. "We're not scavs."

"Course not, dollface," he says, and puckers his lips at me in a disgusting leer.

"Eat me, d—"

"That will be enough," Whitmore interrupts and glances meaningfully at Van Heusen, whose face returns to a scowl.

"Just open it," he says to David.

The inset latch to open the panel sticks for a few seconds before David is able to prise it loose and slide the panel open. He enters his key code and steps a bit to the side, staring hopefully at the hatch. The hydraulics inside instantly begin humming, and the ramp lowers smoothly.

"How did you do that?" Zabriskie asks, suspicion triggered. If they hadn't been able to open it with simple bypass algorithms, there's no way a key code should have worked.

Without missing a beat, David responds, "Facial recognition." I have to stifle a chuckle at the unintended truth of that.

The ruse apparently works. Zabriskie's expression remains doubtful, but he doesn't ask any more questions.

"Before we step aboard," Whitmore says, "I'd like to assure you that we are not pirates and your belongings will not be taken. If there is anything you'd like to share with the city, we'd be happy to have it.

And if you have any weapons aboard"—I look at him sharply, already bracing for the conflict that's coming if he asks that we hand them over—"please leave them be. You may take them when you leave Bogotan, but you understand that we aren't willing to invite the kind of problems they may cause. Aside from that, for efficiency's sake, please separate into three groups, and one of us will accompany each of you."

"That's not really going to do any good, Whitmore," David explains. "Ryan isn't a regular member of our crew. He doesn't have anything aboard and isn't familiar with everyone's property."

Whitmore looks thoughtful for a short, blink-frenzied moment. "I'm sure there's something he can gather for your group." His eyebrows rise questioningly.

David thinks about it, then capitulates. "Sure, yeah. Ryan, can you hit the galley and grab as much of our rations as you can? If you need a backpack, you can pick one up from the crew quarters. Which means"—he looks at Whitmore—"he'll need to go with whomever picks up our personal gear."

Rations? That's a laugh. What's left in the galley could probably be carried in just Ryan's pockets. We'd stored some backup provisions in the cargo hold, just in case, and would have broken them out today if we'd still been on the ship. Before Whitmore had come to escort us from the gym, we'd all agreed that it's best to leave them unmentioned and aboard, mostly for Venus's sake, and in case we have to make a break for it. It's a 140-or-so-hour flight from here to KL, and there isn't enough food to keep all the adults and children well fed (we'd agreed to give the children full rations, but the rest of us would go hungry), but if just a couple of us are able to break free, it will be enough to sustain whoever does.

"Aly and I should both get the crew's items," David says. "I'll take the main bunkroom while you go through the spare and your cabin."

I nod agreement and he starts aboard. Whitmore beckons at Van Heusen to go with him. Ryan follows, Zabriskie on his tail.

"You and me, then?" I ask Whitmore.

"Is that all right with you?" he asks nicely enough.

Without responding, I step inside the hold where the cargo bins are all still tied down exactly as we'd left them.

Van Heusen asks, "What's in all these?"

"Our stuff," David replies bluntly and with finality.

Van Heusen starts to say something, but Whitmore cuts him off with a steely look. The six of us move through the main corridor toward the berthing room. Whitmore and I continue past it as David and Ryan veer inside with their escorts. I enter the cabin Karl and I share, absorbing every detail visible, hoping Venus had left a message or indication of her status.

The room and the rest of the ship are chilly, barely warmer than the outside air. She's not running any power, knowing it would give away her presence. As soon as I think this, I realize that the top blanket from my and Karl's rack is missing and conclude her bunk must already be stripped. Whitmore wouldn't know anything about my blanket, but I hope a bare bunk in the main berth doesn't give her away.

After stuffing a few hygiene items and some clothing in a bag I'd pulled from the under-bunk storage drawer, I suddenly see what I've been hoping for. The digits on our universal clock, which runs on its own battery, flash the hour. The seconds are ticking past in regular time, but as soon as they reach *oo* and the minute should increment by one, it flickers, then returns to the same time it was just on. I move slowly, trying to make it look like I'm searching for something, doing my best to veil the attention I'm giving the clock. Then it happens again. Same time. It has to be Venus, but what's the number sequence for?

"You're a soldier, Ms. Erikson. Aly—if I may. Is that correct?" Whitmore's question surprises me, and I glance to where he remains in the doorway. "Your life experience has forced, perhaps *offered*, you a unique and practical perspective on this kind of situation."

"Yeah, sure. What kind of situation is that?"

"Making choices. Choices that mean the future for humankind."

What the hell is he talking about? I stand up straight and give him my attention.

"The good of one cannot supersede the good of all. If we allow that to happen, even the one will lose. I know you understand that."

"Whitmore, I swear you couldn't have been a dock supervisor before all this. You sure you weren't a teacher, or maybe a priest? If you have a point, would you just get to it?"

He grins with genuine amusement. "A soldier, like I thought, a woman who appreciates directness. So I'll be direct.

"It is vital that we here at Bogotan acquire this soil amendment compound that your, uh, former . . . cohort described. And why? What I propose is doing the greatest amount of good for the greatest number of people—with one caveat. The greatest number of people with *the greatest chance for success.* This is a variable that no amount of numbers, no allowance for attrition, can subvert. And we no longer have the numbers to consider attrition an acceptable factor. We cannot live with an expectation that our gains, our human successes, will accumulate enough in the long term to allow us to thrive. If we don't start thriving en masse right now, *today,* too many will die for us to possibly regain the worlds we came from. We will fall back into chaos, disease, starvation—in short, the return of a Neolithic human existence."

His reference to the Neolithic, reminiscent of my earlier thought about KL seeming Stone Age compared to Bogotan, jars me. His tone of voice is more convincing than his words could ever be, and strangely, I realize I'm paying attention. Acutely. No sharp remarks form behind my lips; no arguments; no naysaying. Am I really listening to this?

"I am no savior, Aly, no beacon of modern mankind, sent to save the world, delusions of grandeur. I am none of that. I am a father aching for the loss of his children, a husband who is tormented by his feelings of gratitude that his wife died before she had to witness all of this, and a believer in the better side of humanity. What we've experienced, this war, it was more than enough to drive anyone to their limits. Those of us who haven't gone a little mad with what we've witnessed must already have been crazy to begin with. And that, that right there, is the new normal."

I move a little to the side and lean against the wall in order to cover the clock. Whitmore doesn't seem to notice. His hands are clasped tightly around his midsection, twisting together in a severe wrestling match, as if he's trying to keep them from flying away. His clear blue eyes almost bug, the intensity and sincerity of his gaze unmistakable. His uncontrolled blink is completely absent. He believes every word he's saying—and . . . so do I? Do I?

"I don't want to hurt anyone. I want everyone who has emerged from this civilization-ending tidal wave to have the same freedom to rebuild everything we've lost. Why else would we have given up so much of our old way of life, the little comforts we had under the Admin's system, to salvage Bogotan? We have running water, we have order, we have the beginnings of commerce, we have satellites to communicate with anyone else who may be able to listen. We are putting the pieces back together. And everyone here knows we're doing what is most important, most vital, for humanity, for our present, and for our future. Our short-term inconveniences mean *nothing* in the face of long-term survival. Long-term thriving. We want to keep going, Aly, but we need every bit of help we can get. We need you and your crew's help. We need your settlement's help. And most of all we need the help of what tools of civilization remain."

He takes a long stride and reaches out to put a warm, gentle hand on my shoulder. We look at each other, me speechless, him searching, and that same sincerity remains in his face. "Will you help us?"

Two thoughts run through my brain in quick succession, the latter snapping at the tail of the former. *This is exactly what Karl was talking about: put aside the fight so we can all start relearning how to live normal lives.* Followed by: *When Bodie first analyzed the data to the soil compound, he found communications about making it commercial. Could we have missed something on KL? Could it actually be used safely? Does Bogotan have people who can figure out how?*

I move my eyes to stare pointedly at his hand, staying silent until he removes it. "Help you how, Whitmore? We already told you the compound is dangerous. No one who created it is still alive, and everyone who's seen it in action says it's deadly—even the data says that. Like Vitruzzi told you."

"And I understand that. But it has incredible effectiveness, according to Quantum."

"The only side effect being the massive kill-everything-else-first issue."

"Science didn't die with the war, Aly, we will of course study it before using it. You can help us by—"

"Convincing my crew to go along with you, right?" I've had this conversation before. He almost flinches at my interruption, unsure how to respond to such aggressive bluntness, so I use the dead air to continue. "And what's in it for me?"

"What do you mean?" He actually seems surprised. He's not an idiot, but the priority list of the criminal-enterprise educated doesn't come naturally to him. So I help.

"Give my team back our VDUs, and let us contact our colony on Keum Libre. You have working satellites; I can't think of a better use to put them to." *And this is your chance to prove you're not bullshitting us. If we don't let the rest of the colony know where we're at, when Zeta gets there, they'll have to assume we're still stuck on Eruo Pium and send out a pointless rescue mission. Or is that what you want, Whitmore? To get more of our people and ships away from KL to thin the herd, make a takeover that much easier.*

His response comes quickly, too quickly for my suspicions to increase. "Can I have you and your crew's word that you won't put our city and people in danger?"

"You have mine," I promise. "And I'll talk with the others."

"I appreciate your candor, Ms. Erikson, and your sophistication." He reaches out to shake hands on the deal.

"Just don't fuck with us," I warn, ignoring his hand.

TWENTY

Hot coffee steams beside me on a table. After a second, I wrap both hands around the ceramic mug and cradle it like a precious gem, trying to get heat back into my body. Once we'd returned to our "accommodations" in the high school and dropped off the collected goods, Vitruzzi, Karl, and I were immediately taken by Whitmore to their satellite link up, this time being led on a walk through the biting cold for about a kilometer along the street. The communications hub resides in an office building like you'd find in any business district on any of the Obals. *Used* to find, that is. I'd lost feeling in my fingers about halfway, despite rounds of blowing on them and then jamming them into my armpits to keep them out of the wind.

Other than letting everyone know we were going to get in touch with KL, I hadn't had a spare second to tell them about Whitmore's and my arrangement before we left to send the transmission. I filled in Karl and V on the way, my teeth chattering to add a dramatic flair to the story. They got the picture regardless, and the relief on their faces about getting back in touch with the colony is as visible as mine. For Whitmore's sake, he better not have been misleading me.

Zabriskie sits beside Korine, a slim, middle-aged woman, at the communication console. The two of them have been sending out hails to KL's satellite frequency every three minutes for the last fifteen, and we're just waiting for Patrick or whoever's on watch to respond. Karl's arm hangs over my chair's armrest, his warm hand on my thigh. Vitruzzi sits to my left, still and straight-backed, as if preparing to give a speech. She hasn't said much since we'd arrived planet-side, and I keep meaning to find a few minutes to check in with her. Something on Eruo Pium had spooked her and sent her even further inside whatever dark mental cave she's been withdrawing into lately. I'm afraid if someone doesn't start to pull her back out, she might stay there for good.

There's no time like the present.

"V, look, I know you're not happy with the plan"—giving up the soil amendment compound—"but I don't really see that we have any other choice. You know? We need to get home. Let them worry about it." I wave vaguely toward the window overlooking Bogotan's city central. "Besides, remember what you and Bodie read in the data logs from the Fortress?"

Pain stabs me deep inside, despite the time that's passed since Bodie was killed. Some people you never get over losing, I guess. The thought makes me glance at Karl, who catches the look and lifts a querying eyebrow at me. Giving him a half smile to tell him I'm okay, I continue, "The data said the compound had commercial potential. Maybe Whitmore's people can figure out how to make it safe."

"Maybe, Aly," she responds. The look she gives me could make a psychopath feel guilty. "Or maybe not."

Had I made a mistake? Taken too much liberty by making a deal that will ripple throughout KL and affect everyone there? No. Vitruzzi has shown that her ability to take meaningful initiative is flawed. If she were operating normally, I could have referred Whitmore to her. If she were operating normally, *she* would have been the one he'd spoken with. But she's *not* operating normally. She's barely operating at all, and someone has to pick up the slack. If my decision turns out to be less than optimal, at least I made one. Someone has to.

"Fair enough," I reply after a second. "But it's not our problem anymore. Let it go; let someone else handle it."

I'm talking about the compound, but I'm also talking about everything Vitruzzi takes on. It's too much, running a colony, a hospital, and everything else. She has to realize she can't hold herself responsible for the way things are or the way things in our system go from here on out, or she's going to burn out. Already is burning out.

"Let it go? You're giving *me* advice, Aly? You know, that's about as meaningful as—"

"Jim, we're getting another incoming ping from"—Zabriskie cuts himself off and glances toward the three of us—"uh . . ." He looks at Whitmore significantly, eyebrows arched.

But whoever's contacting them is not what I'm thinking about right now. "What do you mean, Vitruzzi? My advice is as meaningful as what?"

"Forget it," she says, her eyes as cold and distant as the dark side of a moon.

"No, I want to hear this."

"Excuse me," Whitmore breaks in. "I need a few moments. If you all wouldn't mind waiting outside, just through the door there. The foyer has comfortable seating, and it's warm. This shouldn't take long. We'll get you immediately if your settlement responds."

"Sure," Karl says and rises from his seat, pulling me up by the hand. His grip is tighter than it needs to be. When I glance at him, the message in his expression is as clear as if he were speaking aloud: *Give it a rest, Aly.*

Once we're in the foyer, I pull my hand from Karl's grip and confront Vitruzzi. But I have to give myself some credit; I try to keep my tone benign. "What's on your mind, V? I'm just trying to help."

She seems to deflate right in front of me, like I'd stuck her with a pin.

"Why?" she asks, her expression morphing to neutral, as if we're discussing the merits of eighth-inch screws over quarter-inch screws. "Why are you trying to help? And why should I go along with it? Haven't I done enough?"

"Done enough? What do you mean?" I look toward Karl, the question *Do you know what she's talking about?* in my eyes.

She sighs. "Maybe you're right. Give it to them. Give them anything they ask. I'm out of this. Done. It's not up to me, and I . . . I can't be responsible for things anymore."

I can feel my mouth hanging open, but nothing comes out. Am I really hearing this? Her . . . confession? Is that what it is? Because that's what it sounds like—and it's exactly what I'd been thinking moments ago. But her words do nothing to relieve me. Instead, her newfound flexibility, or rather, disengagement, sounds like defeat at a visceral level. Like she's giving up. Vitruzzi, giving up? It just doesn't compute. Can't be true.

"I . . . what do you mean you need out? Vitruzzi, there *is* no *out*, not of this. People need our help. The compound might be it."

"*Our* help? What happened to 'survival is as good as it gets'?" She looks at the palm of her hand, as if examining it for profound truths that she no longer believes exist, apparently. Then she chuckles. "Survival isn't even that good anymore, Aly. If you don't believe me, ask those corpse-eaters on Eruo Pium what they think."

This conversation has moved beyond surprising to outright weird. "The cannibals? What—?"

"Dr. Wyss. That's who I'm talking about."

Karl and I exchange glances, both of us equally clueless.

She goes on: "We worked together in the Medical Sciences Research facility on Obal 10. His work on developing neurological recombinations was one of the breakthroughs that helped us build cyber-prosthetic limbs. The big joke in the lab was that he put the mind in our matter. Ha-ha, funny, right?"

I have to take a step back. She's not going to be talked down from this ledge until she's gotten whatever it is that's jacking up her frequencies back to a manageable level. If that means letting her brain download a bunch of crazy, well, it's not like Karl and I have anywhere to be at the moment.

A tornado of apprehension brews in the back of my mind, but I nod quietly. Vitruzzi is a boulder—has *always* been stable and strong —that's finally showing signs of cracking.

"He was brilliant. And his family was beautiful." Vitruzzi circles the ring of chairs ringing a center table as she talks, her movement keeping me off balance and fidgety. "Marie, his wife, and their twins, Sammy and Margriet—they'd have been about sixteen or seventeen now. They would come to our neighborhood cookouts, and the twins showed Evie how to ride a magbike. Evie would never listen to John or me when we tried to show her things like that. She was too stubborn."

Evie and John? That's right, her husband and daughter who'd died in the Crowers Croup outbreak before the Soldier's Rebellion. Giving it one last shot, I try: "V, now isn't really the time for a trip down memory lane." Her black eyes hit mine and hold them, and I give up. There's no reasoning with that empty space.

She stops pacing and grips the back of a chair, facing me. "He had a brilliant and capable mind, Aly. A solid career and family. There was nothing monstrous or depraved in him." She sits, collapses really, into the overstuffed seat. "But that's what he became and now he's dead and it's *my* FAULT."

Karl's turn. "Calm down, Eleanor. I don't know what you're talking about, but I'm sure we can, uh, we can fix this, okay?"

Dammit, I wish Brady was here. This is a level of loony that I'm not used to. Her eyes are more focused and severe than I've ever seen them, not like the eyes of someone about to lose their shit, but her voice, what she's saying—this isn't the Vitruzzi I know. I'm damn certain this isn't the Vitruzzi *anyone* knows.

"I had to shoot him, you know. You were there." She stabs me with another black look. "He was going to gun us down in the middle of nowhere and serve us up to those cannibals as if we were wild game. But when I saw his face and realized who he was, it all suddenly became clear to me. There was no way I could ignore the truth anymore. No matter how fucking ugly it is."

"You mean that guy in the hovercraft?" I ask, who it is she's talking about finally dawning on me. "The one who tried to run us down as soon as we got out of the emergency pod? You knew that guy?" The odds are almost impossible. "V, that had to be someone else, someone who just looked like the doc you used to know."

"Do you think I could make a mistake like that, Aly? We worked together for ten years. His kids used to play with Evie. I know his face as well as I know my own, and I shot him because if I hadn't, he'd have killed us."

"I've killed a lot of people, and believe me, when it's either you or them, it gets easier. Trust me on that."

Her short laugh is brittle. "You know what never gets easier? Losing your kid. But when I think about what I let happen, what I *caused*, I'm—" Her body contorts; her arms cross her chest, and she crunches forward like some huge weight has been dropped onto her shoulders. The anguish in her voice in the next sentence scares me more than any words I've ever heard. "I'm glad she isn't here. I'm glad she's dead."

This is the part where I'm supposed to walk over and hug her and tell her everything is going to be okay. Except—I don't even know where to start. Looking at the suffering and pure battle fatigue hacked into every groove of her face, I realize: if everything is going to be okay, it takes a more creative imagination than mine to figure out how.

"V, I'm not sure I understand what you're talking about. But whatever it is you think you let happen, there's time later to figure out what to do about it. But right now—"

She cuts me off. "What I let happen is the war. Medina was right when she said it was my fault. *You* were right when you told me not to trust Rajcik. If I hadn't believed any help fighting the Admin, even from a psychotic criminal, was better than none, the war wouldn't have happened. *I'm responsible for the war, Aly.* I'm the reason so many people are dead."

When she stops speaking, the silence draws out the same way it does after a dying person's last gasp of breath. She thinks she's responsible for the war, for the millions dead. She holds herself accountable for something that's so far outside of her ability to control that it's absurd. Crazy.

Unfixable.

"Eleanor, you are so completely wrong about that," Karl says, disbelief straining his voice. "The war was coming whether we worked with Rajcik or not. He was the catalyst, but you were not the cause. You have to be cra—"

I grab his arm to stop him, but Vitruzzi breaks in first. "Crazy?"

The sound of an incoming ship, something bigger than an intra-atmosphere shuttle, cuts off whatever disaster heads our way. We all instinctively look toward the ceiling, tensing against the possibility of an air assault. But it isn't needed. The ship passes, flying west toward the landing field.

Just as it glides over, Whitmore exits the com room. He catches the looks on our faces, drawing the conclusion that the ship must be the reason for our troubled expressions. "That was another of Bogotan's associates, and I need to go and meet with her. But first, your call to Keum Libre. A man named Patrick Brady is waiting to speak with you."

Finally, a break.

BRADY'S FACE LOOKS like the man went twenty rounds with the devil and lost every single one as Vitruzzi fills him in on everything that's happened to us since getting separated on Eruo Pium. Inexplicably, now that we've reestablished contact, a sudden feeling of calm, even optimism, settles over me. Knowing Zeta and the settlement are safe, and just a few days' flight time away, I start to think we could actually get out of this okay.

"I thought . . . Christ, I thought we might have lost you, Eleanor. When Zeta got here with just the 'Bo, and the story she told us . . ."

"I know. I know, Patrick. But we made it. We're fine. All of us. No injuries. And the *Orika* is still sound."

"Good. When are you coming home?"

Vitruzzi doesn't look at Whitmore, and I have no idea what she's thinking. We haven't had any time to regroup or discuss our plans or options. Everything is happening with the speed, but not the predictability, of dominoes falling.

"Listen, we'll come home as soon as we can. But I want you to do one thing first. Copy everything in the data storage from the lab at the landing platform that has to do with the soil compound. Take that and the compound and the cargo from Karl and David's last run and bring it all here, to Obal 6."

"Are they holding you hostage? Is that what this is?" The transmission's static and fluctuating volume as it bounces through fields of space debris give the rage in his voice a raw, primal edge. "Because if it is—"

"No. We're free to go. It's just a matter of trade. We give them the compound"—she turns her dark eyes on Whitmore—"and they give us what we want in return."

Brady is smart and he knows Vitruzzi well. There's more going on here than she's letting on—even I hadn't anticipated her turning this into a barter—and he's picking that up. "We've discussed at length the issues with that stuff, with what it might do. Why are you considering turning it over to this other colony?"

The obvious answer: we don't have a choice. If I know Brady, he's already assuming that, but Vitruzzi offers a different angle. "They have more of a chance of making it viable than we do, Patrick. I think it's time to get rid of it—and I'm . . . tired of being responsible for . . ." Her voice loses its momentum and she lets the sentence hang.

Her sudden silence isn't like her, and Brady's expression shows his confusion at first. "We're getting a bit of breakup, Eleanor. Repeat that last."

"That's it," she says. "It makes more sense to give it to them than to keep it."

Brady's eyes stray past her to Karl, who leans close to the video feed camera with a hand on the back of Vitruzzi's seat. "What do you think, Karl? Is this a good idea?"

"If it's not, the KLers aren't the ones who need to worry about it," he says matter-of-factly. "We're just ready to get home. If you can send the *Teibo* back, we'll load both ships up with supplies and come back. Soon as we can." He pauses to let Brady process this, but the time is taken up by a sudden disturbance out in the foyer.

"Motherfucker, you better be ready to shoot me, because you're not going to like what I do to you if you don't."

Oh shit. Desto.

Whitmore rises quickly from the chair he'd taken near the back of the room and rushes out to the foyer.

"Wait one," Karl tells Brady, then follows Whitmore, with me right behind him.

Zabriskie stands outside the double door, partially blocking it, his pistol aimed center mass at Desto.

"What are you doing here?" Karl asks.

Desto's expression is grim, and he stares at Whitmore as he responds. "Let me talk to Zeta. And I'm not asking."

"Jono, lower your weapon," Whitmore demands. Zabriskie's face is as blank as a dead monitor, but he drops his arm, his thumb resting on his pistol's safety, but not engaging it. "Of course. Of course. I understand completely. Korine"—he turns to face inside the com room—"please keep Mr. Brady's connection active. Mr. Desto, come inside. And I apologize for not considering your situation."

Desto looks surprised. He'd been ready for a fight, not an agreement. But that doesn't slow him down. Seconds later, he's seated in Vitruzzi's vacated spot.

"Pat, how's Zeta? Can I talk to her?"

"She's completely fine, Bomani. Don't worry. She's over at the platform right now, just taking care of postflight details. I know she'll be upset she couldn't be here to talk with you herself."

"Well, tell her . . . tell her I'll see her as soon as I can. And thanks, Pat."

"No problem. You okay?"

"I will be." There's a sinister undertone to this statement that I catch, even still standing in the foyer.

He stands, leaving the chair pulled out for Vitruzzi to reclaim, and walks out to where the rest of us wait. For the first time since

Desto had woken up on Eruo Pium after Zeta had been kidnapped, the ferocious grooves carved across his forehead have relaxed.

"So, uh, everyone okay back at the gym?" I ask him, knowing that his presence here means one of two things: he'd been lucky enough to sneak out while whoever was left to guard the rest of our crew at the high school had their pants down, or that guard is meeting his or her maker as we speak. I hope like hell it isn't the second possibility.

Desto swings an arm loosely around my shoulders. "No one got hurt that didn't need to be."

"What—?"

"It's all good, Aly. Our sentry just had a demonstration of some hand-to-hand he didn't previously know, but he's not hurt. Much."

Whitmore and Zabriskie look alarmed at these words, but Desto merely stares at them. "Korine, send Stybar over to the school to check on Rodriguez," Whitmore says, and no one else speaks until Vitruzzi comes back into the foyer a few minutes later.

"Whitmore, Patrick is sending our ship back with the compound and the people you had accompany Zeta. They'll be here within four days. Now, let's talk about what you're giving us."

"No, Dr. Vitruzzi." The words come from someone new. "Let's talk about what else you can do for us." Five people have entered the foyer. The first is Commander Medina.

TWENTY-ONE

"You've got to be fucking kidding me," I spit.

The group of us who flew with her during the war grow instantly mute, our surprise at this unexpected reunion cutting off any other reaction like a guillotine. She seems to realize the effect of her presence but keeps her military bearing as stiff and unreadable as ever. Van Heusen and one other soldier enter with her. I recognize his face as her apparently still next in command, Lieutenant Steward. Then comes the next backhand.

Quantum.

Oh how we've waited to see this betrayer again, a walking bag of viscera that needs to be spilled. Karl's hands clench into fists beside me as I involuntarily twitch forward, but I stop myself before doing anything that will lead to nothing except a bottomless pain cave. Desto, however, doesn't have the same hesitation.

"Strahan, stop him!" Vitruzzi's voice echoes clearly through the bowl-shaped foyer.

Karl tackles Desto from behind as the enraged father-to-be stalks toward Quantum with single-minded purpose, his stride amplifying his dead-set intent on revenge. But for Karl it's like gripping an elephant, and his assault results only in Desto's sharp elbow connecting with his collarbone as the larger man tries to shake Karl off.

Hardly seeming to notice what he's doing, Desto promises, "I'm going to kill you, Quantum. Say your fucking prayers."

"Jesus, big guy, you gotta get ahold of yourself," Karl says, his teeth clenching against pain as he maneuvers between Desto and the newcomers. "Little help here, people!"

That's all it takes to galvanize Vitruzzi and me. She rushes up and grips Desto's shoulders from behind, while I use my body to help Karl block him. Karl links his right arm with my left to create a barrier. Vacantly, I realize every weapon in the room is pointed at Desto, and there's no telling how much military discipline this security force has. A single nervous finger is all it will take to send a flurry of projectiles that will turn us into a collection of holes surrounded by blood and bone.

"Out of my way, so help you," Desto grunts, his eyes wide and unwaveringly focused on Quantum.

"Think about this," I say as calmly as I can. "The only way this ends is with you dead."

"I don't care."

"Yes, you do. Because you're going to get us killed, too. Is that what you want?" His eyes leave Quantum for a split second and bounce to my face. "You just heard Brady—Zeta is okay. So lock this revenge shit down before she has to bury an empty goddamn box."

An evil-sounding chuckle oozes from my right, and Van Heusen stands a couple meters away, grinning. He catches me looking and says, "We're this close to having us a roast."

My stomach twists into a sickened knot. *A roast?* This man, whatever kind of soldier he may have been before the war, is now pure monster. I don't even want to consider what he may have done to survive, yet my brain shoots up a high-contrast memory of foul-breathed Twitch the Cannibal from Eruo Pium—sometimes my imagination is a curse.

Desto takes a deep breath and lets it out, then puts a hand on Vitruzzi's, still on his shoulder. "It's all right, V. I'm good." But his face shows the moment is merely an intermission, not an end. He steps back toward the com room door and crosses his arms over his wall-like chest, and the rest of us relax. Slightly.

Quantum hasn't moved at all, choosing to stay at a safe distance outside the potential crossfire of the security team. Medina watched the entire seconds-long encounter with patient reserve, just waiting for the right moment to continue talking.

And that hopeful feeling I'd had when I heard Brady's voice transmitting from KL?

That's gone.

"I DIDN'T ANTICIPATE our paths crossing again so soon, Vitruzzi, Strahan . . ." Medina's eyes take in the room, lingering for a moment on those of us who'd served under her. "Everyone. And under these circumstances. It's only been what? Six months?"

Our initial shock drains out of the moment, and the four of us find a suitable place to sit, stand, or seethe. She displays a calm and appropriate smile that seems to imply, *We are all friends here. There's nothing but water under the bridge between us*, and continues. "I suppose the good news is that the war is truly and unequivocally over. And we are at a new frontier in human history."

Dramatic, but also the truth.

"What are you doing here, Medina? What's this all about?" Karl says from his seat near the foyer's deserted central desk. Desto is parked behind him, leaning against the counter, and I stay close to him just in case. He has returned to normal—or as close to it as he's likely to get with Quantum in the room and still drawing breath.

"That's a question I'm about to answer, Tech Sergeant," Medina says, "if you'll let me."

"I'm not a soldier. You can stop calling me sergeant," Karl cuts in.

Her eyes hold his steadily for a breath before she continues, but none of us need to have it spelled out: something bigger than a straightforward exchange of resources is about to go down. Medina is obviously the person pulling strings in the colony. Whitmore had faded into the background the minute she'd entered the foyer, and Van Heusen is looking to her, not the former dock supervisor, for orders. What we'd all originally assumed was a citizen settlement is nothing but a land base for Medina and anyone still serving with her. Which changes things. How, though, remains to be seen.

"Let me just give you the highlights. Shortly after your group de . . . camped"—I'm sure she was about to say *deserted*—"the volume of fighting engagements, as you probably know, began to diminish, fewer and fewer Admin and Corps Loyalists stayed that way, and those of us controlling the larger forces began disarmament talks. In these last six months, we've achieved a peace of sorts. We don't have the system-wide organization to celebrate this victory with the proper gravitas, but we can all finally draw a breath unburdened by continued destruction. And now we have to look to rebuilding."

Her posture isn't exactly guarded, but still as stiff as ever. Thinking back, I realize I'd never even seen the woman sit down anywhere but at the command bench or let her shoulders drop or wear anything but her uniform. Along with this awareness, the memory of something Vitruzzi had said to Medina back on the *Celestial* just three months into the war surfaces. *"We can continue to fight our brothers and sisters who fell on the wrong side of the rift, or we can begin the process of laying down our arms, laying down our differences, and picking up the pieces together. Rebuild. If we don't, no matter who survives, we've all lost this war."*

So Medina is finally seeing the wisdom in peace over force—at least that's what she seems to be saying, but right now, I feel like I'm choking on the message instead of swallowing it.

Vitruzzi speaks up, voicing what I'm sure we're all thinking: "Understood, Commander, but I don't remember ever voting to put you in charge."

Medina's response is quick and final. "Democracy died when János Rajcik dropped a terra-shattering bomb on Obal 10."

Vitruzzi flinches.

Karl responds sharply, "Then let's restore it."

Medina shifts her gaze toward the wall, as if searching for an argument that will put an end to this off-topic, at least to her, debate. "Serg—Strahan," she starts, looking up again, "if it were as simple as a quick show of hands, we'd all be happier. But since it isn't that simple, and won't *ever be that simple*, we need to start talking about what is, not what was. Hmm?"

The condescension packed into her last statement could only be missed by a deaf person, but it has her desired effect. Our attention cements to her.

"Good," Medina continues. "The crew of the *Celestial* and I have been hard at work throughout the system helping to find and secure everything we need to create and sustain a viable new home. A safe and ideal place to begin a new centralized government, or at least, centralized within limits. With the remaining human population widely scattered and badly organized, Whitmore and I have agreed to make Bogotan that location. We've been working together for these last few months, and we have one hundred percent agreement about what steps to take to get this quadrant of the system back on its feet. I'm sure you've worked out for yourselves that we see the seed sequencer and the soil amendment compound as necessary assets for the fastest and most efficient means to feed a new and growing population."

"What kind of population do you mean, Medina? We have refugees on KL that were turned away from Bogotan because of minor handicaps," Vitruzzi says, her voice finding that old edge. "Doesn't your 'efficient' system have room for people like that? Or is it just for those who are willing and able to march to your fife?"

Whew! I've been known to be abrupt and stubborn, but I think she just won the award for being the most deliberately antagonizing non-cit this side of the war. It's clear now that Vitruzzi hasn't forgotten Medina's actions that led us to leaving the *Celestial* in the first place, or forgiven her for them. The medical station on Broon; the way Medina had ordered its annihilation instead of trying to help the injured. The doctor in Vitruzzi couldn't let that slide if her life depended on it.

And given Medina's presence here, it probably does.

Medina's hard shell doesn't crack, but she's no longer giving Vitruzzi even a fragment of her attention. "We need people like you to help us achieve what we're hoping to achieve. More importantly, we need your cooperation." She lets that sink in, then goes on, dropping the commander's voice and sounding like a regular, needs-driven, hope-filled person. It's a tone as bizarre coming from her as an opera singer's voice coming from Desto would be.

"Erikson, Desto, Strahan . . . Vitruzzi, it's not about fighting to win. We're all fighting to survive at this point, and none of us can do it alone. Your colony on Keum Libre, while noteworthy for lasting even this long, isn't going to last forever. You don't have the human resources, nor even the means to enforce any kind of security, to support the colony indefinitely. You must see that. Bogotan has factories, textiles, metals. Munitions. But what we need now is *people*.

"We need to get together on this. If we couldn't do it during wartime, I pray to any potential powers that may be that we can do it while we have some peace."

She's sounding eerily like Whitmore had when trying to convince me to help sway my crew to his point of view earlier. The two of them are as thick as thieves. Another brief memory surfaces, something Medina had said as soon as the main Corps posts on Obal 8 and Obal 3 had fallen. Some of the *Celestial*'s crewmembers had started advocating for an armistice, but Medina, the unyielding military tactician, had commanded the fight to continue until all regions of resistance were broken—or as she'd put it, *"burned in the refuse pile of dogma and antihuman apostasy."* She might have been in the uniform of a Corps officer, but her true core seems to be made of an almost Straussian idealism. I can see from my crew's expressions that they know it, too.

She goes on: "What I propose is that we all join in one colony and bring the rest of your settlers on Keum Libre to Bogotan. And yes, before you ask the question, I do mean everyone, even the disabled and sick."

She finally winds down, giving us a second to absorb her proposal.

"Maybe we're happy where we are," Karl says after a few ticks of the clock.

Medina reacts, but not in words. Her body instantly transforms from friendly and collaborative to her default rigid military decorum—stance aloof, back rigid, and eyes as unreadable and glassy as an artificially generated human avatar.

"Why should we agree to relocate to Bogotan?" Karl continues, not in the least deterred by her visible frustration. "What's in it for us?"

"Let me make it easy for all of you to understand." She deliberately unzips her Corps-issued officer's jacket and pushes the material back, revealing the tactical vest, holster, and pistol beneath. "I let your crew leave the *Celestial* because I didn't think you had a chance in hell of surviving on your own. I considered it to be cutting dead weight. Now I can see I was wrong, but that doesn't matter. And believe me, I'm not going to make the same mistake again.

"The Admin was an experiment that failed. If the war is going to mean anything more than the destruction of hundreds of years of civilization and progress, we cannot fail like that again. Bogotan is where we're restarting; it has to succeed. And to succeed, we—and that means all people—have to be unified."

"With you in charge," Desto states and flashes the kind of smile at Medina that a large predator shows its prey just before sinking its incisors into its throat.

"Order can only be achieved through the rule of law, with someone to facilitate. Do you think it's possible to keep peace between hundreds of divergent groups of scavengers when they're all competing for the same last resources without unification, without shared goals? Do you have any idea what people have become, what's going on in this system?"

My eyes flick back to Van Heusen, catching his stare of unconcealed contempt for the four of us. I *do* know what's going on in this system, and looking at the sadistic guard, I can guess what would be going on in Bogotan if people like Whitmore, who at least seems reasonable, ever lose the initiative.

Medina's next words hit like an ambush. "I am not going to let everything fall apart, regardless of the resistance—whether from your colony or any other. I'll kill anyone who tries to stop or gets in the way of what we're trying to build." She unsheathes the pistol, and Van Heusen and Steward copy the action. "Make your choice now. We have a lot of work to do."

FOR A SECOND, I think I must have misunderstood her. But the Bhishma 10.3 mike-mike in her hand acts as a bullhorn until her words finally, irrevocably, sink in, and the skin hardens like ice over my entire body.

"Medina, could I have a word with you?"

It's Whitmore speaking, and the sound of his voice gives the rage whipping into a frenzy inside me somewhere to focus. My head swivels jerkily toward him, as if on a broken servo. He'd lied to me, bald-faced and so convincingly. I'd bought every word, and performed like a perfect puppet for him. I'd trusted him enough to convince Vitruzzi and Karl to do the same, and we'd called Brady, asked him to bring the compound and deliver it like an early Christmas present directly to Medina, putting the whole colony in jeopardy. Now we can't even get back in touch with them to warn them. How stupid could I be?

Medina ignores Whitmore's quiet request, her cool gaze riveted to us, waiting for someone to make a hero move so she can sic her dogs Steward and Van Heusen on us. He tries again, "Commander Medina. I need to speak with you *now*."

"It can wait, Whitmore." She never looks at him. Addressing us again, she continues, "I know it's a lot to take in, but I need you to understand your options, and what specifically is at stake. Do you?"

"Fuck this," Desto says, stepping toward our former commanding officer.

"Wait, Desto," Karl warns. "Nothing can go wrong right now that won't be made worse by you doing something stupid."

Clenching his fists, Desto assumes a pose of quiet, simmering deadliness.

I'm about to open my mouth and say something, though I'm not sure what it will be besides categorically offensive and probably suicidal, when Vitruzzi says, "Let me guess, Medina. Anyone who isn't an asset is expendable. That's what you told me, right?"

"Not anymore, Doctor. Anyone who isn't an asset is a liability. And we no longer have the luxury of allowing liabilities."

Vitruzzi doesn't hesitate. "We'll cooperate."

Medina is too smart to believe our subservience will come that cheaply, but she relaxes the finger cradling her pistol's trigger. "Of course," she goes on, "it would never come to that. I don't want to turn our new social order into a dictatorship or even an oligarchy any more than anyone else. I had no doubt you'd see the reason and inevitability of our two separate colonies joining together. We have to remember, I know you'll also agree, that the next few decades aren't about us, they are about creating and protecting our future. I'll let Jim fill you in on our plans." She dips her chin at the former dock controller, then motions to Steward, and the two of them exit. Quantum, who's said nothing this whole time, disappears with them.

My mouth is as dry as the engine housing of an overheated skiff as I say, "Vitruzzi, you can't seriously be willing to go along with this."

"Do you have an alternative proposal, Aly? One that doesn't get everybody on KL killed?"

My eyes jerk away from her, knowing she's right, but my rage isn't going anywhere. I turn it back on Whitmore.

"You double-dealing bastard. You knew about this, didn't you?"

His face is unreadable, but that blinking tic of his eye is going full throttle. "I-I . . ." he starts, but quickly stops himself. One hand goes to the side of his face and rubs near his twitching eye, trying to force it to calm down, but the effect is just the opposite. Abruptly, he turns to Zabriskie. "Jono, escort them back to their quarters. I need to talk to Medina."

Zabriskie nods and opens his mouth, but Van Heusen cuts in and gives the order. "You heard the man. Everyone back outside. And don't do anything I'd love to make you regret."

TWENTY-TWO

Night has spread its blanket over the city by the time we leave. The walk back is a little over ten minutes long, and I mentally prepare myself for the biting cold before heading outdoors. It's easy enough. My inner supernova of fury at Whitmore and Medina keeps me warm. As the others pace ahead, I find myself in step beside Zabriskie, whose stare is no warmer than the weather.

"Help me understand this, Zabriskie. How can a whole postwar settlement think massacring others is the solution to a new system of the worlds?" The cold breeze pulls most of the fire from my words, and I hear the underlying confusion and fear that are hiding in them. I hadn't even known they were there.

For a few seconds, it seems like he's going to ignore me. But then: "You fought in the war, right?"

I nod. Almost everyone fought in some capacity or another.

"Then you must get it. People are scared. There's no such thing as situation normal anymore. You find your tribe and you watch each other's backs. Sometimes that means others . . . well. More than a few of us here have learned the hard way that nothing can be counted on now." His jaw goes taut for a second, as if he's clamping it closed on something he doesn't want to say, but then he continues. "Not even people you thought were allies."

"What do you mean?" I ask, but his face has reverted back to brick-wall blankness. After another few steps, I blurt, "You realize that there's four of us and two of you, right? We can escape anytime we want."

"And you realize we're not the only ones watching you while we enjoy this leisurely stroll, right?"

We're passing an alley, and the wind screams down it with a freight train's whistle as he speaks. But I hear him. Loud and clear. Plenty of rooftops and high windows make our trip down the street a sniper's wet dream. Changing the subject, I ask, "So what's your story? Are you from Bogotan? Were you in the Corps before?"

"No, I was a citizen. Worked here with Whitmore in the shipping yard."

"You have a family?"

He doesn't answer that question. Which leads me to wonder, what exactly had happened to Bogotan during the war? The image of the damaged landing-field berm comes to mind. What had they been fighting against? "Was Bogotan Admin-friendly during . . .?" He knows during what.

"We were just trying to keep from getting wiped off the map."

"Is that why you tried to disable access to the city from the landing field?"

He looks at me sharply, not expecting my insight into their tactics. After hesitating for a second, he answers, "We thought we were under attack, so we took action to try and protect ourselves." He goes silent, again with the tight jaw, before saying, "Turns out things aren't as discrete as good-guys–bad-guys anymore."

I'm still pondering what he means by that when we reach the high school. As we step up to the front doors, they push open and two guards exit. The second one sports a swollen-shut eye and the start of what will be a bruise on his temple that would make a prizefighter wince.

"Asshole," he mumbles as he passes Desto and makes for a land trans parked on the street.

"Zabriskie, make sure they're locked in tight. Don't want them doing more of this, do you?" Van Heusen asks with a nod of his head toward the battered guard.

"Who's on watch tonight?" Zabriskie asks.

"I am. Back in a couple of hours to relieve you." Van Heusen's steel-blue eyes fall on me and he gives me a wink. "And you too, dollface."

Before he gets to the first riser on the stairs, Karl tackles him gut level like a rhino. Van Heusen had no idea it was coming, and his breath exits his body in one heavy expulsion. They fall sideways on the building's stoop almost at Vitruzzi's feet, Karl on top of Van Heusen, slamming his right fist into the man's nose and breaking it. The crunch is amplified by the crispness of the air, the wind having ceased to blow for a minute.

"Hey!" Zabriskie yells.

Karl jumps off the downed security guard just as Desto is about to intervene. He spits on the concrete as he glowers over Van Heusen, every muscle in his body daring the man to retaliate.

Van Heusen sits up and grasps his nose between his palms. Two streams of blood cascade down around his mouth, giving him a clown-faced sneer, and his squinting eyes seek out Karl's face, landing there and digging in like a pit bull's teeth. Zabriskie has his hand on the butt of his pistol but hasn't drawn it. For the first time, his face shows something besides neutral detachment as his lips tighten, and he glances around the group quickly, taking it all in.

With a casualness that completely belies the intensity of the moment, Van Heusen puts a hand to the ground and pushes himself to his feet, leaving a bloody handprint behind. I step forward a pace, ready to jump into the fray if needed. Four of us and four of them, but we can get to their weapons almost as fast as they can in such close proximity.

Van Heusen is enough of a soldier to realize this. Wiping the back of his hand across his top lip and smearing the cold-thickened blood across his cheek, he promises, "See you soon, scavs."

Karl opens his mouth and I grip his arm to try and stop him from speaking, but he says anyway, "Looking forward to it."

"GODDAMMIT, DOES SHE look like she needs a knight in shining armor?" Vitruzzi hurls the words at Karl as soon as we're inside. "What the hell were you thinking?"

I don't need anyone to speak for me, but keep quiet on this. No need to add fuel to the fire. And speaking of fire, Vitruzzi's anger is a good sign. Like she lanced a boil back at the satlink room and has new freedom from her self-induced burden of guilt. Let's hope it lasts. We're going to need everyone operating at full capacity in the coming storm.

"What am I thinking? Where were *you*, V? They're blackmailing us and holding us hostage. This is bullshit! Patrick is getting ready to walk into a trap, and Medina has turned into a primitive warlord that's about to put her enemy's heads on pikes. We have to make plans, to figure out . . ."

"That's what I'm talking about, brother," Desto says. "We need to bust the hell out of this rat hole and get back to KL before something happens."

"Jesus, people!" Mason snaps. "Did you forget about them?" His hand waves toward our four fugee kids, who sit as a group on his bunk, their eyes eating up the scene with the same avidity with which the kids had eaten every morsel of food they'd been given since we'd found them.

Vitruzzi's anger evaporates instantly, and she goes over to them and crouches. "It's going to be okay. We're just trying to discuss what to do next while we're staying in Bogotan. Everyone all right?"

"Dr. V, we don't want any more bad things to happen," Cassandra says, taking the hand of the youngest boy, sitting next to her on a bunk.

"I know, kids. Neither do we," Vitruzzi says simply.

"You want to tell us what the hell's going on?" David says. "Medina's here?"

The four of us spend the next fifteen minutes filling David, Hoogs, and Ryan in: we'd (well, *I'd*) made a deal with Whitmore to give up the soil compound, we'd contacted Brady to deliver it, Medina turned up and threatened our colony with death or worse, and we're all pretty much fucked if we don't dance to her tune. I'd be the world's best con artist if I could convince anyone that they take it well.

"Can we get Venus to launch an attack from the *Orika*?" David's proposal is the first on the table.

"Maybe, if we could get in touch with her," Karl says. "At least we know she's still tucked safely away."

"Yeah, but for how long?" I ask. "She doesn't know what's going on. She might get some ideas of her own. The longer she's in the dark, the twitchier she'll get. I know I would be."

Karl responds, "But she had to have heard your and Whitmore's conversation on the *Orika*. She'd have turned on the com as soon as she opened the door for David. As far as she knows, right now we're all working together. That should keep her from doing anything too, I don't know, too *Venus*."

Somber nods from the group, more hopeful than certain.

Before the conversation continues, the door opens and we all spin to see what's coming. Korine enters, pushing the same cart from earlier, piled with food, plates, and a couple of carafes, presumably our dinner, followed by four more armed guards: two men, two women. They already have their weapons hot.

Korine pushes the cart to within a couple of meters of us, then says in a voice that barely rises above a whisper, "I'm going to need to ask that those children come with me." She doesn't look anyone in the eye.

"What? Why?" Mason says.

One of the guards, a thick-framed meat bag with a face like a hyena, takes a pace forward and says, "You can ask Commander Medina about that." Casually, he taps the side of his pistol's trigger guard.

Korine looks like someone just told her her mother died. "I promise you, they'll be well cared for. It's just until we . . . you . . . the situation gets settled. I'm not going to let anything happen to them, okay. They'll be safer if they're not with . . . not here. Please, you understand?"

Glancing at Vitruzzi, I can't read anything in her expression. Her face is as blank and shrouded as the surface of the ocean. After a second, she crouches again near the cluster of kids and says, "It's okay. These folks are going to get you out of here and into someplace a little warmer and cozier. We're going to pick you up in a couple of days, after more of our friends arrive."

Cassandra speaks again. "No, we don't want to go with strangers. We want to stay with you and Mr. Mason!" She jumps off the bunk, nimbly avoiding Vitruzzi's hand as she reaches for her, and wraps her arms around Mason's waist as tightly as if he were a raft and she were about to go over a waterfall.

Mason's nutmeg-brown eyes squint in an expression that might be pain or might be hate, it's hard to tell which. But when he pulls the girl's arms away from him, he does it with a gentleness that's nearly reverence. Squatting, he looks into her face. "Don't worry," he says, "a lot of good folks are going to be looking out for you while we sort things out. Okay? Come on."

He stands up and holds out a hand to either side, waiting for the kids to grab them. The oldest boy does, and after a second, Cassandra does too. Vitruzzi walks over and takes the hands of the remaining two. The littlest girl starts to cry when she tries to let go of her hand and pass her over to Korine. Eventually, the four are led out, and the door is closed with finality.

"We're going to make that bitch pay," Mason says, talking about Medina.

The eight of us pick at our food silently, like it's our last supper.

TWENTY-THREE

"Don't make the mistake of believing the war is over, Aly," Quantum had said to me, back on Eruo Pium. And apparently he'd been right.

I lie in my bunk thinking over the past few hours, mostly pondering one simple thought: this is what it feels like to be between a rock, a hard place, and a shit sandwich. Around me, everyone else does the same. I doubt any of them are asleep. We'd discussed as quietly as possible the idea of trying to fight our way out of this holding cell together when the Bogotanites switched guard, but the question had been: Then what? Even if we get the *Orika* off the ground, without La Mer to hack Bogotan's satellite, we can't send a message to Brady in time to stop him from launching from KL and delivering the soil compound as planned. Plus, this settlement has their own armed ships, and none of us are naive enough to think the only things they're capable of firing are engine disablers. And finally, we have to assume whatever remains of Medina's attack forces is stationed aboard the *Celestial*, which can't be too far out. It hadn't taken long for us to decide, reluctantly and with extreme prejudice, to lock down our instincts and sit tight until Brady gets here.

But there's still Venus. After I'd mentioned the numbers she'd left on the universal clock in my bunk to the crew, we'd realized they are a secure transmission frequency. David confirmed this, having noticed she'd done the same in the main berth. If we can get a radio or our VDUs, we'll be able to communicate with her again. Knowing Venus, she feels safest and most in her comfort zone staying aboard the *Orika*, and we know she's keeping it buttoned up tightly. But without the ability to contact her, whatever intel she may be able to glean from the landing field and whatever news we could share with her are useless.

Just like the Admin's tactic in the war, Whitmore and Medina recognize that strictly controlling communication effectively controls just about everything else. I wonder, though, if they get it: the Admin still lost.

IT TAKES FOUR DAYS for anything to happen. And when it does, the sucker punch to the gut is like nothing any of us has ever felt.

Zabriskie, flanked by several guards—the usual situation lately—opens up the gymnasium door sometime in the midmorning, as far as I can tell. "Your crew has arrived."

The flood of relief we all feel, though immense, is so intermixed with anger and fear, it's hard to know if the news is good or bad. It's good they weren't taken captive and then executed, something no one would put past Medina at this point, but bad because now they're as stuck in this web as we are.

I catch a glimpse of one of the other guards; Blondie, the mind-like-an-amoeba ringleader of my locker-room-buddy fugees—the ones who'd stared at me like I'd been giving them their own personal striptease after the cannibal camp escape—stands among the security detail. Medina must be actively recruiting more bodies to help discharge and enforce her rule. Her selection leaves a lot to be desired. The scav carries an unholstered Sinbad pistol and wears a basic Corps uniform kit: tactical equipment vest with ammo pouches, lightweight upper body armor, kneepads. It's as if he's expecting to assault an enclave of dissidents, not a group of salvagers who'd saved his ass from being someone else's lunch, literally. The remaining detail, six total, are similarly attired, making it clear that they are fully prepared for us to be, well, a little miffed.

Karl seethes. "I see you've brought along your kennel mates, Zabriskie."

Zabriskie remains detached, but I forget about him a second later as Patrick Brady, Zeta Abrams, and Jeremy La Mer rush through the door. The gym instantly fills with cries of joy as we swarm each other, hugging with the lack of restraint only the desperate can feel.

Our security detail keeps its distance as we all mingle together, letting us reunite on our terms. It doesn't appear our arriving crew have been mistreated, yet they don't seem at ease. After the initial flurry of welcome, I look at La Mer and my stomach immediately drops into my feet. I rush toward him and embrace him as if our entire lives have led to this moment.

"Keep cool," I whisper into his ear. "I don't know what they've told you, but Venus is safe. She's hiding on the *Orika*, and they don't know about her. We have to keep it that way."

I pull away from him and stare hard into his eyes, making sure he'd heard me and understands what I'm saying. We hadn't discussed what to tell Brady and the crew about Venus, never expecting that they'd be allowed to reach Bogotan so quietly and easily. But La Mer's reaction surprises me. "I know," he says.

"Did—?" I stop myself before blurting out anything that would jeopardize Venus's anonymity. He's nodding at me, confirming what I want to know—she must have been able to get a transmission to them, probably as they'd landed at the airfield.

His cold hand is still wrapped around my wrist. I feel his fingers slip inside the hem of my sleeve, and something even colder is pushed against my arm. It feels small, no bigger or heavier than a bolt nut. La Mer's green eyes stay fixed on mine, waiting for a show of understanding. I nod just enough for him to see. It's either a diminutive explosive or a com device; either way, it's a method of creating organization, or organized chaos.

"Baby, you shouldn't have come," Desto croons to Zeta nearby. "I don't want you putting yourself into danger. Not for me."

He holds her so close their two bodies are nearly fused, making me wonder if she can breathe. But from my vantage it looks like her arms are clamped around him just as tightly. Brady and Vitruzzi stand together, arms laced around each other's waists and their foreheads touching as they share an overwhelmed moment of relief.

This is as all right as it's ever going to get. The thought seeps through my mind, leaving me feeling like a sack that's been filled with lead. Heavy, dull, immobile. I reach over to Karl and grasp one of his hands. Behind us, the gym door closes and we're left alone.

"W E W E R E D E T A I N E D the instant we landed. Medina and her jackboots took over the *Nebula* and started moving everything out and onto a Corps ISPS." Brady and the crew stand and sit in a cluster around the bunks as he fills us in on what they know. "They told us you were safe and, in short, that you'd all agreed to relocate the entire settlement here."

I snort loudly, unable to contain my disgust.

Brady's expression tells me he couldn't agree more. "Yeah. I could tell things were fucked here, more or less, the minute Zeta got to KL and explained what had happened on Eruo Pium, and Whitmore's *envoy* explained his proposal for bringing the compound and data here. When we finally got your transmission"—he squeezes Vitruzzi's hand, which he hasn't let go of since arriving, tightly—"we started planning."

"Planning?" Desto asks. "Planning how and for what?"

"For any contingency. We rigged the soil compound with about twenty kilos of explosives camouflaged inside three extra drums that they don't know are dummies. There's one remote detonator on the *Nebula* and . . ." He turns his head to see if anyone is watching through the window in the door, but it's all clear. Waving to everyone, he draws us closer, then pulls a small device, like the one La Mer had given me, from its hiding place in his armpit. "Most of you should have one of these transmitter pods now. Their effective range is up to about two klicks, though we haven't been able to test them completely."

"It's a detonator?" Ryan asks.

Brady and La Mer look at him curiously, and I realize they have no idea who he is. Zeta breaks in, "We picked the kid up on Eruo Pium; he was one of the fugees." She looks at him. "Glad to see you on the crew."

Ryan nods shyly.

Brady continues, "That's exactly what they are. Of course, we didn't know Medina was a factor in this—"

"None of us did," David adds.

"Yeah, that's what I figured. But as soon as she met us in the landing field and sent troops on board the *Nebula* without so much as a 'would you mind?,' my gut told me whatever's going on here, you've been under coercion since the beginning and she's behind this whole game. I thought about blowing her to hell as soon as we landed, but .. . I don't know what the game *is* yet, exactly."

"It's pretty easy to explain," Karl says. "She wants to turn back civilization's clock to the Roman Empire."

"And we get to be the Christians she throws to the lions," Hoogs adds.

After a second to take this in, Brady says smoothly, "About what we thought. This is the reason we left the *Celestial* in the first place. Too bad we didn't just kill her then . . ."

But no one had ever really believed things would go this far. I suppose this is what metaphysicists refer to as the wheel. What goes around, comes around.

Karl responds, "As I see it, the question is, how are we going to link up with Venus and get the hell out of here? We can blow Medina's ship with the compound you rigged on our way off this rock if we can just get to the airfield."

"What if she's not in it, though? She'll just mobilize the *Celestial* and come after us. And Keum Libre," David says. "Not to mention, if that compound is as deadly as it seems, it could kill everyone in Bogotan if it's spread. An explosion might not render all of it inert."

No one has a response to that. It's a fact.

He looks around. "I don't know about all of you, but I'm not prepared to kill a bunch of bystanders. Enough of that happened in the war. I'm done with it."

Something from Rob Cross's final message, a recording he'd left for me to watch after he was dead, whispers in my head. *It's just the way of the worlds. It's a fucking mess and the best we can do is try to survive.* It had made sense to me at the time, but not anymore. Survival at the expense of so many lives, maybe innocent lives, isn't survival. It's lunacy.

As if reading my thoughts, David continues, "Besides, we don't even know if these people are all on board with Medina's plans, or just as caught up in it as we are. Like those kids from Eruo Pium. Whatever we do, we have to get that compound away from here. For good."

The silence that follows his declaration this time is reluctant, almost grudging. But the faces of my crew show agreement, unanimously.

Finally Brady says, "If we have a chance, we have to try." His statement goes without question. "We have to stop both her and Whitmore, and I propose—"

Karl jumps in. "I really don't think Whitmore is the issue. I don't think he knew about her intentions."

I look at him, surprised. "Whitmore was standing right there when she told us she was going to wipe us out if we didn't serve ourselves to her on a platter."

"Did you see the surprise on his face, though? The way she shut him down when he tried to get her attention?" He's speaking to me, but he looks around at Desto and Vitruzzi, too. "He looked to me like a prisoner under a spotlight, dazed. He didn't know she was going to take it this far. I'm sure of it."

Brady rubs a hand along the gray sandpaper of his chin and

meets my blue eyes with his hazel ones, waiting for Karl and me to suss this out.

I take a second for a breath. "Maybe, Karl. But here's where I agree with Medina—in this situation, whoever isn't an asset is a liability. If he's running this colony, he's going to have to fight for it. Our only goal is to protect our own. If he and his people get in the way, that's not going to slow us down. I'm not ready to wipe out the entire city of Bogotan"—I nod to David, showing him I agree with his determination—"but I'm also not going to stand aside if any one of us is threatened."

Our eyes hold for a moment, and I hope he can read my thoughts in my expression. When he says, "I'm with you. We just don't want to put anyone in harm's way who doesn't need to be. All of us are going to have to make an effort to leave the noncombatants out of this," I know he has.

The rest of the crew nod, but I know at least a few of us are sharing a thought: there are no innocents in this. We—and by *we* I mean *everyone*—have lost the luxury of staying neutral and not picking sides. It's gone too far, too much is at stake, to think in any other terms but black and white.

David picks up the thread. "The biggest problem we have is the fact that the *Orika*, even if we get to it, is low on supplies. We won't make it home."

"The *Nebula* is fully powered and stocked. Enough for us all," Zeta comments.

"Good." Karl nods excitedly. "Then if we can just get control of it, we can get out of here. Venus is just one person, so it may be easy enough for her to slip clear of the *Orika* without being seen and meet us there."

"And then what? Run back to KL and wait for Medina to show up with shackles and bullets?"

At the sound of Quantum's voice, all eleven of us turn our heads toward the door so fast we must appear to be a single remote-operated unit. We've been so involved in our discussion, no one saw or heard him enter. He stands at the door, now closed behind him, arms held out, palms up, showing us he's empty-handed. Yet if I've learned anything from Quantum, it's that everything about him is a threat, from his mind to his intent to his schemes.

"What are you doing here?" Hoogs says, the first to break through the stunned silence.

"I ask again: And then what?" Quantum says, ignoring Hoogs. He takes a couple of steps forward, gauging the group to be too frozen in surprise to impede him. "If I've learned one thing from this war, it's that those who want to win never stop fighting, and those who just want to live end up doing little more than dying. So your crew has to ask yourselves, who do you want to be? The winners?" His thick eyebrows arch in a way that makes his always-smug expression that much more antagonizing. "Or not."

"Are you trying to make us think you want to help us, Quantum?" I watch Desto, wondering what he's going to do. For the moment, he remains standing behind Zeta, his hands resting on her shoulders, the muscles of his jaw straining against his skin.

"Think what you want. If Medina isn't stopped, the system just fought a war for nothing. The Cabinets of Directorates may as well still be in charge of deciding who is free and who isn't, and Kurosawa T'Kai may as well still be treating soldiers and non-cits like lab rats. *I* started this war because I wanted to change things, improve humanity. Maybe I'm too ambitious, but at least I have the balls to try."

"And now Medina is just trying to reinstate the status quo," Brady says flatly. "That it?"

For the first time, Quantum shows something like an emotion. But it's not anger or resentment, which wouldn't have made me think twice; it's the look of a puppy that has been smacked unexpectedly by its owner. He glances around at the crew, uncertainty and hesitancy making him drop his eyes to the floor more than once, and he has to clear his throat. But when he speaks, he's back to normal: cold, calculating, deadly sincere.

He puts his hands down slowly, and lets his stare rest on Jeremy. "And you, La Mer, when you were still Axone and part of the network that almost brought the Admin down in the first Rebellion, I remember you from that time. And I remember all the high ideals you had. Are you still that person? Or did you stop standing for anything when you fell for that loopy pilot?"

Is this his idea of a rallying cry? A glance at La Mer tells me he's on the verge of doing something brash, but he's not a fighter, so it's a guess as to what. I step in to cut it off. "How did you get in here?"

Quantum responds, "Not everyone in this city is behind Medina. In fact, most aren't, but they're too afraid of her to stand up against her. They originally resisted any Admin—former or not—months ago and tried to keep her out. But they failed." Thoughts of the partially destroyed landing-field wall and Zabriskie's earlier state-ment—"Turns out things aren't as simple as good-guys–bad-guys anymore"—run through my head, finally making sense. "Even former citizens are smart enough to know when they are outgunned and outsmarted. I have allies, others who think Medina is taking things to places they don't want to go. Who think she is just the seed of a new Admin. Few want that. They will help us put a stop to this."

Brady, ever the pragmatist, says, "Get to the point."

With a dip of his chin, Quantum steps amid the group and continues, "Medina is only part of the problem. She still commands the *Celestial*, and while a ship that war-ready still flies, it will always be a threat. We need to take Medina down—cut the head off this particular snake—and make the cruiser obsolete so no one can step in to take her place."

"And you have a proposal on how to do that," Karl says.

"I always have a plan," Quantum responds, implying that we are too incompetent to think beyond anything more complex than our next meal, and not caring in the least that every word that comes out of his mouth makes everyone in this room detest him more. "Medina will be coming soon to collect those she wants to take back to Keum Libre to recruit the rest of the settlers for her rebuilt Admin. You'll tell Venus to create a diversion at the landing field, during which time you'll board the *Nebula* and escape."

I start at his mention of Venus—*how could he know she's there?*—then realize he must have known she was still aboard the *Orika* all along. If she's not with us, where else would she be? His shrewdness, as misdirected as it always seems to be, still never fails to catch me off guard. But the fact that he hasn't already given up Venus to Medina or her echelons, more than anything else, tells me he's not playing us. At least, not any more than he's playing Medina. But that doesn't mean we can trust him or count on him as an ally, as loyal. Not for a second.

"We've already gotten that far, Quantum," Karl says. "Have anything better to suggest?" His sneer doesn't hide his loathing, but then, Quantum is used to that.

"Then Aly and I will get aboard Medina's landing ship and take it back to the *Celestial*—which she will obviously marshal to destroy you and make dispatching the rest of the colonists easier—where I will disable the ship and stop her."

"Wait, what?" I blurt. "Why me?" It's not fear that makes every cell in my body resist his plan; it's the idea of being alone with Quantum on a fleet cruiser, forced to follow whatever scheming lead he takes. Not fear at all. Just pure survival instinct.

"Because you're the only one small enough to be hidden inside a cargo box and taken aboard undetected who also has the training to use a bugsuit." He looks around slowly at the rest of the crew, then brings his eyes back to mine. "And you're the only one I trust."

It's at this point that my brain stops engaging and goes into a tailspin while pondering the full implications of the words "small enough to be hidden inside a cargo box." He might as well have said "small enough to count worms in a corpse condo." As I consider the reasons to protest, each less convincing sounding than the last—*I'm not a coward, I just feel like I'm choking to death on my own heart when stuck in small places*—the conversation swirls around me . . . Medina still considers Quantum an asset and confederate . . . he'll have free rein of her ship . . . when it's time to put the plan in operation, he'll vent a nerve agent throughout that will knock most of Medina's troops inert . . . I'll take control of the bridge, using the Goldblum to go on the offense and deal with any remaining alert troops, then he'll put the ship in stasis long enough to give the rest of us time to rally more help from KL and get back to take control of the cruiser, its arsenal, and its multitude of adjunct attack ships . . . if the plan fails, we can blow the rigged compound from inside and destroy the cruiser completely, while Quantum and I escape in evac pods—overhearing this part sends me into a shuddering spasm—and the crew can track our emergency transmissions and pick us up before emergency life support gives out.

As the conversation advances, arguments and counterarguments from the group dwindle until none remain. There is no other way to stop Medina, or to ensure the fatal compound is never deployed. And whether the crew believes Quantum is being honest or not, his plan is our best chance for at least getting back to KL and warning the rest of the settlers about what's coming.

My attention comes back to the moment when I feel Karl tug gently on my arm. "You don't have to do this, Aly." His voice, crackling with emotion, carries throughout the room.

I turn to look into his eyes first, then around at the others. Finally, turning back to Quantum, I ask, "Isn't there another way of getting me on her landing ship?"

He stares blankly at me, not answering. Answer enough.

I take a deep inhale, then let it out, hoping no one notices the slight hitch and tremble as the breath leaves my lungs. "Then I'm in .. . I guess."

Quantum reaches into his jacket, pulls out a radio, and places it on the nearest bunk. "Call your pilot and tell her to be prepared to distract Medina's crew and get herself to the *Nebula*. I'll get prepped to leave."

"Hey Quantum," Desto says and steps from behind the bunk Zeta still sits on.

The wire-rat stands his ground as Desto approaches, and to his credit he barely flinches when he intuits the bone-crushing swing Desto aims at his jaw. No one tries to stop the father-to-be this time. After a moment, Quantum picks himself up off the floor, spits a puddle of blood at his feet, and makes for the door, wobbling slightly. He turns before leaving and says simply, "Be ready. This will happen fast."

Vitruzzi shakes free of Brady's hand and hurries up to the wire-rat. This time, he narrows his eyes and his face tenses, preparing for anything. Instead of striking him, Vitruzzi leans close to his ear and says something, but I can't make it out. Quantum nods his head, then exits.

Of all the questions yet to be answered, the one my mind keeps going back to is: Why would Quantum say he trusts *me*?

BRADY AND LA MER TRANSMIT to Venus, knowing she'll be monitoring all frequencies. When they reach her, they fill her in on everything that's already happened and is about to happen. While they discuss possible methods of distraction, the rest of the crew settles in, the tension and stress of waiting for something to go down already growing unbearable within an hour of Quantum's departure. The hardest thing about a plan, any plan, is the time that elapses before it can be put into motion, the questions that arise, the fears that worm into your guts and take root, feeding and growing fatter on every uncertainty and doubt that fractures your equilibrium. With no outlet to bleed off the infection of nervous energy but sitting and waiting, the situation is even worse.

Karl and I sit side by side on one bunk, enjoying the closeness of being together. We've been talking about every detail we can remember of the *Celestial*'s layout from the fourteen months we were aboard, calling out potential advantages or potential weaknesses of Quantum's plan. Neither of us brings up what might come next, all of the what-ifs: What if I or Quantum is caught before I can take the bridge? What if the plan fails and we have to implement the soil compound backup plan? What if that fails? What if it doesn't but I can't get to an evac pod and escape in time? What if I do, but the crew can't find me in all that vastness of empty space? And worst of all, what if this whole plan is a lie cooked up by Quantum for some ulterior motive?

What if these are the last moments Karl and I will ever spend together?

As the night progresses, our ideas and voices slowly fade, most of the crew grasping at the potential for a brief, though guaranteed to be restless, sleep. I'm stretched out on my side on the bunk, one of my hands lightly rubbing Karl's lower back as he sits and stares absently at the door. Seeming to realize how quiet it's become, he glances around him, then reaches into the inside pocket of his jacket and turns his body to the side, facing me.

"Aly, there's something I want to . . . um . . . I want you to have." He reaches behind him and pulls my hand from his back, then drops something into it.

I open my fingers and see a ring like the one Venus had been wearing, the one La Mer had given her.

Before I say anything, Karl continues, "I had Jeremy make one for us. I want you to know how much you mean to me, how much I love you."

As the full meaning of what he's saying hits me, a shiv of fear pierces the center of my chest. My voice barely squeezes past it. "Karl, what—? We . . . we don't have time for this kind of thing." I know it's not the right thing to say, but the fear—fear of losing him, fear of losing everything that matters to me—short-circuits my ability to think clearly or to say what I mean.

But he knows me, and he can hear the truth of my feelings in my heartbeat. Calmly, he says, "Aly, this may be the only time we have." And he lies down beside me on the tiny military cot and wraps his body around mine while I place the ring on a loop of utility cord and hang it around my neck.

TWENTY-FOUR

Medina doesn't make us wait for long. Only for a few hours after Brady, Zeta, and La Mer arrive, in fact. The inside of the gymnasium is like a vacuum where no noise or outside light penetrates, and when she opens the door and steps inside, we're like newborns that must reacclimate to a world outside our insulated one. Now after so many long hours cooped up—some of us in this holding cell, the rest aboard the *Nebula*—we embrace the knowledge that we'll be leaving Bogotan soon. Alive or dead.

Whitmore and a retinue of eight armed guards, including my favorites, Van Heusen and Blondie, come inside with her. Quantum lingers at the back of the group, scowling. No one seems to be paying him any attention.

Without ceremony, she says, "By now you've all had the time you need to discuss your options."

She flicks a quick nod to the gunmen assembled in a single line along the far wall, and each draws their sidearm of choice. I feel cold sweat break inside my armpits, though I know at this point we're not going to put up any resistance. Karl stands on one side of me, his shoulder touching mine, and David stands on my other. Between the two of them, I feel almost invincible, but I've heard the ticking of enough battle countdowns to know it's only an illusion. The dead aren't winners, just losers who don't have to care anymore.

No one has spoken, but Medina continues as if she already knows the answer. "Dr. Vitruzzi, Brady, and Desto will travel with us to Keum Libre. Takeoff is in one hour. Come with me, please."

She spins around, preparing to leave, but my eyes go to Quantum, anxious for a signal to put this grand plan of his under way. What I see doesn't reassure me. He raises a hand to his chest, pressing it there with one finger lifted in a *stay put* gesture. Easy for him to fucking say.

What happens next is more of a surprise than anything I've seen so far. Whitmore reaches out and puts a firm hand on Medina's shoulder as she takes a step toward the door. He looms over her by at least a head, but his gangly form is still somehow *less* than her stocky, erect military persona.

"Wait, Medina. I won't let you do this."

Medina comes to a standstill, but she doesn't turn around. Van Heusen's feral blue eyes stare at Whitmore, and the muzzle of his raised pistol targets Whitmore center mass.

"We talked about this, Jim," Medina says.

"No. No, *goddammit*. I will not allow you to . . . to make yourself the leader of a new Admin, not after what—"

Medina turns around quickly, knocking Whitmore's hand off of her shoulder and following through with a short chop to his midsection. Whitmore's eyes bulge comically as he doubles over, gasping. For the first time since I'd met her, Medina's face shows something new, a side of her I'd hardly have believed existed if I weren't witnessing it. The animal rage of a pit viper about to strike transforms her usually benign but hard features into something too shocking to be feared, too horrible to be ignored.

As Whitmore clutches his stomach and tries to catch his breath, Medina looks Van Heusen in the eyes and says laconically, "Shoot this bastard. In the face."

"No—!" I yell, beginning to step forward before David and Karl both stop me.

Van Heusen doesn't hesitate. Whitmore is dead before he hits the floor.

Medina faces us once more, but my gaze goes back to Quantum, desperate. He remains as he was, his gesture to wait firm, his eyes meeting mine with a ferocious command to follow his lead. I almost don't listen, almost rush into them, throwing my life away over disbelief that the woman who had started this never-ending war had merely done it out of insanity, not idealism, not something more pure, more rational.

But with Karl and my brother next to me, I'm not ready to die. Not today.

Medina's features are smooth and stern once again, no sign of the monster coiled beneath her skin. "If you had any questions about how far I'm willing to go to ensure humankind's continuity, I hope they have been answered. Follow." The command, meant for Vitruzzi, Brady, and Desto, is incontestable.

The three of them look around at the rest of us, then begin walking to the door. Vitruzzi kneels down and puts her fingertips to Whitmore's wrist before passing by. She knows he's dead, but I read something in the action that gives me a tiny jolt of hope. Vitruzzi isn't too far gone. She still cares, she's still *her* underneath the trauma that's been scrambling her circuits. She is still strong beneath the damaged exterior. I hope it lasts long enough for us to see the end of this.

Two of the security detail grab Whitmore's legs and drag his body out behind the rest of them, leaving a repulsive smear along the floor. As soon as the door closes, Karl grabs the radio.

"Venus, it's Karl, come in."

"Karlie," she answers immediately, "time?"

"Yes. Medina is heading to the landing field with Brady, V, and Desto. When they get there, light up the Venus show."

"Roger. Jeremy?"

He grabs the radio from Karl. "Yeah, babe."

"Love you. Don't forget that I like the vanilla frosting better than the chocolate when we get back, okay?"

"I won't."

THE DOOR ONLY remains closed for a few minutes, the remaining eight of us pacing and holding ourselves back from trying to bum-rush through it and race to the landing field. If V, Brady, and Desto get on Medina's ship, we may never see them again. The one predictable thing we all know about Quantum is that he doesn't waste time on sentimentality. The three of them are as good as dead if they're not part of the plan. And he'd made the plan crystal clear. It's him and me. No stragglers, no flexibility, no loose ends.

As our nerves strain, nearing the breaking point, Mason says, "Venus will be able to slow them down. It's at least one element in our favor."

But is it the only one?

As this thought passes through my head, the door opens, and Zabriskie, flanked by at least two visible guards just outside, steps in. "You all need to come with us. Now."

"Why?" David asks.

"Just come." Zabriskie's eyes are lit by an urgency I haven't seen in him before, and my nerves warn me that our old friend Chaos is about to strike.

"Whose side are you on?" David says, his stance rigid and ready.

Zabriskie crosses the distance between the two of them in four long strides. All of us prepare for a confrontation; even the air seems to be alive with coiled energy. I see David's nostrils flare, but Zabriskie stops short of him, and then—does something totally unexpected.

"Take this," Zabriskie whispers and holds out a VDU, then reaches in his jacket and pulls out two more. "Here," he says, looking at Karl and me, both standing closest to him. "We're getting you out of here."

At the mention of "we" my eyes jerk toward the doorway where the other two guards have entered. Neither of them holds weapons in their hands, but both look nervous as hell.

"Who are you working with?" David repeats, not yet willing to take Zabriskie's com device.

We all feel David's paranoia. Could this be a setup? Is Medina looking for an excuse to ghost us so it will appear to have been self-defense to the rest of the KLers if they're brought back here? Why hadn't Quantum told us to expect Zabriskie if he's in on the plan? Without confirmation, it's impossible to guess what Zabriskie has up his sleeve, which leaves us with one last decision-making tool: our instincts.

Stepping up to the colonist, I take one of the VDUs, then turn to the rest. "What are we waiting for?"

"Aly—" Karl says, alarmed.

"We don't have time to debate this. We have to act."

Zeta takes my cue and grabs another VDU from Zabriskie, and the rest's resistance dissolves like salt in water. Everyone begins grabbing what gear they've brought, and we follow Zabriskie out, moving not quite at a double time. The other two men are already down the hallway and at the front door, peering outside. For what or who, we're stuck guessing.

Zabriskie fills us in on the way. "Whitmore wanted to set you free days ago while we figured out a plan. Now that he's dead"—he makes eye contact with the men outside, who nod an all clear, then pushes through the school's front door without slowing—"we're just improvising. Medina is making unilateral decisions. Trying to run Bogotan without consensus or even discussion. Quantum says you can help us stop her."

"Why should we trust you?" I ask as we rush into the street.

He opens the rear cargo hatch of a transport truck. Inside, I catch a glimpse of a cargo container about the size of a squad arms locker with the words COMMUNICATIONS BACKUPS stenciled on the side. "You don't have a choice but to trust us. We're taking you to the landing field so you can get the hell out of here, and—" He breaks off when his VDU lights up.

Quantum's voice: "Zabriskie, do you copy?"

"Zabriskie here."

"Is she in the box yet?"

"Negative, the crew is loading up. ETA to the landing field is ten."

"Affirmative." My own VDU pings to life and I answer. "Aly," he says, "your crew needs to get your pilot in action. There's not much time left."

"Roger. What did you mean by 'is she in the box yet'?"

My screen goes black without him responding. Not that he needs to.

Zabriskie and one of the men with him open the cargo container and begin pulling out weapons. Carbines, Dergs, a couple of Sinbads. He motions to the crew. "Get what you want and get in the back. You" —he passes me an AK-80, my always trusted weapon of choice, and a few clips of caseless—"jump inside there once we get everything out and lie down. I'll get you on Medina's ship."

I swallow hard, checking the action on the '80 and loading the first clip. My eyes hold his steadily while I shake my head. "I'm not missing this fight."

Wisely, he doesn't argue. The crew grab the guns and get in, Zabriskie pulling himself into the covered bed with us. The vehicle is already moving before he gets the cargo gate closed. "This truck is heading straight for the *Kongjù*, Medina's ship. I'm supposed to leave you on the city side of the landing-field gate before we go through, and your pilot is supposed to do whatever she's going to do. The truck is completely armored, so you can use us as a shield until we get to the *Kongjù*. But no one stays inside except Erikson, or we'll never get her aboard. Everyone clear?"

No one says a word; the only sound now is the dull whump of the fuel cell engine and the tires humming on the road. I look around at their faces, seeing the same severe dilation of their pupils, the same controlled breathing, the same fierce warrior mask as mine. The kid, Ryan, has been through some shit, maybe even had to kill others to survive, but he looks more scared than the rest of us. This is a real battle, with real soldiers. The kind of bloody razing mess that he's used to as a scav fighting other scavs, while it was probably always gruesome, would never have had the same methodical, purposeful intent to destroy as what he's about to encounter. Almost all of us in the bed of this truck, and even more of Medina's crew, were trained by the best to be efficient killing machines. The Corps never stinted on doling out ruthlessness, and no one kills better than its graduates. I just hope the kid is prepared for it.

My eyes fall on Zeta, then quickly bounce away. She was a civilian before the war and had left that behind for her own reasons and joined the colony on Spectra 6, but now she's just a survivor like the rest of us. A fugitive in a system where no one is anything but. Fugitives from reason, stability, maybe even hope. What chance her and Desto's kid has was already limited, but now . . . now I don't want to think about what could, and probably will, happen.

Zabriskie's carbine lies across his knees. He leans forward, leaving his hands on the stock and the barrel to keep it from falling, and says, "You know you're putting the whole mission in danger until you get in that crate."

"I told you, I'm not missing this fight." I don't bother mentioning that I'm more afraid of being stuck in that black box than I am of being shot point-blank. "Another gun could be the thing that keeps the people I care about alive."

His seawater-green eyes stare into mine for several seconds, his face only a puff of breath away. Then he leans back, reaches into his jacket, and pulls free a small plastic bag, which he tosses at me. "Quantum told me to give you those. Vitruzzi asked him for them. Sedatives. If you don't get killed before you get aboard the *Kongjù*, take three. Quantum will come get you when it's clear. Save the rest in case it's longer than . . ." He shrugs.

The bag lies in my lap. I look inside at the handful of white pills, then put three in my breast pocket for quick retrieval. If Vitruzzi were here, I'd kiss her.

Someone from the cab hammers on the divider and the truck slows to a stop—our cue. I promise Zabriskie, "Get to the *Kongjù*'s ramp, I'll meet you there."

"Fifteen of Medina's on the tarmac, looks like the three going to Keum Libre haven't boarded yet. They're standing over by the supply dump with four guards on them," says a voice through Zabriskie's VDU. He glances around to make sure we've all heard it, then slides open the rear door and drops the cargo gate. "Good luck. We'll keep it slow so you can use our cover."

"What about Venus?" Hoogs says. "Shouldn't she be doing her magic trick right now?"

We look at each other impotently. Finally Karl says, "We can't wait. Mason, La Mer, and I will go after the crew. Zeta, just stay low and get your ass to the *Nebula*." Karl's obviously been having similar thoughts to mine. "Aly, you do what you can to help Zeta, and make sure you get back to this truck without being seen. Ryan, you stick with David and Hoogs. Cover us from the rear." He stands and the rest of us do the same. Giving it one last shot, he gets on the VDU Zabriskie had given him. "Venus, I don't know where you are, and don't respond to this message if it will compromise you, but we're about to come in hot. The *Nebula* needs to be ready to launch ASAP." He gives it a second, but there's no return transmission. Nodding once, he says, "Let's do it."

TWENTY-FIVE

Not being able to see anything on the other side of the truck is unnerving. But what's worse is the lack of surprise, the lack of distraction. The lack of the Venus show. What could have happened? If she's been compromised or killed, this fight is already over. I may still be able to get aboard Medina's ship and rendezvous with the *Celestial*, but it may not help Vitruzzi, Brady, and Desto. If they die, and if Venus is already dead, the fallout will be much, much worse than just shattered morale. They—along with Karl and David—compose the core of my world, the people I most care about, the people I will never hesitate to put my life on the line for. If I can't keep them safe, the whole hellish fight will be for nothing.

Locking these fears deep inside, I press forward, following Zeta so closely our hips touch as we shuffle along. The line is Karl, Hoogs, Mason, Zeta, me, David, Ryan, and La Mer at the rear. The truck is long, made for carrying large loads, and conceals us easily. Zabriskie's collaborators informed us that all of Medina's squad is busy with loading a resupply cache to take to the *Celestial* and guarding Vitruzzi and the other two. The cargo brought by this truck is the last expected on their manifest. From our enemy's perspective, the arrival of Zabriskie is situation normal.

I'd had a brief look across that landing field after the gargantuan gates rumbled open. The *Orika* is still where Venus had planted it, its state of disuse and general beat-up condition making it look almost like a monolith from ancient times despite its short tenure in Bogotan. Immediately beside it, only thirty meters distant, sits the *Nebula*, a slightly bigger craft. Towering behind the two of them looms the much larger battle-ready fleet attack ship, the former PCA *Kongjù*. I'd been a navigator on it myself during the war and know full well its capacity for rendering the *Nebula* and *Orika* into scrap without even needing to engage its heavy artillery. Seeing it for that split second had made my guts turn to ice. The only chance Venus has is to outmaneuver it. Karl can fly it if Venus is somehow out of the picture, a thought that sends another freezing stab of anxiety through the middle of me, but he doesn't have her preternatural, sometimes miraculous, talents for making a craft do the seemingly impossible. Yet if the *Nebula* makes it into the air, maybe Medina will just let her go. After all, Keum Libre has no defense against a fleet cruiser and its arsenal, all at Medina's disposal, and she must know that. Whitmore's men, the ones who had delivered Zeta, then returned with the crew, could easily have reconned KL during their stay and figured this out, and Medina surely debriefed them. Even if part of our crew splinters off in the *Nebula* and gets to KL in time to warn the settlers of Medina's coming, there's nothing, not a goddamn thing, the settlement can do to stop her.

That part is up to me.

We can't be more than fifty meters distant of the cluster, and David, Ryan, and Hoogs disengage and silently run behind a vehicle parked toward the edge of the ship takeoff zone to take up long-range backup firing positions. No shouts or words of warning come from ahead to indicate they've been spotted. A relief. The *Kongjù*'s engines start to cycle, sending a low-pitched throbbing rhythm through the ground and up into my feet. The rest of us continue to plod forward, then the truck stops and Zabriskie jumps clear of the back.

A voice from in front of us: "Zabriskie, is that the last of the supplies?"

"Yeah, Quantum's parts."

"Okay, one sec and I'll send the loader over."

Where the fuck is Venus?

Karl turns around to face us, meets my eyes with his for a heartbeat, and I read the go signal coming before he says anything. The slight breeze blowing up from the south feels warm against the coolness of my skin. My nostrils flare as I draw in a deep breath, calming myself and preparing to let the battle-drunk veteran that I usually keep suppressed deep within me once again inhabit my body.

He turns back toward the front of the cab, peers around, and lifts his hand, ready to wave us into action. Just before he does, the sound of voices raised in some kind of confrontation carries to us.

"What do you mean 'shut her down'? The commander wants her up in the air to be added to the *Celestial*'s armada. I mean, who wouldn't want this ship, this *absolutely gorgeous hunk of machine*, among their squadron?"

Venus? Really?

Unable to stop myself, I slide up beside Karl and cautiously peer around the cab. He turns to look at me, his eyes shining full moons of surprise.

It *is* Venus. Dressed in a mishmash outfit that is part Corps uniform, part civvies, obviously trying to blend in with the bustle of security personnel finishing up the final supply run, she stands less than fifteen meters in front of us, just at the base of the *Nebula*'s open ramp.

"Nobody said nothing to me."

If it isn't my old friend Blondie.

"Hmmm, must have slipped her mind," Venus replies, her voice as dismissive as if she were a queen speaking to an idiot serf. And then I finally hear what I'd been too keyed up to recognize over the dull thump of the *Kongjù*'s engines—the *Nebula*, too, is online, her internals whirring into flight mode.

"Don't I know you?" Blondie says, leaning forward.

Those of us who realize the risk Venus had taken to show her face flinch in unison. She must be crazy, but sometimes crazy is the only option. I catch something out of the corner of my eye and turn just in time to reach out and grip La Mer by the sleeve as he tries to pass us and help Venus. *Don't*, I mouth, warning him. She may not have played all her cards yet, whatever the hell those are.

Within sight ahead of us, the pile of supplies Zabriskie's man had spoken of, where Vitruzzi, Brady, and Desto are waiting to board in the company of three guards, sits forward of the *Kongjù* and just between the *Nebula* and *Orika*. A track loader rolls down the *Kongjù*'s cargo ramp. The remaining supplies are small, not requiring a loader, and I realize it must be coming to us. If Venus has a move to make, it *has* to be now.

The onetime fugee reaches out and grabs Venus by the arm. "You're that pilot that came from Eruo Pium, I know it. Come with me."

It all happens as fast as the speed of light, and as slow as drowning.

As I watch, Brady and Desto tackle two of the unprepared guards watching over them, while Vitruzzi opens one of the boxes sitting near her and pulls out several weapons. The cue given, Karl takes aim and fires at Blondie but misses. The guard's reflexes are sharp, and he runs behind the *Nebula* at race speed, leaving Venus behind him. She immediately sprints inside the safety of the ship's hull, out of the line of fire. From behind us, I hear David open up with the rifle he'd taken from Zabriskie's cache. Hoogs and Mason take up firing positions behind and under our truck, and the squadron of soldiers under Medina's command scatter or sprint to the only place that offers them any protection on the mostly flat, open landing field—inside the *Kongjù*.

By the time the last bullet's echo fades Desto, Vitruzzi, and Brady have annihilated their guards and taken shelter in the safety behind one of the *Kongjù*'s external missile chutes. We can't know for sure how many others are inside the attack ship, but no one is leaving its interior without being in direct line of fire from those three. The squaddy driving the loader, the four guards with Vitruzzi's group, and three others are down on the tarmac, and we haven't taken a single casualty. The box of guns Vitruzzi had accessed could only have come from Venus, or maybe Quantum, and while it wasn't nearly the bang-up surprise I'd been expecting, I'm not complaining about the results.

But nothing is stopping Medina from calling for backup, which could be seconds away.

And I still have to get onto first the *Kongjù* and then the *Celestial.*

David, Ryan, and Hoogs read the situation and risk closing the gap by running across the space and rejoining us behind the truck. Zabriskie had jumped inside the rear, and his two compatriots are keeping a low profile in the cab, sitting this one out.

"What do we do?" Ryan asks, out of breath. I can see panic and excitement starting to squeeze in on him, turning his decision-making skills and reflexes into granulated powder. Can't have that.

"Calm down, kid," I say. "We need everyone focused and relaxed. Don't let yourself get distracted, read me?" His jittering eyes cut to me, and I force myself to grin at him, passively, showing no teeth. *Just another day, nothing unusual, no need to worry about it being your last,* my expression tells him. "If anyone comes at us, just pick your targets, take a deep breath, and squeeze the trigger. Remember those three steps. That's all you gotta think about. Okay?"

He nods. If the kid gets killed, I won't be happy, but getting shot with a stray bullet because he can't keep his nerves in check will piss me off even more.

My focus returns to the team as Karl moves to the truck's rear and slams a fist against the gate. "Zabriskie, listen up. You have to get this truck to the *Kongjù.* There's no way that loader is coming our direction. Put yourself in between the ramp and the *Nebula* so our people can make a run for it."

Zabriskie responds, "On it," and we hear him speaking into his VDU: "Medina and Steward, this is Jono Zabriskie. I'm stuck on the landing field with Quantum's supplies. The loader can't get to us, so we're bringing the truck to you. Do you read? Over."

"That's a negative, Zabriskie. It's too hot out there. Stand fast until we give you the all clear."

"Dammit," we hear him growl under his breath, then: "No can do, Steward. We're not going to sit here and wait to get shot. Out."

Fuck me, he's quite the gambler.

Karl says, "We'll give them cover fire from the *Nebula*. Stay low and get up beneath the ramp. That fugee may have a good position from the rear of the ship, so make sure the ramp is between you and him. Zeta, you follow me. Head straight for the cockpit. Venus will need your help. Let's move."

As I get into position to run, he steps in front of me, forcing me to stop. "Except you, Aly."

"Karl—"

"We have this covered. Stay here and watch our backs. Once we're all in the *Nebula*, you get on Medina's ship." He leans forward and kisses me on the lips quickly, before I can argue, then straightens. "I'll see you, lover—*soon*."

David wraps me in a brief side hug. "Good luck, Twig. Give that bitch my regards when you see her."

Then Mason squeezes my shoulder: "You got this," and Hoogs says, "We'll be there when you need us." La Mer: "Luck, Aly." Zeta says nothing, just gives me a long, hard hug, and even Ryan says: "Thanks for what you did for me. Good luck."

I don't know what to say, suddenly realizing I couldn't say it even if I did, the way my throat suddenly feels gummy and stuck fast. Finally I squeak out, "Go get back our crew."

I take a knee and get a bead on the direction Blondie had run. The crew rushes past me, and I watch enrapt as they make a few feints up the ramp. No shots are fired, and soon they've all disappeared into the shadows inside the hull.

I hear Zabriskie behind me: "Time to move, Erikson."

Standing, I'm about to make my way to the truck's cargo bed, but suddenly my legs feel weak, wobbly. I lean against the side of it for a second, fighting back dread, struggling not to believe that I've just said goodbye forever to the people I love, forcing my goddamn game face back on. Remembering the pills Vitruzzi had asked Quantum to get me, I reach into my pocket and dig them out, quickly popping all three in my mouth and dry-swallowing them. It's the only way I'm going to find the will to get inside that box.

A second later, I shamble to the rear. Zabriskie sees me and leans out with a hand extended, ready to help me up. I reach out to take it—

—and he points a pistol straight into my face and fires.

The thunder, so close to my head, nearly blows my eardrum out and I fall backward onto the ground, landing on my ass, reflexively trying to scoot away, wondering why I'm not dead. My hand hits meat and I jerk my eyes down, realizing that I can't push any farther away from the truck because there's a body behind me.

Blondie?

"Erikson, come on!" Zabriskie yelling at me just adds to the confusion, and I turn my stare back to him dazedly. "He must have snuck by them. Your friends are in the clear, but we've got to go!"

I push myself up and stand and shake my head to clear the ringing in my left ear, then turn around to glance back at the very dead fugee. Zabriskie hit him neatly in the temple, leaving a slightly gray, perfectly round, upraised ring around the hole in his head. His eyes are open, the moisture already being sucked away by the dry wind.

Zabriskie has the lid to the cargo box open and waits for me impatiently. Looking into it, I feel like I'm looking into an abyss. But even an eternal plunge into emptiness would be better than a second stuck inside this casket. I can't look Zabriskie in the face, too hard to yank my stare away from that box waiting to swallow me whole. The *Nebula*'s engines begin to whine louder, their departure now only seconds away.

"What are you waiting for?"

His words float to my ears from far away. I try to swallow, but my throat sticks. I pass him the carbine, put my hands on the cold metal side of the bin, stand still for a few breaths, then swing a leg over. Once I'm lying flat inside, a sudden and incredibly welcome rush of calm tingles out from my midsection, like a wisp of pure oxygen flowing through me. Either the sedatives or wishful thinking kicking in.

"Quantum says he'll come get you as soon as it's clear. It'll take about ten hours to get to the *Celestial*, so you're looking at about twelve hours in there. There's a bottle of water and another empty one if you need to piss. Just stay calm, take it easy." Can he see the fear in my face? He passes me the carbine, which I lay beside me. He stares at me for several seconds, his face moving through a range of expressions I previously wouldn't have believed he was capable of. Finally he lands on what I take to be confidence, his brow knit sternly and a twist at the side of his mouth that's part smile, part scowl. "Make your people proud, Erikson. Bogotan's too. We're counting on you."

The nod I give him is abrupt and short, all I can manage in my state of approaching paralysis.

The lid closes and I have the scope light of the carbine switched on before I even realize I'm doing it. Sound from outside is severely muted, but the truck is already moving forward past the subdued roar of the *Nebula*'s engines, then it hits the base of the *Kongjù*'s ramp and starts to tilt.

My heart is trying to explode through my chest. "Count," I whisper to myself, "one hundred, ninety-nine, ninety-eight, ninety-seven . . ."—*breathe, breathe, breathe*—"fucking ninety. Eighty-nine, eighty-eight, eighty-seven . . ."—*just fucking breathe*—"eighty . . ."

We've stopped, but at this point, counting aloud to myself is my only conscious awareness. I block it out, everything, crushing the worries—that the Nebula will never get off the ground, that Vitruzzi, Brady, and Desto won't be able to get to the scout, that the mission will fail and Keum Libre will become the killing field of a tyrant, that I'll die in this box—into a dark corner where I can't think about them, can't think about anything except: "Sixty, fifty-nine, fifty-eight, fifty-seven . . ."

When my brain finally fuzzes out completely, I don't know if it's from panic overload or sedation, but I don't care. The relief is all that matters.

TWENTY-SIX

Is it perverse to have grown bored after being trapped for hours in the dark, just waiting for Medina's crew to either find me and put an end to this slow descent into panic-slash-death or run down the *Nebula* and unleash all hell on them? The crushing terror that gripped me at first once the lid closed dulled to unconsciousness soon, then became a sort of malaise when I awoke that I thought only people who'd consumed horse tranquilizers could feel. Now, after the past ten hours and forty-six minutes in this sarcophagus-sized crate, I can't seem to get worked up by the very real possibility they are going to be my last.

I have Vitruzzi's magic anticlaustrophobia pills to thank for that, which have left me adrift inside my drug-induced subterranean mental maze, and surfacing only brings awareness of one simple thing: my muscles are beginning to feel a little cramped. My hidey-hole is only about 2 x .5 x .5 meters in area, so moving around isn't exactly easy. Other than the capped bottle I'd managed to use as a latrine, the only things in here with me are a bottle of water, the energy bars I still had in my equipment vest, and my AK-80. Plus the last four remaining sanity-saving pills.

I've popped two every three hours, and they've magically transformed the anxiety and panic that would ordinarily have sent me clawing through the steel lid with my fingernails into a blunt-tipped afterthought. The aftereffect has been, besides cramps, flat indifference. And I'll take it. Knowing I only have a few pills left, though, turns the dial on my anxiety meter up enough that I've reinitiated the countdown from a hundred in round after round just to keep my mind off it and ... other things. Like memories.

Some might call this brief calm before chaos an optimal time for introspection, but I try to keep my stampeding-rabbit thoughts in a white-noise cloud, or on things like the bruise on my left big toe that will probably make running a lot harder—if I get a chance—and the way my lips are starting to feel a little like sandpaper. But when the panic starts to creep in and I pop the pills, their power sends acid tendrils through my brain that eat away the barriers between my life now and my life as a child, letting memories I wish I didn't have spill into the present. It's a side effect I find much more unpleasant than stiff muscles.

My father's face—his thick, manicured, rust-colored beard, which always smelled of the acrid tonic he used and always made my eyes water; his murky blue stare, which would land on me with an almost physical thud when he was angry; and his ladder of wrinkles, which grew as deep as caverns at times, cascading from his hairline to his brows—loomed out from the well I'd sunk it in as I'd emerged from the first pill-induced fog. I hadn't thought of him in years, since before I'd even graduated from the Academy and been sent to my first duty station on Obal 8. He'd come to David's ceremony but skipped mine two years later. I hadn't been disappointed. We hadn't spoken since I'd joined.

As I cross my legs and press the back of my head and shoulders against the cargo box to try and sit up some, that phantom smell of beard tonic hits my nostrils out of nowhere, jolting me. The memory trailing along behind it is so vivid, it seems like it is happening again. I'd been eight years old and had just been picked up by my father from a neighbor's house. I don't remember her name, but she'd been the single woman living a few blocks away, just leaving for work, and had found me crying on the street after wrecking my magbike. Harald—the only name I ever used for my father—had been forced to turn around from his own work commute and come get me.

In our kitchen, he'd bent down and put his big, heavy hands on my shoulders and shaken me once, twice, three times, hard enough to make my head snap on my neck—despite the fact that I'd been cradling my broken arm since I'd fallen, gamely holding in the tears that I hadn't been afraid to shed until he came home.

"I told you to take the city trans to your summer classes, and what did you do?" Shake one. "You go chasing after David, trying to follow him to Preflight Club. Again!" Shake two. His muddy eyes stared into mine. "When are you going to learn how to at least act like a good daughter?" Shake three. And finally I'd begun to wail, each shake making the greenstick-fractured bones crunch in exquisite, sparking pain.

"What?!" he'd yelled. "Now you're crying because you know what a useless little girl you are?" He'd shoved me into a chair. "Jesus Christ. You'll never know how badly I wish your mother had taken you with her when she split." He leaned down again, and I could smell the beard tonic even through my sniffling nose, almost strong enough to gag me. "If you're ever going to be any good to anyone, you're just going to have to get tougher. You stay home by yourself today until I get back from work. Then I'll have time to take you to get that arm looked at. Unless you're just faking it." He'd risen, put his jacket back on, and warned me as he walked out the door, "Stay out of trouble, or that arm is going to feel like a love tap if I have to knock off work early."

It had been David, home within a few hours after his Academy-sponsored Preflight Club, that had called a friend's mother to take me to the neighborhood medical clinic. Of course, I hadn't said my father had left me home with a broken arm; I'd made up a story about skipping summer school and breaking it while riding my magbike. In reality, I'd just been grateful David got me sorted out so I didn't have to spend any more time in Harald's presence than necessary.

Memories like this one push me fighting and clawing back to

consciousness. I don't want to think of my childhood. That's long over and long forgotten. Or I thought it had been. I'd risked a lot, taken more chances than a reasonable person should, to get as far away from it as I could. Now, sitting in the dark and still smelling the smoke in my clothes and hair from the brief firefight in the landing field, I'm beginning to wonder if my recklessness hadn't just been about escaping, but had also been a lack of a reason to live. Survival instinct, yeah, I definitely have that. How many times have I shot someone faster than they could shoot me just so they'd fall and I'd still be standing? But what was that for? What had I had to live for that made my trigger finger faster and my aim straighter than all those others?

The answer to that question was never more clear to me than after I'd met Karl and the rest of the Beachers, my new crew. I've always had David to look out for and to look out for me, but back in the Corps and when we worked for Rajcik, he was it, the only thing that mattered. Now I have family—something I've never had before—people and a life and home of my own on KL, even if it is a spider-infested jungle with a downed fleet cruiser for its hub.

And there's more. That instinct to survive hasn't gone anywhere, but it has changed. The addendum "at all costs" that used to apply is gone, just like my fears of being betrayed or hurt—the only "gifts" my father ever gave me. I still *want* to survive, of course, but when I look inside myself—and where else have I had to look in these last few hours?—I realize that I'll do whatever I have to now to protect those who matter to me. My crew. My family. Even if it means I'm stuck on this ship and going down with it. I'll do it. I'll do it for them.

Fully awake for the first time in hours, I notice the way the stale air inside my storage box suddenly assaults my nose much more strongly than before. The pills are wearing off, and my heart does an uncomfortable somersault-y *bap-bap* in my chest. Involuntarily, I rattle my hand, which is closed in a protective cocoon around the last four tranqs. The tiny *tick* sound they make is only minimally reassuring. Almost before I think about it, I pop two in my mouth—then I spit them back out into my open fist, still dry, thanks to sedative- and fear-induced cotton mouth. It's almost time. I have to get my head straight, can't be wandering around out there with only half my faculties activated. I have no alternative than to try and deal with the claustrophobic panic currently trying to rip open my chest wall like a glass-clawed parasite.

A quick glance at the counter on my VDU tells me the length of my captivity: eleven hours, two minutes now. I'd felt us dock with the *Celestial* about forty-five minutes ago. Even in my haze, I think I would have known if the *Kongjù* had pursued the *Nebula*, but the flight had been smooth. A ship this size can't make the type of aggressive, split-angle course changes that Venus and the nimbler *Nebula* could have, so maybe they'd seen no reason to give chase. If they had, and Venus was forced to switch to an evasive flight pattern, she'd have used up so much power at once that she'd have had to scale back on output for several hours after the initial evasive burst. Then Medina would merely have had to stay on course and once again close the gap while they were vulnerable. But there's been no change in the regular hum of the ship's engines until the *Kongjù* docked and shut down, so I believe—pray, more like—that the plan is progressing as hoped. Maybe miracles are real.

I guess I'll find out when it's time to take the bridge.

CLAMMY SWEAT OOZES from my forehead and the palms of my hands, and I can almost feel the air pressure increase as the walls and floor of my box collapse in on me too slowly for the eyes to see. Whether it's time or not, I'm putting the next mission phase into action— before I go batshit psycho.

I've spent the last hour stretching and tightening all my muscles, limbering and waking them up in preparation for moving through the ship. I'm done waiting for Quantum. Rolling to my side, I turn on the VDU glowscreen for some light, put my hand on the latch, suck in a slow, deep breath, adjust my '80 for fast deployment, and press the inner release.

It doesn't move.

Okay, a little stuck, so I push a fraction harder, imagining the relief I'm going to feel when it depresses. But there's no give. Was it . . . is it possible . . . it's been locked? Why would Zabriskie lock it?

I freeze, trying to get a grip on the situation before torrents of adrenaline block my ability to think clearly. A drop of sweat slides down my temple and along my ear and plops onto the floor of the crate, looking through my hyperfocused vision like a bottomless pool; then another falls, and a jolt of electricitylike pinpricks dance up my spine and flush across my back, forcing an involuntary shiver to rip through me. When my hand slides through the cold pool of sweat in front of me, the dike gives out.

I slam my palm against the latch as hard as I can, not feeling the shock run up my arm, then flip my carbine around and hit the latch with the stock—again and again, not hearing the clang, not feeling the vibration, not caring that my breath is coming in loud, raging gasps that surely must be audible, even over the polymer-on-metal noise of the weapon and lid. Suddenly, I'm six again and my father has locked me in the trunk at the foot of my bed as punishment for running off to look for my mother. Terror so extreme and so clear it could almost be mistaken for rhapsody explodes from the center of my body, turning every sense and every perception into a singular desire for escape.

Heaving over onto my back, I bend my knees into my ribs and wedge my feet and hands against the cover, preparing to press as hard as humanly possible against it until either it breaks away or my hips and arms splinter into a million shards. Just as my shoulders begin to scream in protest—it opens! My father's face appears in the space over the rectangle of light above me, and my first instinct is to let a kick fly, then I realize—

"Quah-Quantum?" He barely has time to get out of my way before I propel through the opening and thud to the floor, wheezing in great, rasping breaths.

"Erikson. Would you mind doing us both the favor of calming the fuck down? Someone is going to hear you."

Though his words pierce through my straitjacket of panic easily, my brain takes a minute to catch up to the fact that it's really him, Quantum is standing in front of me—not my father.

Even as I realize it, the only thing I can think to say is: "What the hell took you so long? I nearly started this show without you."

He looks up and down the storage bay as he responds in a hushed voice, "You aren't smart enough to do this on your own. Now come on."

Still too shaken up to be pissed off at his statement, I lean heavily against the wall beside the storage box for a second, trying to regain some calm. Avoiding a last look inside its hateful interior, I reach in and feel around until I clasp the butt of my '80 and withdraw it. With a glance around, I take in row upon row of the soil amendment compound drums, all lined up inside the storage bay like sleeping soldiers of the plague, awaiting orders to inflict mass destruction on innocents. Reaching into my jacket, I run a finger along the tiny detonating unit La Mer had passed me. A click of its button would unleash hell.

Not waiting, Quantum steps outside the exit hatch, then turns and motions for me to follow him. *I'm okay,* I tell myself and tighten my grip on my carbine with slightly trembling hands. But after I take a single step forward, the hatch suddenly slides closed—me on my side and Quantum on the other.

Van Heusen steps into view from behind a row of drums, nonchalantly pocketing the remote hatch controller he carries. "I knew that bastard was up to something, but I'll deal with him later."

The nasal growl of his voice, compliments of the broken nose from Karl, makes my teeth want to grind. My carbine is already aimed center mass, but, insanely, he's stepping toward me.

"Go ahead, Erikson. Take a shot." He sees my indecision and laughs. "That's right. You know this ship, don't you?"

I can't shoot. He knows it. The discharge of a weapon aboard will trigger the ship's alarms, and this mission will be over before it starts.

"Stay the fuck away from me, Van Heusen."

"But that's not what I have in mind at all. I've been waiting to get some time with you for a while. Scav or not, you still look tasty to me."

His words barely register as I assess my options. Between his greater size and his body armor, a hand-to-hand encounter has a low chance of ending well for me. I can't blow what he has for brains out, and there's nowhere to run but deeper into the storage bay, but then where? Fleetingly, I think about the detonator in my pocket. No, not that. Not yet.

He takes another step forward, and I add a little more bend to my knees, the carbine not wavering. Surprise ripples across his face. He pulls a knife from his equipment vest. The overhead lights flash dazzlingly along its tang. I flick my eyes over his shoulder toward the hatch, hoping to see it opening.

"He can't get in," Van Heusen says, reading my glance. "It's just the two of us."

"Do you know what this stuff is, Van Heusen? What it will do?"

He takes a half step forward, but I remain firm. Backing down isn't going to gain me anything.

"Do I look like someone who cares if a bunch of weak citizens get turned into fertilizer? That's all any of us are anyway. Worm food—"

He takes another step as he speaks, and I drop to a knee and roll into his legs, forcing him to career to the side. He reaches out and belays his fall with a hand against one of the compound drums, then spins around. I've already scrabbled to the hatch control panel and jam the "Open" command.

Not happening.

He comes at me fast but light, a boxer's approach. But we've had the same training, all Academy soldiers did. I dance away from a jab from his left to my ribs, and block the knife coming toward my chest with the carbine. The thud of his wrist against the stock tells me the nerves there will be sizzling, and I let his next left make contact against my cheekbone as I drive the carbine barrel into his right armpit and knock the knife in his weakened grip free. It flies toward the cargo crate and hits the side with a dull echo, but my senses are busy trying to come to terms with the buzzing pain in my cheek and temple.

With his right arm temporarily numb, he uses his body to smash into me, forcing me up against the hatch. I can't move enough to strike or leverage my carbine, but there's nothing between my teeth and his face.

He screams as I bite into the skin below his eye and tries to pull away. As he does, I grab him around the shoulders, letting my carbine fall to the side and hang by its strap, and wrap my legs around his waist. He wanted a close-up-and-personal, that's what he's going to get. Stumbling backward with me attached to him like a rabid dog, he loses his balance and goes down on his ass. My weight coming down on top of him pushes him flat and compresses the breath out of his lungs in a high-speed purge, and I release my bite, rear back, and smash my forehead into his injured nose. This time, blood pours from it like a fountain instead of a trickle, and he grips his face with both hands, unable now to even scream, rocking his body from side to side in blunt, brutalizing anguish.

I walk to the knife and pick it up almost leisurely, then move back to him. His eyes, which had been squeezed shut, now open a sliver— in time for him to see the kick I launch into his midsection below the base of his torso armor.

He grunts, and I rear back for another one. "What's that?" Kick to the gut. "Did you say you're enjoying the time we're spending together?" Kick to the wedding tackle. "Well, good. So am I." Kick to the head. This one lays him out cold.

"You done, Aly?" Quantum's voice pulls me out of the moment, and I spin around to face him. The hatch is open again; no doubt he'd found some way to bypass it. After assessing me for a brief moment, he says, "Let's put him in the cargo box."

Van Heusen won't be awake for a while, if ever, and he definitely won't get out of there on his own. The metallic-electric taste of adrenaline coating my throat and tongue is unpleasant, but the surge of it in my bloodstream wiped out the last of my jitters from being stuck in the container. Task complete, Quantum and I speed out of the storage bay and down a corridor toward a bulkhead about ten meters distant. Quantum keeps his eyes forward, and I watch our rear, thankful the remaining area is empty. When we reach the hatch, instead of opening it, he climbs (surprisingly nimbly) up the adjacent wall using the housing of an electrical console and pushes a 1 x 1 ceiling panel aside, then pulls himself up. His hand drops through and waves at me to follow.

"No. No way," I mumble, my throat already tightening the way I imagine the walls will if I get in there.

His head drops through the hole, a sneer plastered across his mouth. "Get your ass up here. Or would you prefer to see all your friends smeared from one end of KL to the other?" His voice is gravelly and uncompromising. "You know I've never liked you, Erikson, but we have a job to do."

The comment almost makes me laugh. Since he and his companions had kidnapped me on the streets of Tunis City almost two years ago, I've never exactly teemed with affection for him either. The scar on my left hand from his oh-so-unsubtle way of driving his intentions home while interrogating me looks almost like an arrow pointing to my middle finger. Thinking of it, I stifle the urge to put that finger on display in a similarly unsubtle message. Instead, I say, "The feeling is mutual. But I'd say we're in a situation where what we think of each other"—or how strong our urge may be to strangle the shit out of each other—"is irrelevant."

He nods, as if I'd simply capitulated, says, "Then shut up and quit stalling," and retreats back into the vent.

"Wait!"

"I don't have time for th—"

"No, hold on. Do you know anything about my crew? Did they make it away from Obal 6?"

It seems like an hour ticks by before he answers in a voice that betrays absolutely nothing, like the voice of an android, "Yeah. They made it."

I could press him for an answer, make him say something that will assure me of the truth, one way or the other, but a different part of me—the part that might simply give up if they hadn't—isn't really ready to know. Convincing myself that Quantum's strangely toneless response was merely because he doesn't actually care if my crew is dead or alive is easy enough; he has no stakes in their survival. But the other problem isn't so easy to resolve—how am I going to do this? Crawl from one tiny space into another? It's like being liberated from hell just to be flung into an incinerator. *Figure this out, Aly. Too many people are counting on you for you to indulge in phobias. Put yourself in someone else's shoes. How would Karl make this happen?*

Thinking of Karl helps. I imagine his eyes, the way his smile reaches them when I run my fingers through the hair on his chest, and the trick starts to work—helped along by whatever tranq residue still swims in my bloodstream. *It just has to last a little longer,* I tell myself. Keeping a mental picture of Karl's face in front of me, I push the carbine around to hang on my back and grasp the electrical console. *Like getting on an elevator. No big deal.* My knees and the joints in my shoulders protest as I try to copy Quantum's monkey impression, even with my hefty dose of adrenaline. I knew I'd be a little stiff, but if this doesn't fade quickly, I'll be an easy target once the real ship takeover begins. As I reach over the opening's lip to pull myself up, my grip starts to slip on the slightly oily surface. Just before I fall, Quantum grabs the straps on my vest and hauls me over the edge with a grunt. I lie still on my stomach for a moment, listening— almost hoping—for the tromp of boots below us.

"How you like me now?" I rasp.

"Less and less."

"Fuck you, Quantum." The anger helps, and I take a second to wonder if he's provoking me on purpose. The man has never shown much skill in the social interaction department, but right now I don't care. I need to get through this. I *could* get through this.

It could happen.

He rummages through his jacket, then passes me a new VDU. "I've reconfigured it to block tracking signals and piggyback onboard frequencies so we can communicate without being 'seen.' Wear it so I can reach you."

He turns and begins crawling down the vent shaft.

"Wait. Where are we going?"

He doesn't stop. "You'll see."

We push through the ventilation system for twenty minutes, enough time for me to vacillate between panic and control half a dozen times. Every time it starts to get bad, I randomly berate Quantum for leading us on a wild goose chase, for getting us lost, for being too slow—anything I can think of to get him to respond with equal rancor in that grating hiss he has and yank my mind out of its spiraling descent.

He stops crawling all of a sudden. My focus elsewhere, my hand comes down on one of his ankles and twists it roughly.

"Pay attention!" he barks as I shift backward.

"Sorry."

Looking at his VDU, he ignores the insincere apology, then grabs the edge of another panel and pulls it aside. Without a word, he lowers himself. The sound of his boots hitting a metal floor doesn't echo. Wherever we are, the space is small. Fantastic. But it has to be better than this vent shaft.

Once I drop inside, he informs me it's an anteroom to the bridge's main electronics pipeline. The space is tall enough to stand in, with enough room for two people to sit side by side if their arms are touching—except Quantum has filled half the floor space with electronic panels and two portable control terminals. He's brought in an ammo crate from somewhere and uses it as a bench, leaving only enough room for me to stand behind him.

It's clear he's been busy. In the year-plus I'd been a crewmember on the *Celestial* I hadn't even known this was here. "Let me see if I have this right." Though the space is dark, the consoles' screens illuminate enough of the area to give me my bearings. It feels a little like being in the cockpit of a one-person scout between stops on a planet-to-planet hop. "You started setting up . . . whatever it is you've set up, long before shit went down with Bogotan."

"Right." The impatience and sarcasm sizzle on his tongue like nuclear bacon. "I already told you, I always have a plan. Now do you want to play some more catch-up, or are you ready to hear what comes next?"

"There's something I want to know first." A sound in my tone catches his full attention, and he turns, laying reptilian eyes on me. "So why do you?"

"Why do I what?"

"Trust me."

He snorts. "I *don't* trust you, Aly. I don't need to. Because you're predictable. That's why I wanted you on board with me."

A rare moment of thoughtfulness settles over me, and I comment quietly, no challenge or anger in my voice, "Quantum, you gotta know, when this is all over, we can't just let you go. You're going to have to answer for some of the things you've done or let happen."

His pale brown eyes glitter, but no words pass through his thin lips. He's going to play this till the end. Hell, he probably already has a plan for how to escape not just the *Celestial* but the rest of us, too.

So: "What do you have in mind?" I finally ask.

He returns his focus to the consoles, commenting dryly, "Those who cannot use oxygen responsibly will have it taken away."

TWENTY-SEVEN

The plan is impossibly simple. Full frontal assault, take no prisoners. After studying the armory through onboard surveillance cameras, linked into by Quantum, and identifying the security personnel guarding it, I loaded directions on my VDU (this time I insist on making the trek by using stealth and going through regular corridors, not the ventilation system), and now stand before the vault to the one weapon that can actually give us a chance at stopping Medina and saving KL.

The trick will be getting to the bridge, where the most rigorous onboard security is concentrated. But that's where Quantum's wire-rat genius will save the day. With partial to full control over most of the ship's systems, he's managed to route their nerve-agent tank lines—a Corps favorite for maintaining crowd control during a riot—to their main life support air lines. Exchanging the agent for their air, he'll knock out everyone in the main hull of the ship and buy me a surprise-free trip to the bridge, which, with its own separate and unlinked ventilation system, will still contain awake crew. The good news: I'm only going to have to kill the eight to ten people on the bridge. The bad news: I have to make sure I don't damage too many of the ship's controls if we're going to salvage it. KL will never have to worry about defense again if the *Celestial* belongs to us. And once I suppress any resistance from the flight operations crew, between my nav skills and Quantum's piloting and programming skills, the two of us will be able to control the *Celestial* for as long as it takes for the *Nebula* and more settlers from KL to get here and back us up. With their help, we can revive the *Celestial*'s remaining personnel but keep them firmly controlled until we decide the best course of action for dealing with them. No one wants unnecessary bloodshed. If we've learned anything, it's that we have to live by justice, not revenge, not power, not rule. Another war like the last will be the end of us.

Jesus, I'm starting to sound like Whitmore.

As the access door to the weapons vault tries to slide closed, it catches and hangs on the left boot of the crewman I'd assaulted to get inside, now lying unconscious on the ground. He'll have a hell of a headache, but he'll live.

"Dammit, Quantum, this sonofabitch is heavy. Give me a second to get him inside before you close the door," I whisper through my throat mic.

The hatch slides open again, and I give the guard a solid heave. His body clears the door, leaving only a small smear of blood from his split scalp outside. I need a few minutes to suit up. Hopefully no one wanders by and notices it.

And there they are. Fourteen bugsuits hanging in their ready harnesses. But one is all I need to wipe out the crew on the bridge. I haven't worn one in months, but these machines are basically self-operated. It's just a matter of ensuring their plasma catalyzer tanks are topped off. Usually a remote operator runs the bugsuit installation program for outfitting soldiers, but they can be donned solo if one is limber and determined enough.

The interior of the bay is laid out in a minigrid along the fleet ship's bottom level. A cruiser sports twenty to twenty-six bays, ranging in size from a typical shopping-center warehouse to the gargantuan hangar where surface fighting crafts are stored. Each separate bugsuit vault has on hand the quota intended to outfit one attack ship for a quick-assault op, and the contents of a single bay of this size are usually all that are needed to get the job done.

There's no better single-combat weapon for a lone fighter with plans to take on a small army. As long as those plans include potential suicide and a high probability of personal injury.

The suit is made of a lightweight composite breastplate, backplate, and reticulating arm covers with flexible-fiber full sleeves. The fine mechanism and wire system that controls the user's motions nests between a solid outer plate cover made of the same composite construction material, and an inner graphene mesh that covers the user's skin. Individually, the arm units weigh about as much as a carbine—no big deal.

The weapon's weight factor comes from the energy pack in the backplate. The generator, battery, and materials for creating plasma projectiles add about fifteen kilos, and the helmet another eight. It's not that much to carry, but it's a shit-ton when speed and agility are necessary. The designers, of course, knew this, and given the rarity of foot soldiering on the modern battlefield, there's no longer much need to manufacture small arms that prolong firefights. The bugsuit isn't made for drawn-out contact and leapfrog advances. The bugsuit is made to wipe out every living being within a ten-klick radius in the shortest amount of time possible. A suit operator can potentially stand still in a moderately protected location and plant plasma projectiles into walls of opposing forces in no more time than it takes to drink a canteen of water. And the accuracy of each shot is flawless. The suit's full-auto feature takes the guesswork of a human's brain out of targeting and leaves it all up to the helmet's optical processor— which is where it gets the name "bugsuit." Using a system of bug-eye lenses and autonomous computing, the suit identifies objectives and sends signals to the user's central nervous system through sensors and stimulators in the graphene-mesh sleeves and helmet connection points. The lenses have the ability to focus on things panoramically and at different depths simultaneously, much like a fly's compound eye. This allows it to calculate risk and choose optimal targets and evasive maneuvers for the user and then stimulate the body to bring the arm-mounted weapons into position or get out of the way of potential incomings, effectively turning the user into an autonomously controlled extension of the suit.

The firing armatures are wrist mounted, and most of the heat dissipation happens before the projectiles leave the barrels. Yeah, your back gets a bit sweaty, but most of that is from the compact battery and generator inside the backplate housing nestled between your shoulder blades. As plasma projectiles are basically soundless, users' ears aren't damaged from the firing tubes' explosive power, though the helmet includes nerve-sensing soundbuds to gauge the user's inner ear function as a backup balance sensor. All the user's physiological data, from their lifemarkers to the suit's nerve sensors, are fed into the helmet's processors to help feed the weapon's analytics and maximize shots-to-kills ratio.

Bugsuits' manual operations come from either voice-code-recognized verbal commands or the fire control button screens inside protective covers that are mounted along the radial surface of each wrist. By selecting "manual," "semi-auto," or "full-auto" verbally or manually using the control buttons, users can decide the firing directives for either barrel separately. Of course, given the nature of having a suit that can control your arms and targeting, the only way to have it work at full effect is to set it to and leave it on full-auto.

The suits hang from their cradles along a ten-meter stretch of one wall with the helmets mounted above them. Fourteen suits at full charge are estimated to be all that's necessary to fully neutralize a complement of up to a couple hundred conventionally armed units, i.e., soldiers. Plasma projectiles don't have much trouble knocking over fully armored troops and burning them up from the outside in.

Checking the first suit in the row is a bingo. Fully loaded and ready for wear. I step onto the half-meter-high platform beneath it and operate the controls to lower it over my head. Flexing and bending in uncomfortable ways, I finally get the body sections on. The helmet is attached via hinges to the back piece, and I adjust it to get the fit just right—wincing as it bumps against my bruised cheekbone—latch all connections, and engage the calibrating system.

When it gives me the cue, I say, "Manual. Semi-auto. Full-auto. Engage."

A mild *ping* sounds in my helmet to alert me the voice system is online. For forty seconds, more *ping*s of different tones cycle through my ears, then a hollow, robotic voice says, "All systems online and ready for deployment."

Go time.

My VDU reads one minute till Quantum puts the nerve-agent part of the plan into effect. I retrieve a facemask from my cargo pocket and fit it beneath the helmet, then wait for his signal. Pushing the bugsuit mounting controls aside, I begin taking calm, deep breath after calm, deep breath. Karl's and David's faces appear in my thoughts. If they and the crew made it out of Obal 6's airspace and the potential gauntlet of attack ships Medina may have deployed, they would be within range to transmit to KL's satellite from the *Nebula* by now and warn the settlers to prepare—either for self-defense or possibly for evacuation. If I see any of them again, it could be on another world. But it doesn't matter. As long as we put a stop to Medina's madness. For good.

A slow-building, low-pitched warning alert begins chiming through the ship. Someone must have triggered it when their mates began taking unexpected midday naps. I'm anticipating one or two lucky soldiers to have reached a mask before their lights went out. But when they see me, it's their luck that's going to run out. Despite the sparseness of the bugsuit hardware, these beauties do have a way of making a woman feel invincible.

TWENTY-EIGHT

On Quantum's mark, I triple-time like a whirling dervish on speed through the hull, not taking a breather until I reach the main hatchway to the bridge. I pass only a handful of lights-out senseless personnel in the corridors, not a single person lucid enough to engage me. It gives me a second to reflect on how flawlessly every plan Quantum has been part of has gone down. In a perfect world, he should've been an ally. But here, even with a temporarily shared goal, I suspect it's every man and woman for him- and herself. Shaking off this unsettling thought, I contact him.

"At the bridge. Ready to go. Out."

The flight control cadre must know that things in the main part of the ship are not right, but I cross my fingers that no one had time to inform them exactly what was happening. The next phase is up to Quantum. He'll launch a ghost brigade to make the bridge scramble to ready the *Celestial*'s exterior defenses. Of course, it'll just be interference on the ship's radars and intercept systems, but the crew won't know that right away. The surprise will distract them enough for me to make my dramatic entrance. I should be able to achieve 90 percent casualties before they even know I'm inside.

"You have between five and ten minutes, Aly," Quantum says through my helmet's receiver.

"Hold it. You told me you were keeping the crew gassed until we get backup from KL."

"And if the nerve-suppressant tanks had been full, I would've."

I have a second to wonder if this is Quantum's way of fucking with me, but immediately dismiss the idea. No human I've ever met has less of a sense of humor than him.

"Better hurry," he continues. "Remember, I'm opening the hatch thirty seconds after my mark. Ghost brigade in three . . . two . . . one . . . mark."

So Quantum's plans *aren't* always flawless. This is not the moment I needed to have that reality check. "Full-auto," I tell the suit.

The hatch opens soundlessly, as well maintained as everything under Medina's command has always been. The first crewman to see me looks shocked, not understanding how the bridge could be isolated and operating normally one second and overrun by a bugsuited soldier the next. His shock lasts less than a heartbeat.

The sound of plasma guns isn't loud, but it is unmistakable. Almost immediately after the first man goes down, three more fall, then the rest begin diving under anything that might give them cover. A couple have the instincts to reach for their weapons, but the bugsuit's targeting-and-triage system takes them out first.

To their advantage, the bridge is two levels high, and those on the lower deck, generally the flight navigator and two to three operations personnel, are protected—with the exception of the two who rush my attack to try and stop me. And fail. I dart inside and take a position behind a waist-high observatory counter that flanks the commander's bench on the left. Medina. Where is Medina? She should have been right here. Behind me, the hatch closes, locking in the bridge's air supply and locking out the quickly normalizing gassed air from outside. This tells me that Quantum hadn't been exaggerating; time is short.

Unless he's still working with Medina. But no, if that were the case, he's had a hundred chances to kill me since releasing me from the cargo locker, and there's no way Medina would sacrifice the bridge to an assault. *Then maybe he's trying to let the bridge crew finish the job after you do most of the wet work.*

This thought takes my mind immediately off the task at hand. What exactly is Quantum's motive in all this? He wants Medina dead, of course. Her intent to essentially enslave the rest of the settlers to help her build her private world had definitely sent him to the other side, which happens to be our side; but in the end, Quantum has consistently shown who he ultimately sides with: himself. A team player, he is not. And the idea of the greater good doesn't get past his survival filter. Not like Whitmore and Zabriskie. Or even Vitruzzi.

Cool it, Aly. He can't fly this beast without you. He needs you.

We'll see about that. But first, I have to get control of this situation. The dead pilot who'd been at the bench isn't Medina, and neither are the other crewmembers who'd gone down. If she's not on the bridge, she must be in the hull, and she'll be awake soon. I have to get the bridge wrapped up immediately and then regroup with Quantum so we can come up with another plan for dealing with the rest of the *Celestial*'s crew.

Raising my head just enough for the optics on the bugsuit helmet to clear the top of the observatory counter, I let the suit assess the bridge. The eyepiece gives me enough information to tell that no one still breathing is dumb enough to show themselves. They all know what their odds are. A console next to the pilot's bench suddenly sputters, shooting sparks from an electrical fire. The sharp smell hits my nose, and blue-tinged smoke begins to lift toward the ceiling's vents. Less than a second later, an internal foam deploys, ending the fire. Using the sound to cover me, I dash forward toward the upper-deck railing, a solid enough barrier to protect me, and prepare to blitz the stairs to the lower level.

ZING! A bullet strikes the back of my helmet—just a glancing hit —and nearly knocks me off my feet. Using forward momentum, I careen toward the railing and spin around—thanks to the suit's prerogative—putting it to my back so I'm facing the direction the shot came from. The suit's already controlling my arms and has the target in sight, a crewmember near the blown console. She goes down, and, unable to recover my balance, so do I, right on my ass. Breathing hard, I scoot backward until I'm pressed against the railing's half wall and out of anyone on the lower deck's line of fire. That was too fucking close for comfort. The bugsuit is better in wide-open spaces. I'd forgotten about that.

That's seven down, which leaves from one to three to go, unless they had some bigger meeting going on. My monocular system display informs me the helmet's rear optics have taken damage; too much, they're out. Now the suit can only give me about a 240-degree field of visibility. In other words, no one has my back.

I switch over to semi-auto, leaving the bugsuit in control of only my left arm, roll over to my stomach, and get my knees under me in a crouch. With the ample cover afforded to the remaining crew below, and my now limited visual advantage, I'm less keen to drop down the stairs and start a death disco. The nav bench is down there, too, and if that becomes collateral damage, the ship won't be as easy for Quantum and me to manage. There's a backup nav bench, but it's in the ship's belly, which is off-limits until we take the rest of the crew out of commission.

Quantum again: "Aly, what's your status?"

"Typical," I respond in a half whisper. Then, more loudly: "Sixty percent down. The rest are hiding."

"You have maybe three or four minutes before the crew starts to wake up."

"Thanks, that's so helpful. Why don't you come lend me a hand?"

No response. Also typical.

I glance to my side down the stairwell and immediately take fire. They miss. They aren't dumb; they know I can't get to them unless I come down, and I can't come down by any other means than the stairs.

Fucking standoff; god I hate these. My eyes wander to the doused and steaming nearby console. Unless . . .

"Quantum, come in."

"Here."

"Can you reverse the ventilation in here? Send the used air back?"

"Wait one."

"If you can, shunt it all into the lower deck. Smoke them out."

"Wait one," he says again irritably.

No problem. Take all the time you need.

"Done. But you need to create more smoke if you're going to affect them."

That I can handle. "Roger. Just shut off the self-activating fire retardants."

Reaching back inside my cargo pants pocket, I remove the gas mask I'd stuffed in them before entering the bridge and put it back on. From the cover of the railing, I open up on the overhead lights, the nonessential electronics hardware, and anything else that looks like it might pop, sizzle, or melt. At first, all the gray-blue smoke starts leaving through the outflow vents, but then it stops. A few seconds later, a wall of it flumes up from the stairwell next to me, quickly leaving the deck in darkness. I shove away from the railing back toward the observation counter, hoping to get a better view of the stairs and anyone who comes up them. The only way out is through the main hatch, and if they don't want to choke to death, that's where they're going to have to go.

I hear running footsteps beside me. *What the—? How did—?* Before the thought is complete, the observatory counter starts taking direct fire. Pushing off the floor, I roll-stumble to the relative cover of the commander's bench. The floor is a hockey rink of warm blood, and I end up on my stomach when the hand I place down to brace me slides out from under me. Not important. My ears strain for the sound of whoever is still running around in here with me.

A metallic clink off to my left, maybe ten meters. I pop up from the bench—taking a moment of satisfaction from the fact that I know he can't see me any better than I can see him—and let the bugsuit find my target. Its burst of fire is displeasingly short. My stalker didn't stay visible for long. He's good at this game.

"You know no one can access the bridge to help you, right?" I yell. "They're all getting their beauty sleep. If you're smart, you'll drop your weapon and join them. You can still live through this." I count ten seconds while waiting for a response, but none comes. "I don't want to have to kill you. It's your choice." I give it one last shot. Some people have a well-developed sense of reason, after all.

But not this guy. I sense something dropping down over me before I feel the impact against my left arm, which reflexively goes up to block whatever's coming. It strikes my arm—*What is that? A fucking console? It weighs at least twenty kilos!*—and a sickening crunch vibrates up my wrist, to my elbow, and lodges in my shoulder like a cleaver of fire. I fall back with the console on top of me, pinning my, at minimum broken, arm against my body. I have to get the bugsuit off semi-auto. If it spots a target and tries to fire with my left arm, the pain sprinting its insidious journey through my nervous system right now is going to feel like a candy-wrapped peck on the cheek.

"Manual!" My voice cracks, and what would have been a scream comes out a windless shriek. But the tech is flawless, and my visual display unit tells me I've been switched to manual.

New problem. Commander Medina stands above me, the black bore of her sidearm demanding my attention.

"Don't move," she says through her own gas mask and steps with her entire weight on my still-functioning arm. A girdle of pain cinches down, simultaneously shooting from the arm pinned across my chest and the arm she stands on, meeting somewhere in the middle of my sternum and constricting my already burdened rib cage.

Her face and scalp are bleeding heavily from at least three places, turning the navy blue of her uniform a sticky black. She must have caught a spray of broken glass or poly-composite. In a way, it's a relief to see Medina, even if she's the one who kills me. Not everyone who had remained under her command when we'd broken off to settle KL had been bad people. I'd hate to be killed by someone I'd once liked and considered a compatriot.

"I know you're not here alone, Erikson. Where is the rest of your team hiding?"

"If I told you that, you'd kill me." I have to force the words through the heavy weight compressing my chest.

She grinds down with the sole of her boot, making me cry out. "Where?"

Tears of pain and anger spring to my eyes. "Probably enjoying a nice, hot bubble bath."

"*Where?*" This time she puts her free hand flat on the console and presses down. I try to lock my chest against the pressure, not wanting to lose precious air, but the agony of my arm forces me to make a noise that sounds to my ears like the grunt of a dog being hit by a speeding land trans.

She lets up the pressure, and tears start flowing down the sides of my head. I squeeze my eyes shut as battering rams of nausea choke me, and my skin flushes first blisteringly hot, then icily frigid.

"Last chance," she says. My eyes open to the darkness of her pistol's barrel.

"They're ..."

She leans forward at the waist just a hair.

"Right behind you," I finish.

She whirls and fires, facing Quantum, who fires back at the same time. The woman crumples backward, landing beside me, gasping and gurgling through a mouthful of blood. Her head falls to the side and her eyes come to rest on my face, then go blank.

There's a noise like a laundry bag being tossed into a pile. The room is beginning to clear; Quantum must have reengaged the outflow vents before dropping in. Craning my head up, I first see a ceiling panel halfway across the deck that's been removed—Quantum's ingress point—then see him lying on his side at my feet, grasping his midsection.

"No, no, no," I mutter. Bracing my free hand against the side of the heavy console, I give myself just a moment to pre-regret what I'm about to do, then shove the unit off. A nova of pain freight trains through me, and I go black.

But I'm back in seconds, according to my helmet-mounted VDU. Remaining still for a moment, panting and taking bets against myself whether I or the pain-soaked nausea is going to win, I try to get enough of a grip on myself to stand. Winning the fight for now, very, very slowly I sit up.

It takes more time than I'd like to recover from that maneuver. *Harden the fuck up, Aly. This isn't going to get any easier.* Every nerve fiber in my body tuned in, I try to detect other signs of life on the bridge but hear nothing. If there are any more crewmembers, either they're too scared to come out, or they've inhaled enough of the toxic air that they've blacked out. If I'm going to be able to defend myself, I need to get this bugsuit, now rendered useless thanks to my injuries, off. The weight isn't much, but it's enough to hold me back. Gingerly, I disconnect all of the helmet links and remove it, letting it drop beside me. My hand brushes against a bump on the back of my head, which makes me wince, and I feel blood matting my hair. Whatever had tagged the optics must have nicked me too, but the wound is mild. Nothing compared to my arm.

And it hits me—I'm not getting anything off, not with only one functioning hand. The left arm, definitely broken, is also dislocated, though only at the shoulder, not the elbow. That at least is something to be grateful for, but the satisfaction is short-lived. How am I going to fly this thing? The controls can't be handled without authorization, and Quantum—

Shit!

"Quantum, man, you okay?"

No, he's not. He's still on his side, leaking vital fluids at a rate that I wouldn't be able to stop, even with the help of a full medical team. Gutshot.

"Quantum?"

His eyes, sharp and clear and tortured, find mine. "This wasn't supposed ... to ... to ..."

"Wasn't part of your plan, huh?" I whisper, surprised to discover a hint of sorrow, or maybe just regret, in my reaction.

It occurs to me that if I hadn't told Medina Quantum was behind her, she might not have got off the shot that killed him. More likely, though, she'd have shot me point-blank when he had fired into her back instead of her chest. The thought quickly follows: I'm sure Quantum wouldn't have cared. Which in turn puts definitive limitations on my own survivor's guilt.

The problem is, in my condition I can't climb back into the ducting to look over his hacked systems controls and figure out a way to undermine the remaining crew or keep them from carrying out their original mission. Not on my own. When the crew wakes up, whoever's in charge will immediately start searching for the saboteur, and I doubt, after this havoc, they'll be in a negotiating mood. And Van Heusen is still out there. He's proven his appetite for carnage. Which leaves KL still vulnerable. Even if Quantum weren't down, there's no telling how much time I have left to turn the tide of our completely FUBARed plan, but I'm sure it's not enough. It's never enough.

There's only one thing I can do: I have to destroy the ship from here.

The thought provokes a wave of such intense exhaustion that I can't move for a few seconds. Because destroying the ship means I'm not going anywhere. I'm trapped.

My body feels denser, heavier than a neutron star, and I don't have the will to even think about other options. There just . . . aren't any. Is this what Vitruzzi feels? It suddenly seems so clear, so obvious —why keep fighting when there's nothing left to fight for? All I can do now is try to ensure Keum Libre at least has a chance. Leaning against the pilot's bench, feeling the warmth of the blood trickling from the back of my scalp against my neck, I close my eyes and take a minute to let my mind go blank, just let everything go.

A single thought comes to me, a memory of the way Karl's hair had smelled during those three months living at Agate Beach before Cross showed up and betrayed us all, before the Corps killed Bodie, before Rajcik dropped the bomb that pushed Quantum and Medina to start the war, before everything fell apart. We'd worked hard that summer, and his hair had always smelled of warm sand, sweat, and the soap he used, something both musky and sweet. That smell had lingered with me all day, like perfume, like the scent of pure happiness. I couldn't get enough of him. I'd let myself believe it would last forever.

I've never luxuriated in the illusion that anything, any part of ourselves, continues on after we die. If humans had an everlasting spirit or soul, why wouldn't we have come to some kind of enlightenment by now? Why do we continue making the same mistakes century after century? Because it's just one life. One brief, rushed life, and I know, now, that these will be my life's last minutes. The one thing I want to keep with me until my final moment is that memory. The smell of warm sand in Karl's hair. And what he means to me.

A chime pings on the array behind me, jolting my senses back to the present. Am I going into shock? No, got to get on top of this. There is still work to do. Intentionally and abruptly, I grab the pilot's chair and yank myself to my knees. The scream from my arm and shoulder seems to echo throughout the bridge, though it's only in my head. Sweat pops to the surface of my skin, from my scalp to the soles of my feet. Gritting my teeth, fully alert again, I pull myself onto the bench and scan the flat screens arranged in front of me. Vertical holocontrols will make this easier, and the first thing I do is activate them. The glowing blue, red, and green lines of the ship's control system menu rise before me. Without thinking, I select "Communication," wait for it to activate, then input the satlink codes to transmit to the *Nebula*. I want to know what happened to them. And . . . I want to say goodbye.

"*Nebula* crew, this is Erikson." Transmit. Wait. Repeat. "*Nebula* crew, this is Erikson. Do you read?"

Remembering to engage the video-link, I click it just as Karl's face comes into view in front of me.

"Aly!"

He can't see me yet, and for a moment I'm glad about that. I can't speak, the knowledge that this is the last time I'll ever look into his shining sepia eyes rendering me paralyzed and devastated. But I swallow, activate the feed, and reply, "Karl."

"You okay? You must be okay, right?"

"Yes. Right now it only hurts when I bleed." I don't mean to be funny, but how do you tell the man you love that you're going to be dead within the hour?

"Aly, what—?"

"Listen, Karl, it didn't work out here like we planned."

"Okay, but it doesn't matter. You're alive, that's what counts. Aly, I've been going crazy—"

I cut him off again, not liking myself for doing it, but time's getting short. Do you have to hurt the ones you love to save them? I don't like the answer, but I don't have a choice. "Listen, there isn't time. I have the bridge, but I'm trapped and Quantum's dead. It's just me now—the *Celestial's* crew are still in the picture—and I have to blow the ship. It's the only way."

"Okay, get to an escape shuttle and set your coordinates. We'll come back for you."

This time I don't cut in. I want to hear him out because his voice gives me a second of hope. I wish I could live the rest of my life in that second. My good hand goes to my neck, pulling the cord with Karl's ring free from my shirt. My fist clamps around the circle of metal, warm from my skin. "Babe, I-I don't think that's going to happen."

"It'll only take us about a day to get to you, maybe two. You can hold on that long, right? How badly are you injured?"

He isn't listening to me. For once I don't mind. If I don't do this now, I'm going to lose my nerve. Leaving Karl's feed open, I go to work on the pilot's console. It won't be enough to just blow the compound drums with La Mer's detonator. The *Celestial* is a lot bigger than the *Nebula*, where he'd built and tested it, so there's no guarantee it will even work. Even though I can't control flight systems without crew authorization, I can still access maintenance systems. I'm going to sabotage the ship, burn out the engines and force an overload that will start an irreversible series of internal malfunctions and melt this intergalactic death trap from the inside out. I have maybe five minutes until the crew starts to wake up, if that. No matter. This ship is doomed.

"Aly, do you hear me?" Karl's been talking to me while I concentrate on the ship's destruction, but I haven't responded. "We're already turning back. Just send me the coordinates you're at now."

His eyes are so sincere, so calm, but the dark fear—or is it fury?—lying behind them is another face of the Karl I know. The Karl that has seen battles and blood, wars and violence, and has fought through them all with the same stoic and indomitable resolve each time. The steel in him that will outlast any foe or enemy he confronts. It's that hard-burning, powerful rage that I'm counting on to get him through this next battle. I may not have told him enough, but he became my reason to go on, my reason to live and face every new tragedy and fight. He was my strength. Now he has to be that for himself.

"Karl, I can't make it to the escape shuttles. There isn't time. Tell David goodbye for me, okay? And keep the crew safe."

"I don't know what you're talking about. Are you saying you're too hurt? Can you get an IV in?"

He's going to keep denying what he's hearing until the ship turns into frozen space-borne carbon. I don't want his suffering to be the last thing I see, or mine his. "Karl." This time something in my voice catches him, makes him take a breath of silence. "Be strong. And remember that I love you."

I turn off the feed before he can respond.

Leaning back into the pilot's bench seat, I let my eyes fall closed, the thump of pain from my wounded arm settling into rhythm with my heartbeat and dulling enough for me to just sit here for a few last seconds and count them. With no other living people on the bridge, it is completely silent, even the constant ambient hum of the ship's engines and life support systems seeming to have faded away. Most of the bridge's lights were blown out, and behind my lowered eyelids I can almost imagine that I'm suspended in space, already free from the entrapments of my body and its suffering. In another moment I recognize what this feeling is, though I'm not sure I've ever really felt it before. Peace.

TWENTY-NINE

Noise like screws rattling in a plastic box jerks me out of my semiconsciousness as abruptly as if I'd been shot. Before my eyes focus, something hits me in the leg and bounces off. As I bolt upright the shrieking in my arm pitches to a new fervor, and then I see what happened. Quantum is awake, not dead like I thought, and staring at me with eyes lit feverishly bright. A medkit lies at my feet.

"Take it," he says, his voice no thicker than a spider's strand. "Morphone Z. It'll kill the"—he squints and sucks air through his teeth as if in sudden pain—"kill the pain. Get to the . . . to the . . ." Unable to finish the sentence, he waves toward the front of the bridge.

"What, Quantum? I'm not quite prepared to hurl myself through the viewscreens."

"There's a fucking e-pod under the nav bench." Somehow, even dying, his voice still manages to carry the *Why am I surrounded by such towering stupidity?* tone. "I already set the ship to blow from my link up."

It's as if a Glower missile just hit me in the forehead. "You mean you programmed it to self-destruct?" Then another thought smacks me. "How many escape pods are there?"

"One."

So he *was* going to let me do the dirty work, destroy the ship on his own, then take off using the escape pod and leave me here to die. Or maybe he never thought I'd make it in the first place. Which leads back to the fact that he'd set me up to take the fall while he got out in one piece. I've been right about him all along. But . . . but he didn't have to tell me about the pod. Should I be grateful, or just put him out of his misery for good? One look at him tells me that's going to happen within a few minutes anyway, no matter what I do.

"How long do I have?"

He mumbles something, but I can't hear it. The puddle he's lying in hasn't stopped growing, and the strong smell of blood swims in the air like aerosol. He knows he's already dead, that's clear.

My heart speeds up, and it takes me a minute to recognize why. I could still make it through this. There's a chance—a tiny, almost imperceptible one, but a chance—I could still make it out of this.

Decision made, I ease off the seat and try to crouch low enough to get to the medkit. If I bend over, the weight of my busted arm pulling against my dislocated shoulder could make me pass out. Grinding my molars together, I dangle my good hand and scoop up the kit, then straighten. I don't know if I have time to call the *Nebula* back and tell them what I'm doing, but Karl said they'd already started to double back. If I get out in the pod, they'll pick up my emergency beacon. They'll come back no matter what. I know they will.

I hope.

The world wavers in my vision for a second, the edges of it bleeding dry of color, then it comes back into focus. I take the ramp down from the pilot's bench to the main deck and reach the navigator's array, sparing one last glance at Quantum. His eyes remain open, but they don't follow me. After reaching the bench, a few seconds of exploration reward me with access controls to the emergency sardine can—which is basically what it is.

I don't have the time or energy to care if the deck is clear of danger. If there's anyone else breathing down here, they can take their best shot. Right now, I just want to get out. Regardless, a lifetime of surviving prompts me to do a quick scan. Nothing moves.

I gaze through the hatch that's slid open beside the nav bench into the coffin-sized pod and let the idea of staying aboard the *Celestial* until it blows tease through my mind. If this is truly the only escape pod on the bridge, it must have been built to evacuate the last person left in the case of attack or total ship failure. There aren't many weapons powerful enough, with the exception of the Mini-Nova of course, to instantly obliterate a ship this size. Any attack or malfunction would generally give the bridge crew enough time to get to their nearby evacuation-pod bays.

A heavy thump at the bridge's main entry echoes across the deck. They're awake. I only have a minute or two until they find their way through—that's *if* Quantum jammed up the hatch. Acute claustrophobia aside, I'm not fitting into the pod's cradle while still in this bugsuit. It has to come off. Which means I'm about to suffer. A lot.

I drop the medkit on the console display and thumb the release catch to open it, but it won't budge. The kit looks abused and probably hasn't been opened in years. As Desto would say, what kind of fuck salad is this? With my one usable hand, it's hard to get a grip on the box to work the release tab. Squinting in frustration, I end up picking it up and slamming it hard against the console, breaking both the console and, thankfully, the kit's latch. Everything flies out across the console table, but I manage to slam my palm across the morphone syringe before it gets away.

Pulling the cap off with my teeth, I press the flat delivery end against my neck just below my earlobe and hit the button. A tiny spike of pressure against my skin, followed by a moment of what feels like ice running down my neck, then heat. It'll take a few seconds for the narcotic to kick in, but there's no time to wait. I can hear a dull whine coming from the entry. They're cutting through.

I take a deep breath and don't hesitate, yanking first against the chest buckles that hold the bugsuit on, then the sleeves. Before I start to pull my arms through, I use my right hand to grip my left arm just above the elbow, and simultaneously drop to my knees and press the bad shoulder into the nav table's solid edge.

Okay, Aly, just a quick yank and a push and your humerus will be reseated. You're not getting into that tin can with your arm hanging by the socket like dead meat. On three, two, one . . . OWJESUSFUCK-INGCHRISTTHATFUCKINGHURTS . . . SHITI'MGOINGTOPUKE . . . OHHOLY . . . OH, that's a little . . . oh, okay, I'm okay. It's all okay.

The head of my humerus slips back into place with a wet sound just as the morphone hits like a tidal wave of pure bliss, sending the spiking pain to a dark, lonely corner at the very edge of my brain. I'm even feeling a little happy. Until I look into the waiting bucket of terror that will take me into airless oblivion.

A shudder runs through the floor of the bridge, subtle at first, but quickly building in intensity. Quantum's destruction sequence beginning? It has to be. No more time to wait.

I quickly pull my broken arm through the bugsuit sleeve, feeling it but not feeling it at the same time. That hand is completely numb and won't grip the wrist of my right-arm sleeve. So I hold onto the edge of the nav console table and pull myself to my feet, step on the hanging suit arm to hold it down, and perform a wriggling dance maneuver that eventually gets the unit off. It takes less than a minute, but a high-pitched, whining buzz has begun emitting from all the electronics on the bridge, threatening to turn my inner ear into jelly, and the remaining lights waver between off and blazing. I sit on the edge of the open emergency pod hatch, dangling my feet inside, then slowly slide into the tight passenger cradle. The pain and fear of small spaces sing in a deep, fading baritone in my head, but the tune is drowned out under the morphone ocean. If the e-pod thrusters get me far enough away to clear the debris and flak from the vessel's self-destruction, I'll be lucky. But the morphone drowns that anxiety, too.

Once I'm nestled and buckled, I press the syringe against my neck once more. If I don't live through this, I'm not going out screaming. I'm doing it in quiet, unbroken serenity.

Just as my lights start to fade, I activate the release sequence and emergency beacon, and let fate decide what to do next.

THIRTY

F *lutter, flutter, flutter.*

I shake my foot, trying to get the cat at the end of the bed to go away and stop tickling me with its whiskers.

"...awake..."

Flutter...flutterflutterflutter.

"Would you stop!" My eyes slowly peel open, the lids nearly gummed together by what feels like years of being asleep. It's not a cat, it's Karl. He stands at the foot of a bed—a med-bay gurney?—lightly rubbing the tips of his fingers along the sole of my bare left foot. "Whuh...?" The words *what are you doing here?* stick in my similarly gummy throat.

"Welcome back, lover." He smiles, and, whether it's just a trick of memory or an actual sense, I smell the warm sand and sweet soap of his hair drift to me.

Besides the tickle in my foot, my body is gloriously absent of any other tactile sensation. Blinking with the cinder blocks that compose my eyelids, a glance tells me I'm wearing a sling on my broken arm.

"How do...does...look?"

"How do you look? To be honest, terrible. But you'll live." That same mischievous grin.

Apparently morphone doesn't block feelings of annoyance. I scowl, or think I do, it's hard to tell when my face feels like a drenched, dripping sock, and try again: "My arm. How's my arm look?"

"V says your wrist is sprained and you have an impacted fracture of the ulna, but you'll be doing push-ups again in less than a month. We found a hydro cast in the *Celestial*'s medical supplies, and she's going to fit it for you when you're a little more awake."

A subdued but no less disturbing jolt of apprehension slams through me. He sees my expression and says, "Don't worry. We're safe. There's a lot to catch you up on. But let's wait till the morphone wears off. You have enough in your system to knock out even Desto." He steps up and brushes his hand along my unbruised cheek. "I'm sorry I woke you up. I just couldn't wait to see you again, hear your voice. Go back to sleep now, okay?"

It isn't hard to convince me.

DESPITE THE BRILLIANCE that had been behind Quantum's plan, I've never been happier to see one fail so abysmally.

Desto sits cross-legged on the *Nebula*'s galley floor, detailing everything that had happened between the fight at Bogotan's landing field to when they'd picked me up in the e-pod, unconscious but apparently raving about being buried alive. His leans back, relaxing against Zeta's chair and lightly rubbing her calves, which are draped over his shoulders. "It took us thirty-six hours from your transmission to reach you, but you were still out. Once we got you inside, Vitruzzi sedated you with something to counteract the morphone but keep you from totally losing your shit. You kept shouting 'not the trunk, not the trunk, not in the trunk, Harald.' I have no idea who Harald is, but you clearly didn't like the guy much."

He stops there, letting the pregnant pause pressure me into an explanation, but I'm not going along with it. As far as I'm concerned, I'd left my recollections about my father aboard the fleet cruiser. Some things should stay buried.

After a minute, he continues, "I've never seen anyone who's spent so much of their life flying in dinky scout or attack ships so afraid of small spaces."

"It's different on a ship," I start to explain, then stop. Those without phobias just can't understand. That's what makes them phobias; they have no rational explanation. I change the subject. "So you and V and Brady got to the *Nebula* okay. Did any ships follow you from Bogotan?"

"We had one attacker on our tail, but Zabriskie sent one of their own ships after it."

"Zabriskie?" It had become clear to me that most of Bogotan's people weren't keen on being under Medina's thumb, but I'm still surprised they'd get into any active engagement with her and those under her command. What if Quantum and I had failed and Medina discovered their complicity? She'd have done to them what she'd threatened to do to Keum Libre. Maybe the Bogotanites were tired of living with fear and compromised ethics. Sometimes taking a stand, even if it means dying, is better.

"Yeah. The Bogotan scout took care of Medina's attack ship, and we were halfway to KL when you called."

David, who's been working behind the galley counter to try and make something more appetizing than nutrition bars and endurance gels, jumps in, "We thought our nav-system had failed when we got into range of your emergency alert. The sky wasn't filled with debris from the *Celestial* like we expected. The cruiser was just sitting there, fully inop."

"Powerless and dark and as cold as the grave," Desto says.

"We thought you'd been tricked into sending that transmission to Karl, and we basically just floated there, waiting for Medina to send out a squadron to dust us." David sticks a finger in the bowl he's mixing things in, licks the yellowish substance from it, and wrinkles his nose. He comes around the counter and holds the bowl out. "Desto, could you taste this? What's missing?"

Zeta grimaces. "Get that . . . whatever . . . away from the pregnant lady! You do not want me to get sick. It makes me crabby."

"Get it away, quick!" Desto says, making melodramatic warding-off gestures, and Zeta play-punches his shoulder.

"Sorry." He brings the bowl to me. "Help me out, Twig."

"You know I love you, brother, but . . ."

"Gah! Bunch of cowards." He retreats back behind the counter and slams the bowl down.

Desto picks up the thread. "We waited, ran some hull scans, but it seemed like no one was home, then found you floating nearby. After hanging back for a few hours, just waiting to get blown out of the sky, Brady made the call. We picked you up and got you on board. When it was clear you weren't going to be able to tell us what happened for a bit, we decided to go exploring.

"Everything on the *Celestial* was offline. Power, engines, life support. We broke in through the secondary small-ship airlock and tried to minimize pressure loss to make it easier to figure out what had happened. Didn't matter though; one of the aft engine rooms had a small leak from a minor explosion. The whole place was a ghost town.

"Most of us went in, and it took about three hours to reach the bridge. We found Quantum and Medina's bodies, and every other crewmember we ran across was dead, too. Jeremy dialed in to the ship log and figured out what Quantum had tried to do—and he mucked the beast up pretty bad—but it never fully destructed. I guess fleet cruisers have enough stopgaps that it was able to shut down the sequence Quantum programmed to sabotage it. Unfortunately for the crew, not before the life support systems were totally blown."

"So it's salvageable?"

"Jeremy and Mason have been working their asses off to try and answer that question, but we think so. That kid Ryan has been pretty helpful, too."

I repeat, I've never been happier in my life to see a plan fail so abysmally.

·   ·   ·

THE MOST UNEXPECTED thing imaginable happens over the next six months: life goes on. Though the idea of "normal" is never going to mean anything again, unless you consider disorder and random surprises normal, the settlers of both Keum Libre's colony and Bogotan's pick up the pieces and resume.

I heal, as I so frequently spend time doing, and Karl and I return to being partners in short- and long-range salvage ops. Jono Zabriskie takes over leadership of Bogotan, setting up a representative council to oversee daily life and operations there, giving everyone a voice in their own future as well as a sense of stability. Keum Libre and Bogotan set up a system of trade and aid—just like Quantum had originally proposed, but not in the backward, old-school, subversive process he had attempted. Some Bogotanites move to KL; some Klers move there.

David meets and falls in love (finally, the guy had been like a monk during the last few years) with one of the transplants, a former major in the Stellar Corps, thus proving to David that not all officers are self-serving bottom-feeders—while simultaneously proving to me, though David will never admit it, that she can command him just like she'd formerly commanded the lower enlisted serving under her. I *like her*. And though nothing will ever diminish the bond of family between David and me, Olamina, or just Mina, soon becomes like a sister to me, and the two of them join most of the salvage trips Karl and I take.

As for the two of us, we continue to call KL home, completely content with our off-the-grid, seminomadic lifestyle. I've found that the vastness of the ocean just down the cliff from KL and even the trees and neotropical jungle surrounding the settlement still feel more unconfining and open than a city. And after everything, I can't seem to get enough of open spaces.

More importantly, Vitruzzi has started to heal. Less than a month after we returned to KL, Zabriskie's people made contact with another fleet cruiser. Unlike Medina, the man in charge had been both a civilian and pro-Admin—until the war. Whatever the cruiser's crew and inhabitants had gone through, they'd reached the same conclusions as Bogotan and KL—either we all work together or we all die alone.

One of the crewmembers is a psychologist who specialized in combat-related disorders. She meets via satlink with Vitruzzi several times a week. I'm no brain debugger, but I think that whatever had triggered the reverse of Vitruzzi's downward spiral has been helped by seeing the way things are improving between Bogotan and KL, and the weekly discovery and influx of survivors from all over the system who want nothing more than to find ways to put the worlds back together, peacefully and with minimum competition or struggle. It's probably also helped that she and Brady have adopted two of the kids we'd picked up on Eruo Pium. Those kids may be scarred by all they'd been through, but if anyone can raise them, it's someone with scars of their own, someone who can empathize. And Vitruzzi and Brady have plenty. Even Mason took in the little girl, Cassandra, and her brother, their quick attachment to each other a surprise to everyone.

Speaking of Mason, not everything has been roses and rainbows. Both he and Hoogs have moved on, deciding Bogotan suits them better. I miss them, but it hit me even harder when Venus and La Mer decided to relocate as well. It makes sense; La Mer's technical savvy is put to much better use in their colony, which has more intricate engineering needs than ours. And of course Venus wouldn't hear of being apart from him. Fortunately, we've seen them a few times since they departed, the constant traffic between the two colonies making it easy. As a bonus, Ryan has stayed, and no one can claim the kid isn't damn near as adept in the mechanical and electronics arenas as La Mer. We're lucky to have him.

I'M KICKING BACK in the lounge area on the *Andromeda* after a two-week salvage op when David runs in.

"What are you doing?" he asks.

I give him the look I reserve for people who ask stupid questions. "Reading."

"Yeah, but what's that?"

"Uh, it's a book, Bright Light." It isn't as easy as it sounds to make sense of a question that has such an obvious answer.

His expression shifts from curiosity to exasperation, as if I'm the one asking stupid questions. "I can see that, Aly. What I mean is, why are you reading a book made of paper? And where did you get it?"

Ah, now I see. "Venus brought a few boxes of them from Bogotan. She says they have a nostalgia library with at least a few thousand." I hadn't seen a book printed on paper since I was a kid and we'd visited the Tiptree Memorial and Archive Center. David, obviously, hasn't seen once since then either. "I guess they have a thing for vintage. I'm kind of starting to see why."

"Yeah? Why?"

I have to think about how to put it into words for a second before responding. "I don't know. There's something about the way it feels in my hands. The way I can flip the pages and create a little breeze. The smell of glue and wood pulp. It makes me think of . . . simpler times." A little embarrassed at waxing poetic, I drop my eyes to the book, then glance back at him. The smirk I see on his face confirms my instinct to feel a little silly.

"Well, you better keep them locked up," he says through the smirk. "Some of these heathens may be inclined to use them as fuel."

"Noted. So, mind if I . . .?" I wave the book at him, annoyed.

"Yeah, but you may want to come to the med center. Zeta's about to pop."

Three hours later, David, Karl, Brady, and I stand outside Zeta's room. Vitruzzi comes out, tells us she's sleeping, everyone's happy and healthy, and to come back later. She looks more like the old Vitruzzi than ever. I don't know if it's because of that, or because of my gladness that Desto and Zeta and their new kid are all doing well, or because of some other unexpected, even unimagined, relief that we've somehow made it through the worst of everything, still whole, still human, but I suddenly wrap my arms around her and hug her like I've never hugged anyone but my brother. Almost surprisingly, she returns it, and we stand that way for a while.

The door opens and Desto comes out. V and I let go of each other, and I look at the bundled-up little girl in his arms.

"She's as beautiful as her mama," I tell him.

"Aly," he says.

I look into his face and see the tears streaming from his eyes. Tears of such rejoicing happiness, so unexpected from such a lifelong warrior, it's almost hard to look at him. "What?" I manage, feeling my own eyes start to swim.

"That's her name. We're going to call her Aly."

AFTERWORD

Thanks for reading! This concludes the Spectras Arise Series. Will there be more books set in the post-Admin dystopia of the Spectras and Obals? Will Aly be back, bloody, bruised, and just as belligerent as ever? Well, it's hard to say, but there is no such thing as never. I hope you enjoyed this ride into the maybe-one-day future. If you enjoy the fight-or-die style of these characters, you may be held just as enrapt by my newer novels, The Shackled Verities, an epic science fantasy series with magic, monsters, and a Cosmos-crossing adventure.

ALSO BY TAMMY SALYER

SPECTRAS **A**RISE **S**ERIES

When all other options run out, never let go of your gun.

In a few hundred years, the Algol system becomes humanity's new home. The question is: Is it a better one?

THE **S**HACKLED **V**ERITIES **S**ERIES

In a Cosmos-wide war between celestials, humans are as expendable as pawns. Until Ulfric Aldinhuus, leader of the Knights Corporealis, uses the celestials' weapons to fight back.

OTHERWORLD **O**UTLAWS **S**ERIES

A sawbones fae with a supernatural-sized grudge, a necromancer gnome obsessed with pixie dust, and a hoodoo cowgirl with a Sharps buffalo rifle and damn good aim—the Tuatha Dé Danann will never know what hit 'em.

COLLECTIONS

A Scorpion's Heart: Four Twisted Tales of Love and Lust

SHORT STORIES

Artificial Fate * Creepers * No Suede Soles in Hell

Visit my website to see if anything new has been released since this publication.

www.tammysalyer.com

ABOUT THE AUTHOR

Tammy is an inveterate verbarian, who spends her days surrounded by the written word, both hers and others'. As an ex-paratrooper with the 82nd Airborne Division, her stories are often as gritty as a grunt's pile of three-week-old field gear. Her military science fiction Spectras Arise series debuted to acclaim in 2012, and her epic fantasy adventure series The Shackled Verities was launched in 2020. She's currently five books deep in a Weird West series called Otherworld Outlaws, featuring half-fae sawbones, a necromancer gnome, and a hoodoo cowgirl galavanting into mischief in the Old West.

When not hunched like a Morlock over her writing desk, Tammy runs and bikes silly miles with her super-cool weirdo partner in the Pacific Northwest playground and spends an inappropriate amount of time watching Henry Rollins videos on YouTube. Contrary to whatever ideas her last name might conjure, she's never really been much of a Slayer fan.

Fantasy, space opera, satire, and snark fans will feel right at home with Tammy. Learn more about her and her books by visiting www.tammysalyer.com. She hopes you enjoy reading her works and welcomes your reviews.